OUTFOXED

I pushed the bedroom door open and had just stepped in when I was overcome by a sickly sweet metallic odor. My eyes darted around the dim room and came to rest on a bundle on the floor. Gradually my vision adjusted and—I screamed. There, in the middle of the empty room, was a man lying in a pool of blood.

Feeling faint, I crouched down, my hands reaching out to the solid floor for support.

David bounded over and brushed past me. He gasped and stood frozen while I tried to regain my breath. He took a few hesitant steps into the room and bent over the body. "Shit," he said, followed by a long list of other expletives. He crouched and picked up a limp hand, feeling for a pulse. A wave of nausea hit me.

"Is he dead?" I whispered hoarsely.

"Dead as a doorknob," he said, dropping the hand.

The room seemed to tilt, and I forced myself to breathe slowly, regularly. I dared another glance. There was something familiar, something—I squelched another rush of nausea and looked again. "Do you know who— Oh, my God!" I exclaimed, getting a look at the dead man's face. "Is this who I think it is?"

"It's Jeremy Fox," he muttered, and when he looked up at me, his face was as pale as the dead man's. He took a shaky breath and said, "I think he's been murdered."

Looming Murder

A WEAVING MYSTERY

CAROL ANN MARTIN

AN OBSIDIAN MYSTERY

SIGNET ECLIPSE
Published by the Penguin Group
Penguin Group (USA) Inc., 375 Hudson Street,
New York, New York 10014, USA

USA | Canada | UK | Ireland | Australia | New Zealand | India | South Africa | China

Penguin Books Ltd., Registered Offices: 80 Strand, London WC2R 0RL, England
For more information about the Penguin Group visit penguin.com.

First published by Signet Eclipse, an imprint of New American Library,
a division of Penguin Group (USA) Inc.

First Printing, June 2013

ISBN 978-0-451-41360-4

Printed in the United States of America
10   9   8   7   6   5   4   3   2   1

Acknowledgments

I would like to thank the following people for their help and their contributions to this novel: my husband, who took over much of the cooking while I took weaving lessons; all the wonderful people at Obsidian who patiently answered my questions; my wonderful editor, Jesse Feldman, without whose help this novel would never have been; and most importantly, Brenda Nicolson, for teaching this newbie the basics of weaving and for correcting my many mistakes. Any remaining mistakes about weaving in this novel are mine and mine alone.

I thank you all, from the bottom of my heart.

Chapter 1

Sometimes in the middle of the night, I worried that this might all have been a huge mistake—*this* being the leap I'd recently made. At the age of thirty-five, a time in life when—as my mother liked to point out—most sane women were either married with children or just hitting their professional stride, I had left a perfectly good career as a business analyst to become a weaver. That's right. A *weaver*.

But whatever she thought, I hadn't arrive at this decision easily. A year ago, something happened that shook me to my core. I was accused of embezzling from my company, and if I had not been able to prove to the authorities that my boss was the guilty party, right now I would be the one serving a ten-year jail term instead of him. Just as sure as my name is Della Wright.

It had been time for a change.

So, crazy or not, here I was in my new studio, waiting for somebody—anybody—to show up. I glanced at my watch again—six forty-five, and still not a soul in sight.

I looked down at Winston, the French bulldog I'd inherited with the house where I was living and setting up shop. He wasn't exactly the kind of dog I might have chosen for myself. My taste in pooches ran more toward the tiny poodle variety. In fact, I used to have a tiny poodle, and she was a lot prettier than the dog at my feet. Winston was thirty pounds of solid muscle on a squat frame, and he had a flat face frozen in a perpetual grimace. Good God, the dog was ugly. Admittedly, though, for all his vicious appearance, he would have been about as effective as a lamb when it came to protecting me. Winston, or Winnie, as I had nicknamed him, was more likely to lick an intruder to death than to chase him away. He was so sweet that I was beginning to actually like him.

I bent down to scratch his ear.

"You are my buddy, aren't you?"

He glanced up at me with big, mournful eyes and yawned.

"Don't worry, Winnie. People will show up—you'll see." He stared at me, looking less than convinced. Oh, God, people *had* to show up. I couldn't have done all this only to fall flat on my face.

I'd moved here just over two months ago, and so far I'd hardly earned enough to keep me in java, my personal addiction. All the while I'd been spending, spending, spending: three new looms picked up on craigslist (I needed those. Honestly! How was I supposed to give classes unless I had a few looms?); yarn—dozens upon dozens of gorgeous yarns I hadn't been able to resist (what can I say—fate led me to that yarn shop two days before it closed). And then there was the cost of fixing up my new abode.

Last Christmas I'd admitted to my friend Matthew

Baker just how miserable I felt. I wasn't eating. I wasn't sleeping. I was a zombie at work. Being branded a stool pigeon and a whistle-blower by one's coworkers will do that to a person. That's the damn thing about the investment industry; those in it would more easily forgive a person for stealing than for reporting criminal activity by a superior. So rather than applaud me for giving the evidence to the SEC, my coworkers turned on me. It was a nightmare, living in a place where no one trusted me enough even to share *weekend* plans.

Anyhow, after I confided in Matthew, he very generously offered to lend me his house.

"I have just the place for you," he'd said, going on to paint an idyllic picture of Briar Hollow, the small town at the foot of the Blue Ridge Mountains where he lived. He offered to switch places for a little over a week—I would take his house and he'd take my condo in Charlotte. "You'll enjoy a much-needed vacation, and I'll save myself two hours of daily commuting at the same time."

Matthew had recently accepted a position teaching criminology at the University of Charlotte, a job he intended to leave just as soon as he realized his life dream—landing a publishing deal for a book on criminology. What he didn't say, but I suspected, was that he would also enjoy living closer to his girlfriend, Amanda, whom I referred to as Blondie. He had been dating Blondie for a couple of years, and even though she somehow always rubbed me the wrong way, the truth was she was perfectly nice.

I decided to take his offer. Ten days away from my job was exactly what I needed. Afterward, I would go back to work refreshed and reenergized. Except, that's not exactly what happened.

The farther I got from Charlotte, the more I wondered, why just ten days? I'd always dreamed of opening my own weaving studio, a notion that my mother insisted was sweet and romantic but hardly practical. (Poor Mom, to this day she could not accept that I was a grown woman who did not need her advice.) I had long ago folded away my dream and stored it in an almost forgotten corner of my mind. Weaving was fine as a hobby, and that was what it had become. Whenever the stress of my work became too much, I would sit and weave, sometimes far into the night.

It's incredible just how soothing the process can be—the rhythmic throwing of the shuttle from hand to hand and the beat of one's feet walking the treadles, not to mention the satisfaction of the completed project—ahhh, happiness.

In the past, I would've reluctantly packed away the loom and trudged off to my real job in the morning. But when I got to Briar Hollow, I just kept thinking, *Why not?* Why *couldn't* I do it? Maybe it was because I had nothing left to lose: I had few friends in Charlotte (lately, anyway) and no job satisfaction—in fact, hardly a stable job at all, given how things were going.

The old-fashioned gingerbread house was just right. It had a living room/dining room combo separated by an arched doorway. I could open a shop in one, and in the sunny corner of the other, I could have a studio with an AVL loom—the one I'd always dreamed of owning. All I would have to do was convince Matthew that we should make our arrangement permanent.

"You want to *live* there?" Matthew had exclaimed when I told him my new idea. "You mean, full-time?" I could almost hear the gears clicking in his mind. "Well, I suppose we could switch places until you find something permanent. There'd be no rush. I love living in your condo. It's so close to my work." And to Blondie, no doubt. "But Winston would have to stay with you," he'd added. "He'd be miserable by himself in your small condo all day."

We'd struck a deal. I would take care of Winston, and Matthew would stay in my condo until either one of us changed our mind, which I knew meant I could count on living here for as long as I wanted. I mean, honestly, anyone would be nuts to take a two-hour commute over a ten-minute drive—right?

From then on, Matthew's dog became my roommate, and I never looked back.

I named my studio Dream Weaver, and to help generate interest I announced weaving classes for all levels of ability. I also decided to organize weaving groups as a good and inexpensive way to promote my shop. Tonight's group was for a charity project, making baby blankets for the local hospital. Well, it wasn't really the *local* hospital. St. Anthony's was about ten miles out of town, nearer to Belmont than to Briar Hollow, which technically made it the *closest* hospital. I was hoping the charity angle would attract a mix of people, and that those with less weaving proficiency might enroll in my classes. But it was now five minutes to seven and nobody was here. My earlier optimism was fast deflating.

I looked down at Winston. "What do you think, Winnie? People are bound to show up, right?"

He snorted.

"You are such a pessimist."

For the tenth time, I pulled back the lace curtains and peeked outside. And—*yes, at last*—a car was pulling up. I hurried away from the window, coaxing Winston to follow. He lumbered behind me, a puzzled expression on his mug.

"Sorry, Winnie, but you'll have to stay in here." I closed the kitchen door behind him and hurried to the front just as the bell above the door tinkled. A middle-aged woman with Lucille Ball hair and eyes heavy with makeup waddled in, carrying a large knitting bag. She set it down and brushed her hands over her zebra-print capri pants, which made her already large behind look twice its size.

"Hello, hello!" she exclaimed. "I'm sorry I'm late."

"You're actually a few minutes early," I said with a smile. "I'm Della Wright. Welcome to Dream Weaver."

"Marnie Potter," the woman said, fanning herself dramatically with a bejeweled hand. "My, but it's hot in here. Don't you have air-conditioning?" Beads of moisture had gathered on her forehead. I thought it was humid rather than hot, but I wasn't about to argue.

"It is hot, isn't it?" I looked around for a solution. "I'll open a window. That should help. Oh, and I have a fan upstairs." I hurried to the window, but no amount of struggling would get it to budge.

Marnie frowned. "Where is everyone? I thought I was joining a group. We won't produce very many baby blankets with just the two—"

At the sound of the bell, we both turned to see a

pleasant-looking, sandy-haired woman, wearing a gauzy tie-dyed top over a pair of black yoga pants that were hugging what was one of the tightest bodies I had ever seen. I wasn't in the habit of ogling other women's bodies, but this one could have been a walking advertisement for a health club. It wasn't a look I could ever hope to achieve with my short stature and gargantuan appetite—I was just lucky to weigh one hundred and fifteen and not two hundred and fifteen. I glanced at her tiny waist enviously. On second thought, I wouldn't give up eating, not even for a tight body like hers. I studied her outfit. It was interesting—sexy, in a New Age or bohemian sort of way.

I became aware of my own Ralph Lauren natural-linen pants and Navajo-inspired beaded shirt, which identified me as exactly what I was—a city girl trying to fit into her new small-town life by dressing in a designer's version of country duds. I suddenly felt self-conscious.

"Hi. I'm here for the weaving group." She spotted the looms in the workshop. "And it looks like I'm in the right place." She offered her hand. "Jenny Davis." Her smile lit the room.

"Della Wright. I'm the owner."

"Nice to meet you." She looked around and nodded a hello to Marnie. "So you're joining the group too?"

"I am."

"You two know each other?"

Marnie chuckled. "This is Briar Hollow, sugar pie. Everybody knows each other around here."

It was difficult for a city girl to conceive of a town being so small that everybody knew everybody. I really wasn't in Charlotte anymore. That, however, had been the whole point of moving here. I'd wanted to live in a place where one could live life at a slower pace. I'd wanted a home in a town where people said hello to each other on the street, where trust and loyalty existed and where the likelihood of being embroiled in an embezzlement case was nonexistent.

Meanwhile, Jenny had wandered farther into the room. "I've been dying to see what you did with the place. Oh, will you look at those." She made a beeline to the maple hutch I'd salvaged from the garage next to the house. I'd emptied it of car parts and an assortment of tools, and then waxed and polished the old piece until it glowed. Now it was the display case for my fine-linen towels and dishcloths.

Jenny reverently touched one of the towels. "These are gorgeous. Did you make them?"

"I did. That one is a Swedish design called monk's cloth. It's also known as huck embroidery."

Marnie Potter approached. "That is fine work indeed. You're very good." Her tone was almost grudging.

"Thank you. I'm glad you think so. Weaving is my passion. I just hope I can make a living at it." I was about to ask the women about their experience with weaving when the doorbell rang again.

"Hello. I'm here to weave baby blankets," the young woman said, her gaze sweeping over Marnie and me, and then over the store. I had an immediate impression of a laser-sharp mind.

"Welcome to Dream Weaver. I'm Della. And you are?"

Her dark lashes flickered, and she smiled. "Susan Wood." She extended her hand, her eyes focused on mine. "Nice to meet you."

On second glance, I realized that Susan Wood was older than I'd first thought. She looked to be in her mid- to late twenties, with auburn hair in a shoulder-length blunt cut. She wore jeans and an open white shirt with rolled-up sleeves over a T-shirt. That was how I should dress if I wanted to fit in. On second thought, scratch that. With my body, it was easy to look chubby rather than curvaceous. I would stick to Ralph Lauren. My body needed Ralph almost as much as it needed caffeine.

"Susan, why don't you join the others? I'm sure I don't have to introduce you. I'll be right back." I dashed upstairs and retrieved the fan from my bedroom, making a mental note to buy a couple more before the next meeting. When I returned to the front room, Marnie and Jenny were chatting away like old friends—which, for all I knew, they might well have been.

With excitement I heard the bell jingle again, but my cheer ebbed when a man walked in. He was tall and handsome in a business sort of way, in his late thirties to early forties and wearing a gray suit and tie. Surely he was not here for weaving. Everyone grew silent as they turned to stare.

He closed the door behind him and scowled. "Is this the place for the charity weaving group?"

"Yes, it is." I set the fan on the floor. "Are you here to join the group?"

"What else would I be doing here?" he grumbled, looking about as pleased as a bear in a trap.

I sensed trouble. Why was it that every group had to have at least one churl?

Chapter 2

*H*e looked at us like a poker champ sizing up the other players. When his eyes fell on Marnie Potter, the redhead met his gaze with a frosty stare.

She pointed an index finger at him. "Don't take this the wrong way, cupcake, but something tells me you don't have much weaving experience."

"You're damn right, Mrs. Potter," he replied, looking uncomfortable. "And to tell you the truth, I can think of a dozen things I'd rather be doing with my time."

I can pretty safely say that we were all taken aback, except for Marnie, who crossed her arms.

"So what exactly brings you here?" Before he could answer, she added, "And maybe you could show a little politeness and introduce yourself, unless you expect Della here to call you cupcake too." Oddly, Marnie's comments seemed to amuse him. His scowl melted into a cocky grin.

"I've been called worse." He pulled out a business card and handed it to me. "David Swanson, ma'am, at your service."

I glanced at it. COTTAGE AND CASTLE REALTIES, it read, followed by his name and the address and phone number of his firm.

"If you don't want to be here, why aren't you out having a beer, or watching baseball, or doing whatever the heck you'd rather be doing?" continued Marnie. But something in her tone piqued my curiosity. I had the strange impression she was baiting him.

His grin slipped, and he looked pained. "On the off chance that you haven't already heard, which I seriously doubt"—he glared at Marnie, who glared right back at him, and I realized that whatever David Swanson was about to say would come as no surprise to her—"I've been ordered to do community service. They let me choose between some kind of charity work and pulling up nutsedge," he said, naming a local invasive plant. "Call me lazy, but weaving seemed easier on my back than weeding."

This admission was followed by a heavy silence. What, exactly, had David Swanson done to earn himself this penalty? Briar Hollow being such a small town, I suspected I might be the only person in the room who didn't know.

He caught me staring at him. "Hey, don't look at me like that," he said defensively. "A coworker charged me with assault, when all I did was grab him by the collar." He shrugged, looking slightly sheepish. "I guess I did sort of lose my temper. But frankly, I think I deserve a medal for the restraint I showed in just *threatening* to kill him. Instead, they tell me I have an anger management issue." He made quotation marks in the air.

Susan Wood cocked a hip. "As I already told you, Mr. Swanson, I'm not so sure you chose the easier of the two. Weaving can be hard work, maybe just as hard as weeding." She was right. Depending on the yarn used, weaving can be murder on a person's back.

At that moment, the bell above the door tinkled, and a startlingly beautiful woman walked in with a sullen-looking teenage girl.

"I'm Dolores Hanson," the woman said, "and this is my daughter, Mercedes." She gently elbowed the girl. "Mercedes, say hello."

Mercedes mumbled something that might have been a greeting. To say that she looked less than thrilled to be here was an understatement.

Mother and daughter were both blue-eyed blondes, but all resemblance ended there. The mother, probably in her mid-forties, had the kind of perfect complexion one usually saw on soap ads. She was expertly made up and wore a floral dress, strappy high-heeled sandals, a pristine manicure and—wow—my eyes nearly popped at the size of the diamond ring on her left hand.

The daughter—maybe sixteen—had the same coloring and similar height and weight. She might have been beautiful too, but the ghostly foundation and thick black eyeliner made it difficult to tell. She was dressed in top to bottom black: black T-shirt torn strategically to show off plenty of flesh, tight black jeans and black four-inch heels; even her dangling skull-and-crossbones earrings were black. But when I looked into her eyes, I saw insecurity. *So the provocative exterior is a mask*, I thought. I smiled at her and she averted her gaze.

Now, what in the world would bring this pair to my little group? Neither of them seemed the weaving type. But, I reminded myself, who was I to judge? "You don't seem the type," was exactly what my friends had said when I shared my plan to open this shop.

"I'm Della Wright. I take it you're here to join our charity weaving group?"

"We are," Dolores said. "But I have to warn you, we don't know the first thing about weaving. Will that be a problem?"

"Not at all." My eyes were drawn to her forehead, which was probably the smoothest brow I had ever seen. I was fascinated and had to stop myself from staring.

"Hi, Dolores," David Swanson said, brightening suddenly. "I had no idea you were interested in weaving."

She shrugged. "I've been a mental case since my husband's death. I'm hoping weaving will help me relax."

David nodded, looking uncomfortable. "I don't know the first thing about weaving either," he said, ignoring the remark about her husband. As I looked around the room, I saw that Dolores's comment seemed to have cast a pall over the entire group. She either didn't notice or didn't care, because she kept talking.

"Well, that means you and I will both learn something new today." She walked over to him and put a hand on his arm possessively. "I didn't expect to see you here, David. This is a nice surprise."

Something in her tone told me this was not entirely true. As if to confirm it, her daughter rolled her eyes and muttered, "Yeah, right, a big fat surprise." I swung around just in time to see—was it anger?—in the teenager's eyes. But as quickly as it had appeared, the expression was gone, and I was left wondering if I had imagined it. Dolores turned to give her daughter a warning look.

It was time to get this meeting started. I herded the group out of the shop area and into the second room, where I had set up my looms.

"Welcome to our weaving group, everyone. I'm thrilled that so many of you decided to join, no matter what reason may have brought you." I looked at David Swanson and gave him a smile. "There are a few different ways we can do this. We could meet once or twice a week and work together, or we can each decide what kind of blankets we want to make and then weave them on our own. I will leave the decision to you."

This time Jenny spoke up. "How about a combination of both?" She looked around. "Maybe I can do some work on my own, but I sort of like the idea of getting together once a week or so." Her suggestion was met with smiles and nods.

"I think that's a good idea. Those of you who don't have looms of your own can make appointments to come use one of mine whenever you like. As for tonight, there are seven of us, and only four looms, so we'll have to partner up. But I'll try to have enough looms for everyone at our next meeting. Does anyone have a portable loom we could borrow?"

Jenny looked at me. "I have a rigid heddle I can bring. I've only ever used it to make scarves and place mats though. Do you think it'll work for making baby blankets?"

"Of course it will. Weaving on a simple loom is a wonderful way to learn the craft. It will be perfect for our beginners. After they learn the basics, they may want to graduate to a more complex loom."

Marnie Potter cut in. "I've seen some gorgeous blankets made on simple looms."

"That settles it, then," replied Jenny. "I'll bring it over."

Susan raised her hand. "I have two looms at home. One of them is portable. I can bring it over if you like."

"Thank you. That would be great. I'll need help preparing the warps and dressing the looms for the beginner weavers." I looked around, hoping for a volunteer.

"I can do that if you like," Jenny offered. "How about I come over tomorrow morning, say, sometime around ten thirty?"

I wondered if I looked as pleased as I felt. Since I'd moved here, all my concentration had been on setting up and I'd yet to make friends. Perhaps that was about to change. "Great. Maybe we can have coffee together afterward."

Across the room Marnie Potter was fanning herself again. She looked at David Swanson. "Could you do this lady a favor and open that dratted window?" David struggled with the window for a few minutes and managed to raise it a couple of inches. Meanwhile, I plugged in the fan and turned it on, creating a light breeze.

"That's the most it'll go," David said.

"That's much better, cupcake," said Marnie, beaming at him. Apparently it didn't take much to soften her up, because the frosty woman of a moment ago had morphed into a coquettish flirt. "You are such a sweetie pie."

"Who else here is new to weaving?" I asked, trying to bring the subject back to our project. Mercedes raised her hand, grimacing. "I have a suggestion," I said. "Why don't the newbies join my beginner class? Better yet, how about I organize a class for just the three of you? That way, you can learn while working on your baby blankets."

They glanced at each other, looking unsure. The first to nod was David. "I will if you will," he told Dolores.

"You can count on Mercedes and me."

Her daughter scowled. "Oh, Mo-o-om," she said, stretching the word into three syllables. "You know I don't want to—"

"Mercedes, you will do as I say, and that's that."

"Let's get to work," I cut in enthusiastically. "I suggest our beginners join an experienced weaver—just for tonight," I quickly added, seeing Dolores's face fall.

Marnie headed straight for David Swanson, hooking her arm through his. "Don't you worry, cupcake. I know enough for the two of us." She led him toward my AVL, the largest of my looms, and began explaining its different parts to him. "These are the heddles, and every one of them has to be threaded."

"Shit! There must be hundreds of them. It'll take forever," David replied.

Meanwhile, Susan had partnered with Mercedes, who still looked miserable, while Jenny and Dolores inspected my counterbalance loom.

I walked over to my table loom. "This one is only eighteen inches wide, so I think a good solution might be to make blankets of twelve-inch strips joined together."

"That's a great idea," Jenny said. "A sort of variation on friendship blankets. It'll make it easy to work on the project from home too."

Dolores looked at me, puzzled. "Friendship blankets? I thought we were making baby blankets."

"Friendship blankets can be made in any size. It simply means they're constructed of many pieces, usually woven by a number of friends," I explained.

"Oh," she said, looking bored. Once again my eyes were drawn to her smooth forehead, and it suddenly hit me. Botox! That explained it.

"That's why they're called *friendship* blankets," added Jenny. "They can look really pretty with strips of different weaves and colors. They can be less expensive to produce too. They can be made from leftover yarns—of which I have tons, by the way."

I nodded. "That's a good idea. I'll go through my leftover yarns too. I probably have enough for the entire group. I'll supply the warp yarns for the new weavers. You can choose what colors you want to use as weft from this collection." I indicated the basket of partial cones of yarn at the foot of the AVL.

Jenny fished through her bag. "We'll have more than enough if you count mine." She pulled out a number of skeins, showing them to a very disinterested Dolores.

I wandered back to my table loom, where Susan was rummaging through her bag. "I already bought yarn." She pulled out half a dozen spools of lovely pastels— light blue, soft pink, and creamy white. "They're one hundred percent preshrunk Egyptian cotton." She rubbed the end piece of the pink yarn between her fingers. "And so soft."

"If you'd rather keep those for another project, you're welcome to any of my leftover yarns," I offered.

"Go ahead. I'm sure you can find something appropriate."

"No, thanks. I don't mind making my baby blankets in a friendship pattern, but I want to make them beautiful." And then looking contrite, she added, "Sorry. I don't mean to imply that your blankets won't be pretty. It's just that I have my heart set on these yarns."

"No offense taken. Everyone's allowed to make their baby blankets any way they want."

She nodded. "Thanks."

Hmm, I thought. She was opinionated, which I rather liked in a person, most of the time. But something told me that Susan might turn out to be a bit overbearing. Standing next to her, Mercedes looked as if she was being tortured. Her eyes kept darting from the loom to her mother, throwing angry glares her way.

"If you need help, just give me a shout."

She scowled. "Sure."

Soon, all six of the volunteers were discussing different weaves and choosing colors and yarns. I had planned my project earlier, had already measured my warp, and was about to start dressing my dobby loom when the house phone rang.

"I'll be right back." And for the newbies, I added, "If you need help, maybe you can ask Jenny or Marnie."

I hurried into the kitchen, getting almost bowled over by an ecstatic Winnie. "Whoa there, big fellow." I bent down to give him a quick head scratch, then picked up the receiver.

"So, kiddo, how goes the weaving life?" Matthew's deep voice greeted me.

"Matthew, how nice to hear from you."

"You sound good," he said. "Briar Hollow must be agreeing with you."

"I'm happy to report that I'm back to my old self. Briar Hollow is exactly what I needed."

"How's Winston?"

"He's good. There's so much space for him to roam around in the backyard, I can understand why he'd be miserable in the city. He's great company."

"I knew you two would get along. Are you getting rich with your new business?" he asked.

I chuckled. "Hardly! But I already have a few customers, and I'm told the tourist season is just about to start. Also, I'll be starting some weaving classes in a few days."

"That's good. With your business know-how, kiddo, I have no doubt that you could turn any venture into a success."

Matthew's vote of confidence flooded me with joy. "I'm in the middle of a meeting right now. But if you want to chat, I can call you back later." As if—he was probably just calling to make sure I was taking good care of Winston.

"Actually, there is something I want to talk to you about. Give me a shout when you have a minute." Something in his voice told me that whatever he wanted to discuss was important.

"I have a minute right now." I wondered if maybe I should close the door between the kitchen and the front rooms. "What's up?"

There was a pause. "I have good news and bad news. Which do you want first?"

A sinking feeling settled in my stomach. "Give me the good news." *Lord knows I could use some.*

"Remember that book proposal on criminology I sent to publishers?" The excitement in his voice left no doubt as to what he was about to tell me.

"It's been accepted? Oh, Matthew, I'm so happy for you! Congratulations. I know how long you've been waiting for this."

"I can hardly believe it's really happening. I've taken a sabbatical from the university"—his voice became serious—"but I'll never get any work done in Charlotte. I need to be somewhere quiet."

I knew exactly where he was going with this. "You want to move back here, don't you?" I asked, my mouth suddenly going dry. "I guess that means I'll have to move out." What a fool I'd been to think I could go on living here indefinitely.

"I would never ask you to move out." He hesitated, then added, "Have you started looking for a place of your own?"

"I—I didn't think . . . I mean, I thought you would—"

"I know," he interrupted apologetically. "I never imagined I'd want to come back so soon. As long as I was teaching, your condo was perfect for me. Of course, if you don't think it would work, I can—"

"Don't be silly. This is your house. I'll find somewhere else to live." I kept my voice upbeat. I felt almost ill at the thought of all the work that moving and setting up again would entail.

"I have an idea. Why don't we share the house until you find the perfect place? You can take all the time you want—no rush." He chuckled. "Mind you, you might not want me as a roommate, so if you don't like the idea, just tell me, and I'll think of some other solution."

Matthew and me living in the same house might be . . . Well . . . I had a quick vision of quiet candlelit dinners, of cozy snuggles by the fireplace, which might have had a better chance of coming true if there was a fireplace somewhere in the house and if he didn't already have a girlfriend. Besides, I was focused on launching my weaving studio now, not on men.

The person who would be most thrilled at the prospect of Matthew and me sharing a house was my mother. For years, she'd been championing her favorite cause—getting him and me together—and she refused to understand why I wasn't taking her advice.

Matthew and I had known each other all our lives. His mother and mine had been roommates at college and were like sisters. In fact, our families had spent holidays together for as long as I could remember. During all those years, I had never felt anything for him but friendship—maybe because of my mother's constant efforts to match us up. Then suddenly, during his last holiday visit, I found myself fantasizing about running my fingers through his hair, which proved only one thing: It had been far too long since I'd gone on a date.

"How about this?" he asked, sensing my hesitation. "We can give it a try for a week or two, see if it works. If it does, great; if not, we'll think of something. What do you say?"

"That's a good idea." The truth was I was stunned. I'd quit my job. I'd exchanged my BMW for an eight-year-old Jeep Cherokee. I'd listed my condo for sale—which could take a long time considering the current condition of the real estate market. And then I'd spent a month scrubbing and cleaning and scraping and painting Matthew's house until it looked as bright as the first of June, which today just so happened to be. Besides, I liked Briar Hollow. Being here, I felt peaceful and happy. I was *not* going back to Charlotte.

After hanging up, I stood rooted to the spot for a few moments, feeling as if I'd just been hit over the head. "What do you think of that?"

Winston jumped up and licked my hand.

"Do you know what I think, Winnie? I think nobody will ever be as good a roommate as you." He tilted his head, staring at me with that puzzled expression again. Impulsively, I bent down, threw my arms around his neck and gave him a hug. "Sorry, big boy. I'll take you for a walk later. I promise." Ignoring the pang of guilt, I closed the door and returned to my studio.

The volunteers were poring over my collection of weaving magazines, still discussing patterns and yarns. David pulled away from the group and came closer. "I couldn't help overhearing that you'll be looking for a new place," he said in a low voice.

I knew I should have closed the door. I looked around, wondering if everybody in the room had been listening in on my conversation. "I haven't quite decided, but it's a possibility."

"I know of a few places that might be perfect for you. If you have time tomorrow, I can take you around to see them."

Whoa. This was all going so fast. I wanted to think things through before coming to any conclusion. "I—I'm not sure—"

"If you decide not to move, no problem, but you should at least know your options."

I spun that around in my mind. "I guess there's no harm in looking."

I noticed Jenny staring at me with surprise. She wandered over with one of my *Weaver's Craft* magazines. She opened it and, pretending to show me something, whispered, "Did I just hear David say you're looking for another place? I don't understand. You just got here. And you've put so much work into this house."

"The owner is moving back to Briar Hollow."

"Matthew's coming back?" she asked.

"You know Matthew?" I said, just as I remembered Marnie's earlier comment that in Briar Hollow everybody knew everybody.

"He's a friend of my ex-husband's, so I know him very well. He's nice." She smiled, closing the magazine. "It's a small world, isn't it?"

I didn't know about the world, but Briar Hollow sure was small.

Chapter 3

As I tidied the studio later—gathering weaving magazines and books and sorting skeins and cones of yarn—I could hardly believe how many people had shown up. When I'd decided to organize a charity group, I'd hoped for three, maybe four participants. I never imagined I might get as many as six. That all three beginners had registered for weaving lessons was another stroke of luck, and better yet, Jenny and Marnie had both offered to bring in some of their finished projects to sell on consignment. That would bring in more income that would go straight to my bottom line. So why did I feel like I needed Prozac?

Ha! As if I didn't know. Matthew's call had completely unraveled me.

What was I supposed to do?

I could think of a dozen ways living in the same house as Matthew could backfire. We'd always bickered as kids, and in the two months I'd been here, I had turned his house upside down. I had banished all of his downstairs furnishings to the smallest upstairs bedroom. There, sofa, armchairs and dining room furniture were piled topsy-turvy. What used to be the living and dining rooms now held exactly one desk, which I used as my sales counter; one maple hutch and a few tables, which I used to display my wares; my looms and half a dozen chairs and stools. Except for the kitchen, which I'd left unchanged, most everything else was gone.

I didn't mind living this way. It was for the sake of my new business. But this was Matthew's home. He was moving back, expecting to find his house the way he'd left it.

I sighed at the truth: There was no way I could stay here. I had to move out. *Crap!*

I couldn't blame Matthew for my predicament. Our arrangement had been clear from the start—until one of us changed his mind. Since the real estate market was bad now, I knew my condo wouldn't be selling any time soon, but it had been wishful thinking to imagine he'd like it so much in Charlotte that he would live in my condo indefinitely. I pushed my worries away for now, took a step back and sized up the room. Before the meeting had ended, everyone had completed the planning of the blankets. Until the next meeting, patterns and yarns would remain neatly stored in the baskets at the foot of each loom. After making sure that everything was tidy, I wandered over to the shop area and made a cold, objective assessment of it. Sure, it looked pretty, but it was much too bare, which might be why Jenny and Marnie had offered to bring in their wares. Whatever the reason, I had jumped at the chance. More stock would only improve the ambience of the place. It was just rotten luck that I would probably have to move.

"Want to go for a walk, Winston?" He jumped to his

feet, swinging his butt as if wagging a nonexistent tail. "I'm glad at least one of us is happy." I clipped his leash onto his collar.

I closed the door behind us and headed west along Main Street, walking past Briar Hollow Mercantile—a sort of local general store where one could find anything from farm machine parts, overalls and tools to fresh eggs and baked goods. I continued on past the church and past a row of small stores—a vacuum-cleaner shop, a watch-maker, the local grocery store. Winnie, of course, stopped, sniffed and peed at every tree, every lamppost and every fire hydrant.

"There isn't a tree you don't love, is there, Winnie?" He trudged on determinedly to the next one. "Hey! Who's walking whom here?"

All I got was a snort.

The evening was dark, lit only by the occasional streetlamp. I was about to turn back when I noticed a COTTAGE AND CASTLE REALTIES sign in a store window. I paused. Could this be one of the places David Swanson wanted to show me?

"Sit, Winnie." His butt hit the sidewalk. I turned to the store, pressing my nose to the glass and peering in. There wasn't much I could see in the dark, but I could tell the space was large, considerably larger than what I would need. I pulled away. No matter how wonderful this place might be, it was a shop, not a house, which meant I'd need a separate place to live. *Crap!* I couldn't possibly afford two rents.

In fact, even if I found the perfect place, one with a

setup similar to Matthew's house, where I could work downstairs and live upstairs, the cost of moving and settling in would still be more than I could afford. Part of the problem was that I was still paying the mortgage on my condo in Charlotte, and would have to keep paying it until the place was sold. I groaned as another problem occurred to me—furniture. As my agent had pointed out, empty homes sell for considerably less, so I'd had to leave my furniture in Charlotte. That had suited me fine as long as Matthew and I were just swapping places, but if I moved, I would have to buy new stuff. Where would I get the money for that?

I was so screwed.

Unless . . . "What do you think, Winnie? Should I accept Matthew's offer to share his house? Or should I move out on my own?" He looked at me blankly. "Come on, help me here. If I move, you'll go back to living with Matthew. That means no more sleeping at the foot of my bed."

He kept staring, unconcerned.

"You know what I think, big boy? You don't care one way or another. You'll live with anyone as long as they feed you." I could have sworn he looked offended. "Let's go home, Winnie." He took off at a trot, dragging me along.

I was still obsessing about it as I got ready for bed. I picked up my toothbrush and squeezed toothpaste on it. *Look at the bright side*, I told myself, swishing water through my mouth. *Living with Matthew could turn into a blessing. It all depends on the way I manage things. We could get along great, never quarrel, and I could save enough to move into a bigger shop in a year or so.*

I returned to my room, drew back the blankets and climbed into bed, filled with warm fuzzy thoughts.

But what if the opposite happened?

I wasn't exactly Miss Personality all the time. I had been known to occasionally lose my cool. What if, after a few days or weeks of living in the same house together, he and I got on each other's nerves? Matthew might decide he couldn't stand the sight of me. Having a person around all the time could do that. A lump the size of a fist was forming in my throat. *I might lose one of my oldest friends and my new career at the same time.*

"Enough of all this negativity." Winston, who had snuggled at the foot of the bed, looked up. "Go back to sleep, Winnie. Don't worry. Things will work out." All I had to do was make sure they did.

He looked back at me, his eyes mirroring my own doubt.

I envisioned scenario after scenario—two bad ones for every good one—until sometime in the middle of the night I decided that I wasn't accomplishing anything by tossing and turning. I propped myself up on one elbow and glanced at the time—almost five o'clock. It was too late to catch any sleep, so I might as well have a cup—or three—of java. And then what I would do was weave. I always did my best thinking at my loom.

I threw back the blankets and padded downstairs in my chenille bathrobe thrown over my favorite pajamas, light cotton covered with a print of shoes. Winston trotted along, hoping for a treat, no doubt. I fished a liver cookie from the tin on the kitchen counter and tossed it to him. He shot up and caught it in midair in a jump worthy of Shaquille O'Neal.

"So, you're not always a lazybones." I plugged in the coffeemaker. He was so busy chewing that he didn't even glance my way. "Ingrate."

A few minutes later I was back at my baby blanket project, weaving away with Winston lying at the foot of my loom, snoring—lucky dog.

I had decided to make blankets that measured thirty-six by forty-eight inches, made up of twelve-inch strips in a rosepath threading, with weft color and threading changed every twelve inches to make a sampler of variations. After a hundred forty-four inches of weaving I would have enough to cut the yardage into three strips, join them into a finished blanket, and bind it with a satin trim over the raw edges. Satisfied with my plan, I rummaged through my chest of skeins and selected enough white for the warp, and soft yellow and celery green yarns for the weft. Before long I was lost in the joy of measuring out my warp and starting to dress the loom.

I was halfway through the threading when I reached to pour myself a cup of coffee and found my pot was empty. I glanced at my watch. Ten twenty! Jenny was scheduled to stop by in a few minutes, and thankfully the warping board was ready for her. I put it down and was halfway up the stairs when the doorbell rang. I tightened my belt and hurried to the door.

"Jenny, hi."

She stepped inside, looking like a burst of sunshine in a gauzy fuchsia top and feather earrings. Her hair was tied back in an artfully messy ponytail. Damn, she looked good. Over her shoulder was a large straw bag. She looked me up and down, then muffled a giggle. I might as well have been wearing bunny slippers.

"Nice outfit. Am I early?" she asked, giving me a teasing smile.

"No, not at all. Sorry about . . ." I gestured vaguely toward my bathrobe. "I couldn't sleep, so I came down in the middle of the night to do some weaving. I didn't realize it was already morning."

"Don't worry about it. That's one of the perks of working from home. You don't have to get dressed if you don't want to." Her smile was infectious. "I have everything we need right here." She noticed Winston lumbering over. "Oh, and look who's here."

"Winston, say hello to Jenny." He sniffed her hand, unimpressed, and sat—hoping for a treat, no doubt. "Come on in. He's as sweet as a kitten."

"I know Winston. I'm just surprised that he's here."

I explained how Matthew and I had switched places and how Winston had hated being cooped up in my small condo. "But now that he's coming back, I'll probably move out, and then Winston will stay with Matthew." I bent down to scratch Winston behind the ear. "I'll miss you, Winnie." And then to Jenny, "Would you like a cup of coffee? I was just about to make a fresh pot. I'll run up and change while it drips."

She followed me to the kitchen. "You must be a mind reader. I'm dying for a cup of coffee. But why don't we get started measuring the warps and save the coffee for later?"

"That's a good idea. Have a seat." I offered her a chair. "How much do I owe you for the materials?"

She set the yarn on the floor and waved my question away with a flick of the wrist. "It wasn't much. Consider it a shop-warming gift. Besides, you'll be making me money, selling my goods." With that, she plopped her bag on the table. A minute later, my small kitchen table was covered with piles of woven wall hangings, rugs and place mats.

"These are wonderful," I exclaimed, picking up one of the rugs. It was so beautiful that I momentarily forgot about wanting to get dressed. Studying it, I saw it was made of rows of turquoise cotton strips interspersed with jute yarn.

"I tore up an old summer dress that I always loved, but was a bit out of date. This way, I can still enjoy it." She chuckled. She ran her hand over the rug. "I was trying for a casual, beachy effect. What do you think?"

"I think it's great. This is so creative. I would never have thought of mixing rows of cotton strips with rows of jute. It's beautiful."

"How do you like this one?" She pulled out a wall hanging made from the same materials, and I noticed the small shells and bits of sea-glass beads threaded throughout. "I have coordinating place mats too." She sorted through the pile until she found them, and laid them out. "I made different color groupings in this style. Do you think they'll sell?"

"I'm sure they will. They're great. Show me the others." I put the place mats down and riffled through the rest of her projects, pausing to admire each one. "This one is gorgeous," I exclaimed over another rug, woven from an assortment of heavy yarns and cotton strips intermingled with occasional strips of faux fur.

"I'm glad you like them. I'm a bit unorthodox when it comes to weaving. I just use anything I have—outdated clothes, old curtains, even an old tweed coat and a faux-fur jacket."

"I can't believe how creative you are. I'll take as many of your pieces as you'll let me have." I put down the rug I was admiring. "Let me run up and change. I'll be back in a second," I called over my shoulder as I hurried away.

I returned, having copied Susan Wood's outfit of the previous night, a pair of plain jeans and a white shirt with rolled-up sleeves—but with my four-inch wedge sandals, I didn't quite pull off the casual country look. What can I say? I prefer looking at the world from a height of five feet four rather than five feet nothing.

I stepped into the shop and stopped in surprise. All of Jenny's items were already displayed. A few were on the table in front of the window. Some hung from the doors of the hutch, and others still were nicely folded on the seat of a chair. I looked around, delighted.

She spun around to face me, looking embarrassed. "I hope you don't mind—"

"Are you kidding? I love it. I didn't have near enough stock. In fact, this place could use even more merchandise."

"I thought it looked very Zen." I caught the amusement in her eye and laughed.

"That's just your way of saying I'm right. It still needs more merchandise, doesn't it?"

She smiled. "Those are your words, not mine." She was just being too nice to admit the truth.

"I have a few boxes of yarns in the garage. I might as well get them." Winston appeared heartbroken as we left the house by the back door. He whined.

"I'll be back," I promised. He slunk back to his favorite spot and plopped down on the rug, looking wounded.

Jenny followed me to the garage. She looked around at the shelves upon shelves of car parts. The cement floor was covered with countless oil stains. In the far corner was a jumble of tools, car jacks and dollies.

"Wow. Will you look at this place? I knew Matthew was into antique cars, but I had no idea he collected all this stuff." She chuckled. "You know how he is. He likes to do most of the repairs himself."

Actually, I hadn't had a clue, and for some reason it bothered me to know that she clearly knew him better than I did. I went to the stack of boxes against the far wall and began opening them, looking for those with the yarn.

"Let me help," said Jenny, tackling the next stack. "Looks like he keeps his man cave neater than his house. So, when is he moving back?" she asked casually—maybe too casually—as she handed me the drill.

"He's driving down today. He said he'd be leaving sometime this afternoon." I shrugged. "I expect he'll be here around four."

She paused, an opened box at her feet. "How do you feel about it?"

"What part?" I asked. "Him moving back? Or my moving out?"

She laughed and picked up another box. "Both."

Just as casually I said, "I hate the idea of moving. It means having to set up all over again." I picked up the next box and opened it. "Here they are." A minute later I had found both boxes of yarn. She followed me back into the house and we set up in the studio.

"What about staying here? Don't you think the house is large enough for two people?"

Much as I liked Jenny, this was a subject I felt uncomfortable discussing until I figured out my own feelings about sharing a house with a man—even though the man in question was one I had known my whole life. I shrugged. "I don't know. I've been living on my own for a long time."

She started measuring a cone of yarn. "I'm just learning to live alone again after ten years of marriage, so I totally understand. There's something to be said about not having to share the television remote, isn't there?" Then she abruptly changed the subject. "I'm not sure how I feel about David Swanson—you know, about his anger management issue. I kept trying to interpret his aura, but I couldn't get a reading on him."

"You see auras?" I half expected her to be joking, but when I glanced at her, I saw she was serious.

She smiled, looking embarrassed. "I know what you're thinking." I shook my head, but she went on, "I'm not crazy. I've been seeing auras since I was a child. In fact, until I was about ten years old, I thought everybody saw them." She chuckled. "You have no idea how much I can tell about a person just by reading their aura. I know when they're lying." She said this as if it were self-evident. "I can also tell if a woman is in love, or if she's pregnant. I can tell when someone is sick, when they're in danger. Sometimes I can even sense death." She hesitated, then went on. "Just between you and me, I knew something would happen to Dolores's husband about a week before he died."

I gasped, shocked. Could she really be serious about sensing death? Now this was more than weird. It was spooky.

"You don't believe me."

"No, no. It's just that—you knew he was going to die?"

Jenny tilted her head, looking pensive. "Well, I didn't know that he would die—only that he was surrounded by danger."

Call it silly, but I found that a lot less unnerving than her claim of being able to predict death.

"I didn't know him well, but I happened to see him at Bottoms Up a few days before he died," she said, naming a local restaurant. "He stopped by my table to chat, and his aura was so dark it was almost opaque."

She turned and peered at me through her lashes, as if she were trying to read my mind.

I squirmed. "You're staring at me."

"Don't move. I'm trying to get a reading."

I grimaced. "Please don't tell me I'm going to die."

She chuckled, and to my relief the spell was broken. "You have a very nice yellow aura with a tinge of orange, which means you are a creative person and that you have a sunny disposition. And, just in case you wondered, you're not pregnant," she added with a smile.

I chuckled. "Now *that* would have been a real surprise." As for the rest of her reading, anyone who met me would know I was creative, but I decided to be nice. "Wow. You're really good."

"Thanks. What sign are you?" she asked, and then, "Wait, wait. Don't tell me. Let me guess." She leaned in and studied me, her eyes boring into mine. And then she smiled victoriously. "You are a Capricorn—no, no, you're an Aries. I'm right, aren't I?"

"I am." This time I was sincerely surprised. As long as she stuck to horoscopes, I didn't mind playing along. "How can you tell?"

She giggled, shrugging. "Oh, I don't know. It's just one of those things I do." She dismissed the subject with a wave. "But getting back to David Swanson, the atmosphere got so gloomy after he showed up. I've rarely felt such negative energy. It felt almost evil."

"Evil! That's a pretty strong word."

"I know. I have to admit that sometimes"—she tilted her head thoughtfully—"in a room full of people, it can be difficult to tell where a particular energy is coming from." She raised an eyebrow. "You wouldn't believe the stories I've heard about him."

I paused, cone in hand. "What kind of stories?"

"Different versions of what happened between him and Jeremy Fox—he's the man David threatened," she explained. "Don't get me wrong. David had ample reason to hate the guy's guts. Jeremy broke his sister's heart by two-timing her with David's own wife."

My jaw dropped. I must have looked shocked because she said, "That's right. Rather sordid, isn't it? The first account I heard was exactly as David told it yesterday—that he grabbed Jeremy by the lapel and threatened to kill him. But there's another one going around—that Jeremy had to be rushed to the hospital after David nearly strangled him to death. And if that one's not bad enough, I just heard another one while I was waiting in line at Mercantile's this morning—that he was waving a gun in Jeremy's face and that it had to be wrested away from him."

"Oh, my God. Did he really have a gun?"

She shook her head. "Of course not, but Briar Hollow is a small town. I swear, sometimes I think gossiping must be the number one form of entertainment around here." She gave me a sheepish smile. "I hate to admit it, but I'm sometimes guilty of it too."

"I can't imagine you being mean in any way. But getting back to David—he seemed very charming yesterday. I told him I wasn't sure that I'd be moving, but he still offered to show me a few places."

"He's a real estate agent. It's his job." She grinned. "Did you see the way Marnie Potter grabbed his arm and pushed Dolores out of the way?"

I laughed. "I sure did. And I also saw the look on Dolores's face."

"For a widow who lost her husband just a few months ago, she sure seems to have recovered fast, don't you think?"

"That recently?" I asked, surprised. For some reason, I'd imagined it had happened years ago.

"In mid-January—just a couple of months before you moved here." She paused, then said, "Greg Hanson was a well-respected businessman—real estate holdings all over the state. And filthy rich," she added in a whisper. "The strange part about it is that he was an avid hiker. He went hiking by himself one day and never came home. A search party went out the next day and they found his body at the bottom of the Devil's Courthouse."

"The . . . what?"

"The Devil's Courthouse—that's the name of the mountain. It has a really popular trail, maybe half a mile long. People climb all the way to the top to enjoy the view. Sometimes people have picnics there. The point is, the trail is moderate to difficult, and Greg Hanson was an expert hiker. When Dolores was told that he was dead, she cried 'murder' to anyone who would listen. According to her, her husband could have hiked that trail blindfolded, and the idea that he would fall to his death from such an easy trail was preposterous."

I shuddered at the mental image of a shattered and bleeding body at the bottom of a cliff. "But it really was a hiking accident, right?"

Jenny shrugged. "Just between you and me, I'm not sure what to think. On the one hand, Dolores Hanson claims he was murdered, but she's a drama queen— always vying for attention." She looked thoughtful for a moment. "I sometimes wonder if maybe she's right."

"But you just—"

Looking as if she regretted her words, she shook her head. "That's true. Forget what I said." She paused for a second. "On the other hand, Greg Hanson was a very rich man, and rich men sometimes make enemies. You know who had the most to gain from his death?" She paused for a beat before answering her own question. "Dolores."

I tilted my head. "Are you going to tell me you have a feeling about this?" She remained quiet, avoiding my eyes. "Crap, I wanted to live in a nice, safe town. I sure hope there isn't a killer running around loose in Briar Hollow."

Jenny slapped a hand over her mouth. "Oh, damn. I didn't want to say anything that would turn you off Briar Hollow, but I've been doing exactly that for the last half hour." She looked at me, embarrassed. "You must think I'm a real bitch."

I laughed. "Not at all. You didn't frighten me one bit."

A twinkle lit her eyes. "I didn't? Oh, well, let me try again." She giggled, and in the next breath she stood up. "The warp is done. We're ready to dress the student looms." Half an hour later, we had everything under control.

Jenny brushed her hands off. "Now how about that cup of coffee you promised?"

Chapter 4

Jenny followed me back to the kitchen and propped herself on the stool at the counter. I pulled out a bag of dog treats and gave one to Winston.

"There. Friends again, right?"

He didn't even look up, chewing his beef jerky with relish. I got the coffee from the cupboard and was measuring it out into the filter when the doorbell rang.

"I'll get that for you." Jenny hopped up and hurried down the hall with Winston in plodding pursuit.

I heard the door open and close, and voices growing closer. A second later Jenny appeared, followed by Marnie Potter. Today the redhead's hair was tied in an old-fashioned Katharine Hepburn bun, which contrasted sharply with her checkered pink shirt and floral print pants. She carried a straw basket full of fresh muffins. If not for her outrageous outfit, she would have looked like an older, overweight version of Bree Van de Kamp from *Desperate Housewives*. I stifled a chuckle.

"I brought you some home-baked goodies." She set the basket on the table. She pointed her chin toward the coffeemaker and said, "Is that freshly ground coffee I smell? Got enough for an extra cup?"

"Sure do." I measured a few more tablespoons of coffee into the filter.

She pulled out a chair and sat down so hard I had a sudden vision of Marnie sitting on the floor surrounded by chair debris. She had barely sat when she jumped back up and hurried to the back door, swinging it open. "Good God, why is it so hot in this house?" She fanned herself, looking from Jenny to me. "Aren't you two hot?" And then seeing the surprise on our faces, she smiled crookedly and, leaving the door propped open, returned to her seat. "Oh, never mind. I came over here for a reason. There's something I want to run by you, Della." And with no further preamble she went straight to the point. "What would you say if I offered to work for you? I'm looking for part-time work, and I was thinking, you're in your shop all by yourself every day. Maybe you could use some help. I wouldn't charge much."

I turned on the coffeemaker, searching for a kind way to let her down. "That's nice of you, Marnie, but business is really slow so far. I haven't enough work to keep even one person busy right now."

She rolled her eyes. "I am not being *nice*. I need the work." She folded her arms, scowling. "I made a bad investment and unless I find some work soon, I might have to move out of my house."

"Oh, no. Poor you," Jenny said.

"Keep your sympathy. It was just plain stupidity on my part. I let that jerk Jeremy Fox talk me into investing in his condo project. I should have known better." She shook her head ruefully.

I paused, coffee container in one hand. "Jeremy Fox—isn't he the fellow David Swanson attacked?"

"One and the same," said Marnie, absently patting Winston, who had sidled up to her, probably in hopes of a muffin—the bum. "This dog reminds me of my Brutus," she said. "I had him for eleven years." She was quiet for a moment. "Much as I still miss that old dog, the person who was most upset when he died last year was Mercedes. I never saw anyone cry over a dog as much as she did."

Jenny turned to me. "Mercedes walked that dog before and after school every day since she was ten years old." She turned back to Marnie. "Don't be too hard on yourself about investing in Jeremy's project. From what I hear, you're not the only person he took for a ride."

"Please, let's not talk about him," she said impatiently. "I get upset every time I think about how gullible I was. I swear I'd kill that man if I thought I could get away with it."

Chapter 5

Seeing the alarm on my face, she said, "Oops. I didn't mean to shock you."

Jenny folded her arms. "Believe me, you're not the only person around here who would like to see Jeremy disappear. In fact, I'm surprised he hasn't skipped town."

Marnie passed the basket around, turning the conversation back to her initial subject. "Don't you take a day off once in a while?"

I selected a lemon and poppy-seed muffin. "I'm sure I will at some point. But I can't afford to hire anyone until business picks up." She looked so disappointed that I felt compelled to add, "How about this? The minute it does, I'll give you a call."

"I'd like that." She gave us a forced smile.

"But in the meantime I can sell your weaving," I reminded her, breaking into my muffin.

Her face fell. "Oh, shoot. I plumb forgot about that. I'll bring it by tomorrow."

"You can drop if off anytime during shop hours. Otherwise I might not be here."

"Okay, I'll do that." Now that she'd completed her business, she looked at Jenny and then back to me, changing the subject yet again. "So what were you two talking about before I so rudely barged in?"

"Nothing really," Jenny said, munching on something that looked like a caramel-pecan muffin. "Oh, my God, this is so good." She flicked a loose strand of hair behind her ear, sending her feather earring fluttering. "Della was telling me all about her plans for the store." That was a complete fabrication, but better I supposed than admitting we had been gossiping about members of the weaving group, including Marnie herself.

I was sinking into a comfortable sugar high. "I want to stir up more interest in my shop. I know there must be something I can do other than sit around and wait for customers to show up. I just haven't figured out what yet."

"What did you do before moving here?" Something in the way she looked at me made me believe she already knew all about me. After all, the papers had dragged my reputation through the mud for weeks until the real embezzler was caught. It was a miracle nobody in Briar Hollow had recognized me from my pictures in the media.

"I suspect you already know, don't you?" I waited for her reaction.

Marnie had the grace to blush. "I'm sorry. You're right. I recognized you immediately, but I can't say that I read any of the articles."

I seriously doubted that. In fact, I was willing to bet she'd practically memorized every libelous word written about me.

Jenny's eyes darted from me to Marnie and back again. "What is she talking about?"

"You'll probably hear all about it, so I might as well tell you myself. To make a long story short, I used to be a financial analyst for an investment firm. Six months ago I came across evidence that my boss was embezzling from the company. When I confronted him, he begged me to wait twenty-four hours before calling the SEC." I scowled, remembering. "He said he wanted to make restitution before turning himself in. And—fool that I was—I believed him. Of course, to the SEC, the fact that I didn't report him until the next day made me look guilty."

"Poor you." Jenny sounded genuinely shocked.

"But then he disappeared, and that made her look even guiltier," Marnie chimed in. I was right. Marnie did know every detail of the case.

Jenny's head swiveled from Marnie to me. "He disappeared?"

"He pulled a fast one. The next day, when I called the SEC, he had vanished. He was apprehended three weeks later, trying to cross the border into Mexico—three weeks during which I was questioned, charged, arraigned and released on a one-million-dollar bond, borrowed from my mother. Even after he was caught, a lot of people still thought I was guilty. In the end, I was able to clear my name only by providing evidence against him."

Jenny's eyes widened. "Oh, my God!"

I let out a long sigh. "Testifying against my boss, as it turned out, caused another set of problems. In the financial industry, blowing the whistle on a superior is professional suicide. It's almost worse than embezzling."

Marnie laughed ruefully. "Maybe because they all seem to think it's okay to steal from clients."

I gave a half smile and said, "Rather than look for another job in the industry, I decided it was time for a change." I shrugged. "So, here I am, doing what I always wanted to do—operating a weaving shop and studio."

The women were quiet until Jenny said, "I'm not sure I'd have the guts to just pick up and go like that. It was incredibly brave of you."

I smiled crookedly. "A few of my friends said the same thing, but they made the word 'brave' sound more like 'crazy.' I wouldn't be surprised if they placed bets on how long I would last here." I grew thoughtful, remembering how overwhelming the decision to move had been.

Marnie leaned forward to pat my hand. "I'm sorry I asked. It was really none of my business."

I waved her apology away. "I don't know why I wanted to keep it a secret. It's not as if I did anything wrong."

Jenny nodded. "That's right. You didn't. In fact, what you did was heroic."

"I feel exactly the same way," Marnie said. "The fact that you turned him in, in spite of the problems it caused you, makes me respect you all the more."

"Thank you. That's nice of you."

Marnie got a faraway look in her eyes. "Crazy, isn't it, the way life is a continuous string of starting-overs? You get divorced—people tell you you're starting a new life. You go through the change, they say, 'This will be the better half of your life.' You make a bad investment—" She shrugged. "They say, 'Don't worry. It's not too late to start over.' So here I am. I'm fifty-four, single, and look-ing for a job." She said all of this with a bright smile, but suddenly the smile cracked and tears hovered on her lashes. She fished in her pants pocket, pulled out a lacy handkerchief and dabbed at her eyes. "I'm so sorry. I don't know what's come over me."

I looked around for a box of tissues. "Can I get you anything?"

"I could sure use that cup of coffee. Is it ready yet?"

"Coming right up." I hopped off my chair and brought the pot to the table. "Here you go." I poured coffee all around.

"I'm sure everything will work out somehow." Marnie took a deep gulp from her cup. "Doesn't it always? Anyhow, enough about me." She looked around as if searching for a new subject to talk about. Her eyes fell on me again. "I know it's none of my business, Della, but have you ever been married?"

"No." I picked up my coffee. "Don't you just love this coffee?" My attempt at changing the subject was not successful.

"Ever been in love?" The woman didn't know the meaning of minding her own business.

I felt the heat rise to my face.

"You're in love right now, aren't you?" Jenny leaned in as if trying to read me. "I can see it in your eyes."

"Not in the least." I held back from adding that she obviously wasn't very good at reading auras after all. "My last relationship was a long time ago."

"What happened?" Marnie asked.

I chose an orange-cranberry muffin that looked good enough to die for, and passed the basket around again. "It's the old story. I loved him, and he loved somebody else." I said this in a way meant to change the subject.

"How long exactly?" Jenny was clearly also oblivious to hints.

I shrugged. "Oh, a couple of years ago."

"Does he live in Charlotte?" *Good grief, will she never stop?*

"In Charlotte—yes—and now let's please change the subject. It's over and done with and I'm here now. As you said, I'm starting a new life."

Jenny poured herself another cup of coffee. "Do you want a refill, Marnie?" The redhead shook her head. Jenny stirred milk into her coffee and said, "Did you know that Matthew is moving back to Briar Hollow and now Della has to find a new place to live?"

I took another long, steadying swallow of coffee.

Marnie nodded, her double chins quivering like gelatin. "So I overheard last night. But why would you have to move out? I mean, from what I gathered, you and he are childhood friends."

"Where did you hear that?" I asked, surprised.

"Oh, people talk," she said vaguely, and I realized my name had already been fodder for the gossip mill. It was a disconcerting thought. "Besides, this house has more than one bedroom, doesn't it?"

"It has three bedrooms, but my shop and studio have taken over the living room and dining room, and all the furniture is piled up in one of the rooms upstairs. Unless Matthew spends all his free time in the kitchen and his bedroom, there's nowhere else for him to go. It just wouldn't be fair. Besides, it could be a bit awkward for him and me to live together. For one thing, he'll probably want his privacy when Blondie—I mean Amanda—

comes to visit." I must have blushed, because Marnie gave me a slow, knowing smile.

Jenny's eyes widened. "Oh, didn't you know? He and Amanda broke up."

What? How come I hadn't heard about this? "When did that happen?"

Jenny looked thoughtful. "I guess it must have been early in the new year. He told me that he had feelings for somebody else. When I asked who, he refused to say."

So he was already involved with someone else. Why was it that some men could not be without a girlfriend for a second? "Hello-o." Marnie waved a hand in front of my face.

I snapped back. "Oh, uh, did you say something?"

The older woman must have taken pity on me because she gave me an almost imperceptible nod and changed the subject — at long last.

"By the way, you're right. This is really good coffee."

"Jamaican Blue Mountain — it's crazy expensive. We might as well enjoy it because when this bag is finished, I won't be able to afford it again anytime soon."

Jenny poured in another drop of milk and stirred, looking pensive. "I used to dream of starting my own business too, you know. I wanted to start a tea salon where I could do aura and tarot readings."

I almost laughed. *Tarot readings? Really?*

"But I have no sense when it comes to numbers. I'd go under in no time."

To my surprise, Marnie was nodding enthusiastically. "I think that's a brilliant idea. I love having my fortune told. And I know a lot of women who see astrologists and clairvoyants regularly."

She had a point. Just because I scoffed at that kind of stuff didn't mean others didn't believe in it. Besides, if this was Jenny's dream, who was I to laugh? My own dream sounded just as nutty to a lot of people. "You don't have to be good with numbers to run a successful business. Most successful business owners don't do everything themselves."

Marnie jumped in. "That's what employees are for."

Jenny looked doubtful. "Maybe."

"Marnie's right. Why don't you make a business plan?" She looked at me as if I'd just sprouted a second head. "I can help you if you like."

Marnie seemed to be getting more and more excited at the idea. "If you open a tea shop, you'll need cakes, and muffins, and cookies. I can bake all of that for you. You do like my muffins, don't you?" She slid the basket across the table toward Jenny. "Here, have another."

She put a hand up in protest. "I love them, thanks, but I'm full."

Marnie pulled the basket away almost regretfully. And then her eyes twinkled. "Here's what I'll do. I'll make a list of all my favorite recipes and you can pick whatever you want for your menu."

Jenny rested her chin in her hand. "Whoa. Not so fast. Let's see. I'd need to hire an accountant. I'd also have to rent a space, buy tables and chairs and dishes and . . ." She smiled. "I *could* do all that, if I only had the money." She let herself fall against the back of the chair, chuckling. "I guess I'll have to stick to what I'm doing now.

There's nothing wrong with working part-time at Franny's."

Marnie pouted. "Oh, well. It was a fun dream."

"What's Franny's?" I asked.

Marnie's eyes widened, "You've never been to Franny's? Oh, you must go. I buy all my clothes there."

I almost laughed. I *so* didn't see myself wearing floral or zebra pants like hers, or for that matter, yoga pants and gauzy tops like Jenny's—unless I was willing to give up eating, which I was not. And to punctuate that thought, I took another bite of my muffin.

Jenny nodded enthusiastically. "It's at the other end of Main Street. I'm there three mornings a week. If you come by, you can tell me what you like and I'll get it for you with my employee's discount."

Marnie said, "I'd ask you to do the same for me, but—" She patted her ample stomach. "We're hardly the same size. It would be difficult to convince Francine you were buying them for yourself." I didn't bother pointing out that being almost a foot shorter, I wasn't exactly Jenny's size either.

In spite of the fact that Jenny was rather flaky and Marnie was more than just a little pushy, there was something so forthcoming about these women that I really liked them. As the conversation wound down, I found myself making them promise to drop by again the next day.

Chapter 6

After washing the dishes and putting them away, I returned to my project, finished warping the loom and soon lost myself in the rhythm of my work.

I had just wound a bobbin with blue yarn and was starting a point twill when the doorbell chimed. I put down my shuttle and was walking toward the door when two women stepped in. I glanced at my watch—already past one. Time had flown.

The first woman was a middle-aged blonde in a business suit. "Hi, I'm Kate Radley." She strode purposefully over to me and handed me her business card. I glanced at the second woman as she turned toward one of my display tables. It was Susan Wood from my class.

"I've been meaning to drop by," Kate went on. "I understand you've just moved into town. Welcome to Briar Hollow."

"Nice to meet you, Mrs. Radley—"

"Oh, please call me Kate."

At that moment Susan turned toward me. "I was telling Kate about all your beautiful linens and how much fun I had last night."

"Thank you. I had a good time too." Returning to

Kate, I introduced myself. "I'm Della Wright. Call me Della." I glanced at the card in my hand, recognizing the logo of the company. "You're with Cottage and Castle Realties."

"Yes, I am. If you ever want to look at properties, give me a call." I couldn't help but wonder if Susan hadn't told her I had already promised to go house-shopping with David.

Susan put down the tablecloth she had been admiring and crossed the room to look at the items in the maple hutch. She picked up one of my dish towels. "These are the towels I told you about," she called over her shoulder to Kate.

Kate went to take a look. "They're almost too nice to use." She turned over the price tag, her forehead furrowing. "That's a lot of money for a dish towel." She closed her eyes, calculating under her breath. "But I suppose it's reasonable for something that's handwoven." She turned to Susan. "You're right. These would make wonderful housewarming gifts for my clients." She counted out the pile of towels, picked them all up and brought them to my desk. "I'll take all of these."

"You just made my day." I carefully folded each one in tissue paper. "I'm glad you like them. I made them myself."

"You did?" She looked thoughtful. "Do you think you could add a small card saying something like 'Handmade by Della Wright'?"

"Already done." I unfolded one of the towels and indicated the thick cream-colored tag tucked inside. I had spent a small fortune on those tags, but they looked so rich with their gold lettering, they made each of my items seem more precious.

"Would you like me to gift-wrap these for you? It's no trouble."

She beamed. "That would be perfect." She glanced at her watch. "I don't have time to wait right now. How about if I pick them up in a few hours?" She turned to Susan. "Or maybe you can pick them up. Susan is my office assistant."

"I didn't know you worked for the same company as David."

"I've been there for years."

Kate leaned in, whispering dramatically, "When Susan told me that David had joined your group I couldn't believe my ears. I can't imagine David taking weaving classes." Her eyes narrowed and she smirked as she searched my face. "Did he happen to tell you *why* he joined the weaving group?"

"Yes, he did." I was beginning to suspect the real reason for this shopping excursion—gossip. Something else occurred to me as well. If it was common knowledge that David would be joining my group, that could explain why I'd had so many volunteers. Some of them might have been there looking for new gossip—a small town's favorite activity, or at least this small town's. My heart sank a little. Hopefully they wouldn't leave when nothing eventful happened.

Susan wandered over to join us.

Kate continued her tale, bubbling with excitement. "I was there when it happened," she gushed. "I couldn't believe it. I thought he was going to kill Jeremy. If I hadn't stepped in, I swear he might have."

"Oh, come on, Kate. I was there too, remember? All he did was grab Jeremy by his shirt collar. And you didn't exactly save Jeremy either."

I laughed. "And to think that I moved here believing Briar Hollow was a sleepy little town."

Kate's eyes lit up again. "Don't you believe that for one second. If you heard the stories about a few of the folks around here, your hair would stand on end. Why, even the chief of police was saying that—"

"Don't you have an appointment in a few minutes, Kate?" Susan asked. "We'd better go. You don't want to be late." They were halfway out the door when Susan called over her shoulder. "I'll be back to pick up the towels. If I don't make it today, I'll be by tomorrow."

"I'm open from one to six on weekdays," I reminded her. A moment later, the doorbell tinkled behind them. Through the window, I noticed Kate turning to say something to Susan Wood. From the look on the assistant's face, I guessed she was getting a tongue-lashing. I chuckled. Jenny was right about one thing. Gossip was a popular pastime in Briar Hollow. If not for her office assistant's interruption, I suspected Kate would have regaled me with juicy stories about every Briar Hollow resident and his uncle.

I became aware that my stomach was growling, and when I looked at the time I saw that it was already one thirty. Yikes! Matthew was due to arrive in a few hours, and I hadn't even started moving my things out of the main bedroom. There were sheets to change and my new room to set up. I had to get going, but first—food. I hurried to the kitchen and, keeping an open ear for the doorbell, made myself a hero sandwich — salami, cheese, tomatoes, lettuce and jalapeños with a side of potato chips. I carried it to the desk. All at once, a sleepy Winston became alert. He stumbled to his feet and lumbered over, licking his chops.

"Sorry, Winnie, this is people food." Other than his ears flickering, he didn't budge. "What is this, a staring contest?" I took a bite, trying to ignore his soulful gaze. "Go away, Winston. Shoo." He stood rooted to the floor, ogling my food.

"Oh, all right — but just a little piece." He raised himself on his hind legs, trembling with anticipation as he watched me tear off a piece of Monterey Jack.

I held it over his head, ordering, "Sit." His butt hit the floor with a thump. "Good boy." I released the cheese and Winston snagged it in midair. A dog after my own heart — he liked food just as much as I did. I ate the rest of my sandwich, sharing the occasional bit with my buddy, who strolled away the minute it was time to clean up.

"Just like a man," I called after him. "As long as there's a possibility of food, you hang around. But when it's time to clean up, you're nowhere in sight."

Chapter 7

The afternoon flew by in a frenzy of moving, organizing and cleaning—unfortunately without a single client coming to the door. I was looking forward to seeing Matthew again and for the occasion had changed into my favorite outfit—a short red linen dress, dangly gold earrings and my hottest shoes—red high-heeled Kate Spades. *This proves it*, I thought. *The city side of me is not entirely gone.* I posed in front of the mirror behind my bedroom door and sighed. Designer shoes were another luxury my new life would no longer allow. I put on some lip gloss and smacked my lips together.

At four o'clock I was back at my loom, hurrying to the window every time I heard a car. By six o'clock, I'd concluded that Matthew would not be arriving today. I was sure that any minute he would call to tell me he'd get here tomorrow instead. I had just resumed weaving when the doorbell rang. I slipped my shoes back on, hurried over with a beaming smile and flung open the door.

"Oh, er, hi." I tried to cover my surprise. It wasn't Matthew but David Swanson.

"Hi there, I hope I'm not too early?" I gave myself a mental head thump as I remembered our house-hunting appointment. He gave me a quick once-over, his eyes lingering at the edge of my short dress. "Wow. You look great."

"Thanks," I said, hoping he didn't think I'd dressed up for him.

I glanced at my watch, feigning shock. "Is it six thirty already? Sorry, I was weaving, and time just flew by. Let me grab my purse and I'll be right with you." Winston followed me expectantly. "Sorry, Winnie. You'll have to stay here." Under his reproachful glare, I closed the kitchen door and hurried back to the front.

A minute later David helped me into his Volvo and we took off.

"The first place I want you to see is half a mile down the street. It's a little house very similar to Matthew's. You could set up the front rooms for your business, the same way you're set up now."

"How much is the rent?"

"The owner is asking five hundred a month for a minimum two-year lease. That's low even by Briar Hollow standards." He slowed to a stop in front of a ratty-looking place. "Here we are."

I took in the house, its peeling paint and rickety front porch. "Good grief, it sure needs a ton of work." But for all its neglect, enough charm and character filtered through to make me think it was a possibility. I hopped out of the car and hurried across the street, as fast as my stilettos allowed. David unlocked the front door and we walked in.

"I don't think I've ever seen so much junk." I was startled at the amount of furniture in the room. It was so crowded with old bric-a-brac that I could hardly visualize how it would look once it was cleared of everything. I took a few steps, wondering how I was going to make my way through without getting dust all over my sexy dress.

Next to me, David nodded grimly. "Tell me about it. I've been begging the owner to get rid of everything for months, but he lives out of state and doesn't want to be bothered. Too much old stuff only makes the place less attractive to prospective buyers."

I wandered farther into the house, sidestepping an old table piled high with chairs, almost stumbling on a rocker. Upon closer inspection, I realized the furniture wasn't junk. It was just worn. A fresh coat of paint, a few sanded edges, and it could be transformed into perfectly attractive and serviceable shabby chic.

I walked through the rooms, noting the original tongue-and-groove walls, the scalloped trim in the fifties kitchen, the small maid's room at the back. On the second floor, I was pleasantly surprised at the claw-foot tub in the tiny bathroom.

"Does the house come furnished?" I asked, as an idea began forming in my mind. Instead of buying new furniture, I could refinish the pieces I needed. If I could paint walls, surely I could paint furniture. However, I'd hate to go to the trouble unless I owned it. "I'm not sure about the house, but I have an idea. If the owner wants to get rid of all this furniture, I might be interested in buying it."

David's eyes lit up. "I think that could be arranged. I know he doesn't want any of it. The only reason it's still here is that he doesn't want to pay for movers. I can probably get it for you for free."

"It'll depend on whether I move or not. I haven't quite made up my mind just yet. Anyhow, I'll think about it and let you know."

I followed him back downstairs, and at the front door I turned to look at the crowded rooms again.

"I like it," I said, more to myself than to David. The front room was large enough to accommodate a weaving studio at one end and my shop at the other. And the big bay window facing onto the street would be perfect for displays.

"I knew you would."

"But it sure needs a ton of work."

"I know, I know." He leaned against the doorframe. "That's why the rent is so low. But the location is perfect for a business. I really think this place could work for you."

I glanced around one last time before leaving. "If I do decide to get a place, maybe, but all that work would cost a—"

He put up a hand to stop me. "If this one isn't right for you, don't worry. I still have two more places I want you to see." He ushered me out, locked up and led the way back to the car. A few minutes later we pulled up in front of a bungalow on one of the side streets. The house was small, but the paint looked fresh and the lawn was perfectly manicured. It was certainly in better shape than the one I had just seen, but other than that, everything about it was wrong, starting with the location.

"This house is modern. It's in good shape and wouldn't need any fixing up. And the price is also really low."

I shook my head. "It won't work, David. It's already challenging enough to attract customers when I'm on Main Street. If I were to set up here, where foot traffic is almost nonexistent, I might as well admit defeat and return to Charlotte."

He chuckled. "Well, we don't want you to do that now, do we?" He turned the motor back on. "I have to admit, I would have been surprised if you liked this one. But as your agent, I have to show you every place that has even the slightest possibility. That's the only way you can make an informed decision." He put the car in gear and we drove on. "There's one more listing I want to show you." He turned onto Main Street again. This time he parked in front of the empty store I'd noticed on my walk last night. "I wanted you to see this one last, because it's by far the best."

I followed him to the entrance, where he struggled with the key until the front door creaked open. He reached along the wall and turned on the light.

The store consisted of one large room—larger even than I'd imagined last night—with gorgeous wide-plank floors and old-fashioned schoolhouse lights hanging from twelve-foot ceilings. I walked to the middle of the room and pivoted slowly, taking in the rest of the details. There were two large windows, both directly facing Main Street—nice for displays. Near the entrance was a built-in antique wood counter that cried out for an old chrome candy-shop cash register. Behind it, the wall was exposed brick, giving the room the kind of country charm that lovers of rustic decor spend fortunes trying to copy. This, however, was the real thing. It had the kind of patina that is almost impossible to replicate.

"How big is this store?"

"Twenty-five hundred square feet."

"Wow! That's huge." I pictured handwoven throw rugs scattered about, rocking chairs piled with throws and blankets, in one corner an antique cupboard stocked with kitchen cloths. I could have one window display with more-traditional woven goods and the other stocked with Jenny's more-modern work. My imagination was running a mile a minute, but I put a halt to it. There was no way I could fill all this space.

"I love it. It's wonderful. But it's way too big. I'd never—not in a million years—have enough stock to fill it. I need something half—correction—a quarter of this size. Besides, this place has to be a lot more than I can afford."

"Don't be so sure about that. The previous owner had a private mortgage and when she went bankrupt, the lender foreclosed on the building." He handed me the listing, and I glanced at the amount. Suddenly I noticed the words "For Sale" at the top.

"This isn't a rental," I exclaimed, handing him back the sheet of paper. "I can't afford to buy, David. You already know that. Why are you even showing me this place?"

"I know, I know. But I think you might want to consider it. Look at the asking price." He held the listing in front of my eyes again.

I hesitated. The idea that a monthly payment would

eventually result in owning a property was tempting, but I shook my head. "I'm already stuck with mortgage payments on a condo I'm trying to sell. I listed it almost six months ago and I still haven't had a single offer. So not only do I not have the money for a down payment, but even if I did, I would never qualify for a mortgage. I can't exactly show proof of regular income. Since the whole subprime crisis happened banks are extra careful in evaluating mortgage applicants." I shrugged. "If things were different—" I opened my hands helplessly.

"That's too bad." He slipped the listing back into his folder. "This will be the deal of the century for some lucky buyer. It comes with two apartments upstairs." He paused. "You know, with a thirty-year amortization and the income from the two apartments, your monthly payments wouldn't amount to much more than what you'd pay in rent."

I planted my hands on my hips. "Didn't you hear a word I just said?"

"I know, I know. But this is a small town. We don't have much available right now. I guess the first house I showed you is the only place that has everything you're looking for. It needs work, but the price is right." He nodded toward the door. "Shall we go?"

I was suddenly reluctant to leave. It was such a beautiful space. If only I could think of some way to make it work. "You said there are two apartments upstairs? How much would they rent for?"

David paused with his hand on the doorknob. "The larger unit has two bedrooms." He thought briefly and quoted a figure that made my eyes widen. "The second apartment is smaller. You'd get about half as much for that one."

"And they're included in the sale price?"

"Of course they are. The entire building is for sale, not just the store space. Do you want to take a quick look at them?"

Why I said yes, I'll never know. Not only was buying not a possibility, but the shop area was way too big. Still, I followed David up the old staircase, trying to think of a solution to those problems.

"Careful on that step." He pointed to a nail that was sticking out. "I should get a hammer and fix that before somebody breaks their neck." He glanced at my shoes. "I should have told you to wear flats."

"Don't worry. I won't trip." I'd been wearing high heels practically since I learned to walk, and stilettos were as comfortable to me as running shoes.

He stopped at the top of the stairs and fumbled through his key ring for a moment, then unlocked the door. He stood back to let me in.

I gasped. I was in a round foyer with beautiful old inlaid-wood floors. Beyond, I could see a living room with tall, slender windows. I walked farther and my hand went to my mouth. At the far end of the room was a fireplace with a mahogany mantel. Adjoining the living room was a dining room with built-in china cupboards, a plate rail all around the room and a coved ceiling. Just when I thought it couldn't get any better, I walked into the kitchen and stopped. I was looking at a forty-inch gas blacktop stove. It could have been the same model my grandmother used to own. "Oh, this is amazing!" I exclaimed, running my hand along the black counters with chrome edges. This kitchen brought back memories of Nana's pancakes, and of her secret-recipe dream cake, to this day my favorite. My mouth watered at the memory of the sweet dessert. "This looks as if it hasn't been renovated since the forties."

David leaned against the doorframe. "I know. Whoever buys this place should gut it and build a brand-new modern kitchen—tile floor, stainless-steel appliances, microwave fan. Maybe put in a laminate floor in the other rooms."

"Oh, no. I wasn't complaining when I said it was old. It's absolutely gorgeous. I love this place just the way it is."

His eyebrows bobbed. "You do?" He surveyed the room again, as if trying to see the place through my eyes. He nodded, slowly. "I guess it does have a certain charm, if you go for that kind of stuff."

"I take it you don't."

He shook his head. "I like modern. But to each his own."

"Will you look at that?" I was drooling over the old porcelain sink complete with drain board. "It would be terrible to tear this place down. Believe me, if I could afford it, I would buy it in a New York minute. I could definitely live here."

"Want to see the bedrooms?"

I just knew this would only torture me more, but I couldn't stop now. I followed him down the hall. The first bedroom had old yellowed wallpaper, but in spite of the faded walls, it still looked pretty. The second bedroom was small, more like a nursery than a full-size room, making it perfect for an office or a small den. I popped my head into the bathroom and noted the claw-foot tub with the large chrome showerhead. *Damn it! I* love *this apartment.*

As if he could read my mind, David said, "I told you you'd love it. Come, I'll show you the other apartment." I didn't need any coaxing. I was dying to see what other treasures this building held.

He fumbled with the key for a second, and then to his surprise the door swung open. "Somebody must have forgotten to lock up."

I had just walked in when I heard voices coming from the back room. "There's somebody here." I turned to leave.

"Don't worry. It's probably just another agent—" And then the blood drained from his face. I turned to see a couple step out of a room.

The woman—a sexy, pouty blonde—stopped and sneered. "David! What are you doing here?"

"I could ask you the same thing," he replied, his face a mask of cold fury.

"I don't have to tell you anything." She looked amused rather than frightened.

The tall, handsome man, who until then had not said a word, wrapped a possessive arm around the blonde. "Well, well, will you look at who's out of jail? Do you still want to kill me? Come on, Swanson. Take your best shot. I dare you."

I had a sudden vision of fists flying and noses getting bloodied. I grabbed David by the arm. "Let's go." He stood his ground, hands fisted, jaw clenched, but regardless of his frozen stance, I could feel him ready to pounce.

"What's the matter? Not so brave anymore?" The man's lips were stretched into something that looked more like a snarl than a smile. He laughed, and then, looking bored, he said, "Why don't you do yourself a favor? Turn around and get the fuck out of my sight, unless you want to get arrested again."

So this was Jeremy Fox. I studied him, not liking anything I saw. But who was the sexy blonde? And all at once, any concern I might have had about David Swanson having an anger management issue vanished. I didn't even know the Fox guy and I had a crazy urge to wipe the smirk off his face. He made my skin crawl.

"Come on, David. Let's get out of here. You can show me the apartment some other time."

His face underwent a range of emotions—rage, uncertainty and finally acceptance. When he turned to leave, I had to restrain myself from patting his back in sympathy. We scampered down the stairs and across the street. I barely had time to close the car door before he stepped on the gas and we took off, tires squealing.

"Thanks for getting me out of there," David muttered, breaking the heavy silence. "I came this close to losing my cool." He held up his thumb and index finger half an inch apart.

"What did he mean about you being out of jail?"

He shook his head, looking pale. "He was just being stupid. I was only in custody for a couple of hours, until my sister posted bail." He was silent for a moment, and then he shuddered. "I don't feel so good."

No sooner were those words out of his mouth than he swung to the side of the road and screeched to a stop. He rested his forehead on the steering wheel, his breath coming in gasps. "Sorry." His voice was shaking. He sat up abruptly, stumbled out of the car and around to the back. Poor guy. The confrontation had upset him more than he wanted to let on. I waited in the car, a dozen questions rolling around in my mind—questions I would never ask. They would only embarrass him more.

A few minutes later he returned, looking slightly jaundiced. "Listen, Della, I want to apologize about what happened back there. It was completely unforgivable on my part to put you in the middle of it. I would understand if you—"

"Don't be silly. You didn't do anything, David. That man is a jerk."

He answered my silent question. "That was my ex-wife, by the way."

I turned to look at him. "She's . . . Really?"

He nodded. "That's what the argument with Jeremy was about. He was involved with my sister and broke her heart by two-timing her with my wife." He grimaced. "He's a real piece of work." He added, "As it turns out, so is she."

I was slack-jawed for a moment, reeling from this revelation. It was too awful for words, and I couldn't imagine how betrayed he must have felt. "Wow! No wonder you lost control. You *do* deserve a medal for the restraint you showed."

"Thanks for saying that. God only knows why Jeremy was showing her that apartment."

"Is Jeremy a real estate agent?"

"Yes," he said, sounding bitter. "Which, as far as I'm concerned, is completely unethical on his part. He is also a developer and should not sell his own project—conflict of interest. An agent is supposed to represent his client, not himself."

There was an uncomfortable silence during which his eyes bored into mine. He must have seen what he was looking for, because he let out a sigh of relief.

He started the car and turned onto the road. When we neared the house, I spotted Matthew's antique Triumph TR6 behind my Jeep, and my heart did a somersault.

"Looks like you have company. Is that Matthew's car?"

"Of course you would know Matthew."

He chuckled. "We were in high school and played football together. Besides, this is a small town. Everybody—"

"—knows everybody in Briar Hollow."

He attempted a smile, but it didn't reach his eyes. "Say hello to him for me."

"I'll do that," I said, stepping out of the car. I closed the door, waved good-bye to him and watched his car disappear down the street. *What a nice man he is*, I thought, feeling sorry for him. David probably wanted no more than what anybody else wanted—to have someone who loved him, somebody he could love back. I felt sad for him. Was he going home or heading to a bar to get drunk? And for some reason I couldn't explain, I had the bad feeling that David Swanson's troubles were about to get much worse.

Uh-oh. I'm starting to sound like Jenny, I thought, chuckling.

Next, I'd be seeing auras too.

Chapter 8

I shook off the pall that had descended on me and crossed the street.

"Hello-o, anybody home?" I called out, pushing the door open. A second later Winston came galloping over, almost knocking me down in his excitement.

He whipped out his tongue, giving me a sloppy kiss. "I love you too, Winnie," I said, wiping my cheek with the back of my hand. "But please spare me those wet kisses."

From the kitchen, I could hear music and the sound of laughter—Matthew on the phone. But to my surprise, when I walked in, Matthew was not on the phone, but clinking glasses with—of all people—Jenny. And right there, in the middle of the table, was *my* bottle of sparkling white wine—the one I'd bought to toast his new writing career. I struggled to keep my smile from evaporating.

He grinned and raised a glass toward me, saying, "Hey, there you are, kiddo. Come join the party."

Matthew was good-looking in a clean-cut sort of way, more of a Tom Hanks than a Tom Cruise. He was almost six feet tall, with dark hair and eyes that kept changing color. I'd seen them get very dark when he was angry and almost golden when he laughed. At this moment they were golden.

He tore his eyes away from Jenny, who had changed into a white off-the-shoulder sweater that she kept tugging back up, making her tanned shoulders all the more noticeable—and poured a glass of wine for me. He gestured to the bottle. "Hope you don't mind I helped myself. I'll replace it tomorrow."

"No, no. That's okay. I got it for you, to celebrate your publishing contract."

"Matthew was just telling me about his book deal. That is so exciting," Jenny gushed, looking at him with something I read as fawning adoration.

I lifted my glass in his direction. "You deserve it. And may this be the start of a long and successful career."

Jenny beamed at him and said, "I always knew you would be a successful author. Didn't I tell you that?" Matthew looked at her, surprised. She went on, saying, "Don't you remember when I gave you a reading last year?"

"Oh ... er ... right," he said, clearly remembering no such thing. He rose and pulled up a chair for me.

Turning to me, Jenny set her glass on the table. "After I left this morning, I realized that I'd forgotten my loom in my car. I came by to drop it off, and who opens the door but Matthew?"

I wondered briefly if that was just her excuse to see Matthew, but when I glanced at her, she looked sincere. "I'm glad you're here and Matthew didn't have to wait all by himself."

"I only arrived a few minutes ago," he said.

Jenny turned back to me. "Did you see anything you liked?" For a second my mind blanked. "Weren't you out looking at houses?"

"Oh, right." I nodded. "I was. Actually there's one place I sort of liked and one I absolutely loved. But that one is listed for sale—not for rent—which makes it impossible." I shrugged. "It's really too bad because it's absolutely gorgeous. I wouldn't have had to do a thing . . . except get a whole lot of stock. It's huge. The other one I saw is a little house almost identical to this one. It's at the other end of Main Street."

"Oh, I know the place you're talking about. That used to be Mrs. McLeay's house. She lived there her whole life, until she went into a respite-care facility about a year and a half ago. Now it belongs to an out-of-town nephew of hers." She crinkled her nose. "But doesn't that house need a ton of work?"

"It sure does, which is the main reason I'm hesitating. Most of the work would be cosmetic, mind you, but it would take a ton of plaster and paint. I doubt it would be difficult, just time-consuming—so I could probably do most of it myself."

Matthew picked up the bottle, offering refills all around. "Speaking of plaster and paint, I can't believe all the work you did on this house. It looks great. But where did my living room and dining room furniture go?" He looked a bit worried.

"It's all upstairs in the third bedroom, including a really ugly green La-Z-Boy I had half a mind to throw out. As for the painting, don't worry about it. I didn't do that much."

Jenny's eyebrows jumped up. "What are you talking about, you didn't do much? You did a lot. I remember how this place used to look."

Just how often has Jenny been here? I wondered. Meanwhile, she was looking at Matthew apologetically. "Sorry, Matthew. No disrespect, but you have to admit, when it comes to housekeeping you're the worst. What Della's done is nothing short of a miracle." She pointed a finger at him. "And just so you know, if it had been up to me, that ugly recliner would be landfill by now." She turned back to face me. "He never notices when something needs fixing. The roof could leak, the walls could be falling down, and he'd have his nose stuck in one of his books, completely oblivious to the disaster around him." She shook her head in mock exasperation. "A typical absentminded professor, that's what he is."

Matthew smiled at the description. "Now I can be an absentminded author."

Jenny rolled her eyes, and out of nowhere she said, "You're in love, aren't you? I can see it in your aura. So tell me all about her. Who is she? How did you two meet?"

Matthew looked momentarily stunned, blood rushing to his face. "I'm not seeing anyone right now," he said sharply.

She frowned. "What do you mean? You look—"

"Whatever you think you're seeing, you're reading it wrong." His tone was meant to end the subject.

Jenny continued. Whether she was being obstinate or just oblivious, I wasn't sure. "Well, then," she said, grinning, "that's a problem. What you need is a woman in your life. I know lots of nice women—clients at the store. I'll set you up with one of them. Don't worry. I'll find you someone wonderful." Her eyes were gleaming with excitement.

He was already shaking his head. "Thanks, but I can find my own dates, Jenny."

"Give me one good reason why not."

"At the moment, all I'm interested in is getting this book written." He turned to me. "Jenny's right about one thing. I had no idea how much work you put into this place. When you asked me if you could do a little painting, that's what I expected. But you repainted the whole house. And you refinished the floors." He sounded impressed. "Am I wrong or did you also paint the outside of the house?"

I waved away his concern. "Not the entire outside. Only the front door and the window casings."

He rolled his eyes, and looked at Jenny. "'Only,' she says, as if she only worked a couple of hours." He turned back to me. "You must have spent a small fortune in paint alone. Just tell me how much I owe you."

"Oh, come on. I don't want your money. I was happy to do it." I looked around at the soft yellow walls. "You don't think the place looks too feminine, do you?"

Jenny interrupted. "Don't ask him anything about interior decorating. Do you really think he notices things like the color of the walls?"

"I did notice. Didn't I just tell Della what a nice job she did?"

"Only because I pointed it out."

I laughed. "I hate to tell you, Matthew, but I think I'm with Jenny on this one."

He looked sheepish. "Still, I can see you did a lot of work. Tell you what. When you move, I'll paint, fix, and do anything that needs doing in your new place. How's that?"

"When you move," he'd said. Obviously, he wanted me out—not that I could blame him. I'd want my living space back too if I were him. I put on a smile. "That's an offer I'll gladly accept. Thank you."

Jenny set her glass down. "Well, I think I'll call it a night. I have to get up early. Fran has a dentist appointment tomorrow morning, and I agreed to take over the store for a couple of hours."

I glanced at my watch. It was only a few minutes after eight. "What time does the shop open?"

"At ten, but I do an hour or two of yoga first thing in the morning. It's like meditation for me."

An hour or two of yoga! I swallowed hard. Well, that settled it. I would never—in a million years—have a body like hers. Even on the off chance that I took up exercising, I wasn't about to give up any of my favorite dishes—fried chicken, buttermilk biscuits, corn bread, pecan pie . . . The list was a long one.

"You should join me sometime," she added. "You'd love it."

Sure, I would. "I'm afraid I'm not into yoga. My joints are so stiff I can barely touch my toes."

A horrified expression descended on her face. "That's terrible. Maybe you could do Bikram yoga."

"What's that?"

Her eyes grew wide as if she could hardly believe her ears. "You mean you've never even heard of it? It's yoga done in a hot and humid environment. It makes you sweat like a horse, but it also makes you lose a ton of weight. And the heat also increases flexibility. It's really good for you."

I could think of another, much more pleasurable way of getting hot and sweaty, which didn't involve twisting my body into a pretzel. I decided to change the subject.

My eyes darted to Matthew. "Did you have dinner yet?"

"No, actually I haven't. Jenny, why don't you stay and have a bite with us? I'll just go pick up some pizza or Chinese food."

I jumped to my feet and headed for the fridge. "Don't be silly. I'll make something. How about—"

"You sit," he ordered. I moved away from the fridge and sat. "Now, what would you ladies like? You can have anything you want."

Unfortunately what I really wanted—a successful business and maybe a nice place to move into—was not on the menu.

Chapter 9

"Anything we wanted" meant exactly that: anything ranging from Chinese, to Italian, to Greek, to Japanese. And I was probably forgetting half a dozen other choices. Briar Hollow had only a couple of restaurants, which specialized in nothing but had menus offering dishes from every country in the world, none of which they had mastered. So when Matthew returned from picking up dinner, we sat down to dry nori rolls and soggy tempura, and the conversation wound its way back to the two properties I'd just seen.

Matthew slathered enough wasabi on his rolls for an atomic brain explosion. "So explain to me why you can't get the space you really like?"

I watched, wide-eyed with morbid fascination, as he dipped the roll into soy sauce and then popped it into his mouth. He chewed, swallowed—and his eyes never even watered. The man must have been made of steel.

I said, "It's for sale—not rent. Until I've sold my condo, I can't even think about buying a property. And with the state of the economy, who knows how long that will take. Also, I'm just starting a new business, and it's not exactly profitable yet."

Jenny leaned toward Matthew. "What she's saying is she's like me, broke."

"I understand." I could see the wheels turning in his mind. "I think there might be a way around that."

I helped myself to another roll, squeezing on the teensiest dollop of wasabi. "You wouldn't say that if you saw my bank account."

He ignored my comment, continuing patiently. "As bad as the real estate market is in Charlotte, it's ten times worse in Briar Hollow."

Across from me, Jenny was already nodding. "He's right. Mrs. McLeay's house has been empty ever since she moved out." She tilted her head. "So, where is this gorgeous place you can't afford?"

"It's the empty store right past the watchmaker." I went on to describe the shop and the two upstairs apartments in salivating detail.

Matthew put down his chopsticks. "I know the place you're talking about. That's been empty for a long time." He turned to Jenny. "Wasn't it some kind of women's clothing store?"

"How can you not remember? It used to be Sally's Salon. She went under—let's see, oh—about two years ago."

He shrugged. "It's not like I ever shopped there."

"Two years? And it's been empty ever since?" I was surprised. "How come?"

Jenny pushed back her plate. "The shop part has been empty, but both apartments were rented until recently."

Matthew said, "The owner probably wanted the apartments empty in case a buyer would want to occupy one."

That made sense. My agent in Charlotte had told me

much the same thing—that my condo would sell more easily untenanted. I said, "Two years is a long time for a store to be empty."

"In this economy, people aren't rushing out to start new businesses," he said.

I grimaced. "Unless they've completely lost their minds—like me."

Matthew leaned over and patted my hand. "I can't think of anyone who's more levelheaded than you. I have an idea. Why don't you offer a lease-to-own deal? Who knows, in this economy sales are so hard to get that the seller might accept. You would have to pay a premium on top of the monthly rent, but at the end of the lease period, that amount would be credited against the purchase price."

I leaned against the back of my chair, thinking. "What's the catch?"

"The drawback is that if you decided not to buy, the premium you paid would be forfeited."

I mulled the idea over. "A lease to own—it's an interesting idea. I wonder why more people don't think of that."

"Sellers prefer a straight sale because they get their money right away. But when real estate markets go flat, an imperfect deal is better than no deal."

I frowned. "I wonder how much rent I could get for my condo. It might be enough to cover the mortgage payments—" Another thought occurred to me. "But if my condo is tenanted, it will be even more difficult to sell."

"That may be true." Matthew helped himself to a few

more nori rolls. "But that might be a good thing in the long run. The market is bound to turn around at some point, and when it does, your condo's value will go back up."

"What if the market drops even lower?"

He shook his head, dismissing my concern. "Then you simply keep it rented until things turn around."

Jenny was studying me, a gleam of excitement in her eyes. "Are you thinking of making an offer?"

"I don't know. A lease to own would eliminate the need for a down payment, but I don't know that I can afford rent plus premium. It really depends on how much it would add up to."

Jenny wagged a finger at Matthew. "You sneaky devil," she said, laughing.

"Why? What did I do?"

She crossed her arms. "You don't fool me one bit, Matthew Baker. You only want Della to buy that place instead of Mrs. McLeay's old house so you won't have to help her fix it up."

Matthew burst out laughing. "Busted." He winked at me. And for some odd reason my heart fluttered.

I forced myself to focus on how I could make this work—instead of losing myself in Matthew's eyes. "You know what else is great about that place? I could live in one of the apartments and the rent from the other would help cover some of the expenses."

For the next few minutes I calculated the potential income of the building, the probable costs, and the amount I would likely earn from my new business. "I think I could just squeak by. But I'd have to live in the smaller of the two apartments."

Matthew plucked the last roll from the carton and dropped it on his plate. He looked at me in disbelief. "How can you even question it? That place sounds amazing. You have to give it a shot. If you don't, I just might put an offer on it myself."

"Trust me, I know it's great. The problem is I'd be living dangerously close to the line. I have to find a way for the shop to make a lot more money. I'm afraid I'm in for some lean times ahead. I have no one to blame but myself. I knew, getting into this, that selling handwoven goods wasn't exactly going to attract the hoards."

Matthew crossed his arms and gave me his don't-be-silly look. "Don't you think you're being hard on yourself? You've been open—what—two months?"

"Actually, only about a month. It took me a while to get set up."

"You, of all people, should know it takes time for a business to get running. You can't expect to make a million dollars the first year."

I laughed. "A million dollars—as if a weaving shop could ever make that much." I took a sip of wine and thought out loud. "There must be something I can do that will attract more customers. Maybe what I need is some other product that would tie in with weaving."

Matthew leaned in. "Knowing you, Della, I have no doubt you'll come up with something." A moment later he pushed away his plate, and even though it wasn't even ten o'clock, he pled fatigue and headed off to his room, leaving Jenny and me to do the dishes.

"Hey, how about lending us a hand here?" Jenny yelled as he went upstairs.

"He who provides the food doesn't have to clean up," he called back over the banister.

She planted her hands on her hips and shook her head. "Typical."

I laughed. "You said it." I turned on the hot water, squeezed in the liquid detergent and handed her a dishcloth. "I'll wash. You dry."

"Works for me." She stacked the plates and brought them to the sink. "That man is so hardheaded—typical Taurus." Funny, I'd known him for years and had never asked him his astrological sign. Jenny said, "I don't understand why he won't let me set him up with one of my friends." She grew quiet. "It's too bad it didn't work out with him and Amanda. She was nice."

If you like tall blondes with big smiles and even bigger boobs, I thought. But all I said was, "I didn't know her very well, but she did seem nice." I rinsed the suds off a plate, feeling guilty for being happy about Matthew and Amanda's breakup, an event that had probably caused him some pain. I handed the dish to Jenny.

She wiped it dry and set it on the counter. "I wonder who the other girl might be—the one he had feelings for. Do you have any idea?" I asked.

My eyes met hers, and all at once I wondered if it could be her. It would explain a lot, like the fact that Matthew was still unattached. Being close to Jenny's ex, he would not have acted on those feelings. Also, just now, when Jenny had asked him about his mysterious love interest, Matthew had blushed. Maybe it was only my imagination, but I had the impression that he'd avoided her eyes. The more I thought about it, the more my theory made sense.

"I haven't got a clue."

Jenny picked up the stack of clean plates and put them away. "Whoever she is," she said, turning to me, "it sounds like that relationship didn't work out either." She paused, dish towel in hand, and then said, "You know what I wish?"

"What?"

"I wish love didn't have to be so complicated. Take Mike and me, for example. Do you know that he and I started dating when we were still in high school? He was my first boyfriend, my only boyfriend. We got married right after he graduated from the police academy. You would think that after a decade of marriage, a woman would know her husband." She shrugged, looking miserable. "But just out of the blue one day, he tells me that he knows I've been cheating—believe me, I never, ever was unfaithful—and that he wants a divorce." Tears hovered on her lashes. "Funny, isn't it? I can read perfect strangers, but when it came to the person I thought I knew best, I read him all wrong."

"Oh, Jenny, you still love him, don't you?"

She blinked away the moisture in her eyes and gave me a brave smile. "I'm completely over him. As a matter of fact I wouldn't have him back if he begged." Something in her voice told me otherwise.

"Why was he so sure you were seeing someone else?"

"I don't know. The reason he gave me doesn't make any sense. I told you—didn't I—that Greg Hanson went door-to-door to collect signatures for a petition against Jeremy's project?" I shook my head, "Oh, well, Greg took it upon himself to stop Jeremy from developing that parcel of land. When he came by my place for my signature, Mike happened to drive by in his police cruiser at the very moment I was letting him in. When Mike came home later, he asked me if I'd seen anyone that day and I said that, no, I'd stayed in and hadn't seen a soul. I wasn't lying. It just clean slipped my mind that Hanson had dropped by. Mike served me with the divorce papers one week later. I can't help but believe there was another reason. But whatever it might have been, I have no clue." She sighed deeply. "After ten years of marriage. Go figure."

My heart went out to her. "Was he always the jealous type?"

She shook her head. "I don't know why I expected our marriage to be different from other people's. Look around. Couples break up all the time. Take David Swanson. He idolized that wife of his. Nothing was ever too good for her. Whatever Marsha wanted, Marsha got." She made a face. "The problem was, Marsha didn't want David. She wanted Jeremy Fox. She didn't care that the man was involved with her own sister-in-law. She went after him, and she got him. Or maybe he went after her. Whatever." She shook her head. "I swear there are more broken hearts in this world than people who are happy."

How right she is, I thought morosely. In fact I had never been happy in love either. "Tell me about David's sister. What's her name?"

"Leanne—she was Jeremy's girlfriend for—oh—

about a year. She fell head over heels in love with him, so much so that she invested her entire inheritance into Jeremy's condo project. Of course, the minute he had his greedy hands on her money, he dropped her like a hot potato and moved on to the next woman—in this case David's wife."

"No wonder David can't stand the man. How's Leanne now?"

"I hope she's all right. She took off right after it happened. Last I heard she was in New York." She glanced at the dish rack. "Oh, will you look at that," she said, surprised that the dishes were done. "It's almost ten. I guess it's time for me to get going." She folded her dishcloth and planted a kiss on my cheek. "I'm sorry for dumping all over you this way."

"Don't be silly. What are friends for?"

She smiled and I detected a little shyness. "We are becoming friends, aren't we? I'm glad."

Chapter 10

The next morning, I decided on a little floral sundress that accented my curves—of which I had plenty. When I looked at myself in the mirror, I was happy with the results. I didn't have Jenny's lithe body, but some men preferred women with a little more meat on their bones.

I strapped on a pair of tan sandals with four-inch heels, which meant the top of my head would reach Matthew's shoulder. I fluffed up my hair and went downstairs.

"You coming, Winnie?" Winston rose from his spot on my bed and lumbered down behind me.

I was at the stove, turning over bacon strips in the frying pan, when Matthew strolled in, wearing blue jeans and a pin-striped shirt with rolled-up sleeves. He hadn't shaved and his dark stubble only made him look sexier.

"I've wanted to do this for a long time," he said, sweeping me into his arms and covering my lips with his.

Actually, Matthew did not say or do any of this—except in my suddenly rampant imagination. I gave my head a shake. Where had that fantasy come from? It was definitely time for coffee. What he actually said was, "Hey, kiddo, if you throw two more eggs in the pan for me, I'll make you my famous barbecued ribs for dinner tomorrow night." And he said it with the same teasing tone he'd been using since I was ten and he was twelve.

"Oh, well, for barbecued ribs, sure." I cracked two more eggs and scrambled them with a bit of cream and some freshly chopped chives. Granted, I wasn't much of a cook, but one thing I did do well was scrambled eggs. "But how about you make those ribs another day than tomorrow? That's when I'm giving my first weaving class."

"Fine by me. What can I do to help?"

I handed him the bread knife and indicated the loaf on the cutting board. "How about putting a couple of slices in the toaster?" I pointed to the coffeepot. "Coffee's ready if you want some."

"How did you sleep?" he asked, leaning lazily against the counter, looking sexy. "I hope I didn't wake you up when I went out?"

"You went out?" I asked, not surprised. I'd heard him go down the stairs shortly after I climbed into bed.

"I was looking for Winston. Hey, Winston, where did you sleep last night?"

"He was in my room." I dropped a pat of butter into the frying pan. "He's been sleeping at the foot of my bed every night since I moved in."

"I finally figured that was where he was, but not before I walked up and down the street for half an hour. I almost woke you up to help me look for him. I was worried to death."

"I'm sorry. I should have—"

"Don't worry. I'm surprised I didn't guess right away. Winston always did like the pretty girls." I had the unbidden and unpleasant image of Winnie curled up at the foot of all Matthew's exes' beds.

"And I thought you had feelings only for me," I said reproachfully. Winston didn't so much as flick an ear.

Matthew poured himself a cup and turned to Winston. "Hey, buddy, didn't you hear me calling you?" Winnie opened one eye, snorted and closed it again. "Winston. Come," he ordered sharply. But Winston played deaf. Matthew looked at me. "He's always been obstinate, but never this bad."

"Don't look at me. I didn't spoil him," I said, slipping a small piece of bacon into the palm of my hand. "Winston," I called, and he instantly jumped to his feet and scampered over, his nails clicking on the worn wooden floor. I scratched his head with one hand and sneaked him the treat with the other.

"What the hell?" For a moment I thought he'd caught on, but no. "Who is that dog and what have you done with mine?"

"I don't understand why he won't listen to you," I said, smiling innocently. "He always comes when I call him. Don't you, Winnie?" I knew it was childish on my part, but showing Matthew that his dog obeyed me more than he did him gave me a small measure of satisfaction. Winnie stared up at me, hoping for more bacon. I tore a small piece off another strip and made him sit for it. At least *somebody* around here was paying attention to me. Too bad that somebody was only a dog—and not a very pretty one at that.

"You know," I said, "I was thinking about your suggestion. I think you're right. I should make that offer." What I didn't tell him was that I had come to this decision after hours of tossing and turning.

"So?" He waited expectantly. "You'll do it?"

I nodded. "I think I'd be crazy not to at least try. I've even thought of a way I can get all the furnishings I'll need for next to nothing. David has been trying to talk Mrs. McLeay's nephew into getting rid of all the furniture in the house. But he lives out of town and can't be bothered to come down here and sort through all of it. So I got to thinking. Even if I don't rent that place, I can still offer to buy the furniture. I'm pretty good with a paintbrush. I could paint it myself." I smiled prettily. "Maybe you can help."

"I told you I would."

Encouraged, I said, "And whatever I don't need for myself, I can use for store displays. What do you think?"

"I think it's a great idea. I have to hand it to you. You sure think on your feet." He glanced down. "By the way, nice shoes. But how the hell you can walk on those is beyond me. They're like stilts."

"They're perfectly comfortable." I scooped the crisp bacon strips onto a spatula and dropped them on a plate. Winnie, who hadn't left my side since his first taste of bacon, suddenly lunged for the plate, almost knocking it out of my hands.

"Winston! Bad boy!" shouted Matthew. "Bad, bad

boy." Winston skulked away, glancing back at me with an expression screaming of being misunderstood. I set the plate in the center of the table, and soon we were sipping coffee, eating and chatting. I wasn't sure why—maybe just for something to talk about—but I found myself telling him about David Swanson's anger management conviction and the tense confrontation between him and Jeremy Fox last night.

"You're kidding," he said, looking more amused than shocked. "David's a friend of mine. I've known him my whole life. We went to school and played football together. I know he has a temper, but I wouldn't go so far as saying he has anger issues."

"I'm happy to hear that. He seems like such a nice man."

He studied me, and then said, "I think you like him. You do, don't you? I couldn't help but notice that you got all dressed up for him last night."

I was at a loss for words. Had I dressed up last night? I suppose I had—but certainly not because of David. "Sure, I—I like him." I blushed as I realized how that must have sounded. Matthew probably thought he was right in assuming that David and I had a thing going on. "But he's just a friend—"

His smile didn't quite reach his eyes. "You don't have to explain."

Winston chose that time to come sniffing for another handout, and the chance to explain was lost.

Matthew leaned back in his chair. "Nobody could accuse Jeremy Fox of being a saint. He is a sly one—a real snake. I wouldn't trust him farther than I could throw him. He's handsome and charming, and he's a real smooth talker. He bought up a large parcel of land on the outskirts of town for some big condo project, and then brought in investors from all over the country, not to mention a good number of local suckers," he said, and something in his tone sparked my curiosity.

"Please don't tell me you invested with him too."

He grimaced, looking embarrassed.

I leaned back in my chair. "You didn't invest a lot, I hope."

"No." His expression made me suspect it had still been too much. "Still, I should have known better. He made his project sound like the best thing since sliced bread. Good thing I'm conservative when it comes to investing. A couple of months later, an environmental study reported that the land is dangerously contaminated. Getting our money back has been like trying to get water from a stone. According to him, he's lost more than anybody on this project and he's as good as bankrupt." With a smirk, he added, "Some people claim that he knew all along that the land was contaminated, which is why he got it for such a low price. If that's true, the whole project was nothing more than a swindle. Good thing that report came out when it did—otherwise a lot more people would have lost their money."

"How did the report become public?"

He shrugged. "Somebody—nobody knows who—printed copies and mailed them to every investor. Whoever it was, that person saved a lot of people from losing even more."

I was silent while I digested this. "How come Jeremy's not in jail?"

"Believe me, Mike Davis would have arrested him in a second if he could. But unless we can prove that Jeremy intentionally swindled people, he can't be prosecuted. Some of the investors are talking about a civil suit, but that could be expensive." He looked pensive for a second before continuing. "The problem is, when a victim has already been bilked out of a small fortune, he isn't exactly eager to spend any more of his hard-earned money on lawyers unless he's damn sure to win. For all we know, Jeremy could be sitting on a ton of cash, but if it's all hidden somewhere like in the Cayman Islands, the chances of finding it are slim to none."

I let out a breath. "Where does he get the gall to go about his business as if he didn't do anything wrong? If I were him, I wouldn't dare show my face in public. I'd be worried someone would come after me."

"Don't underestimate his charm. Jeremy has always had the ability to talk himself out of trouble."

"From the short encounter I had with him, I can't say I found him very charming."

"Then you, my dear, have better judgment than most other people."

Hopefully this applies to my business acumen also, and I'm not making a huge mistake. But all I said was, "I like to think so." I glanced at my watch. It was eight thirty. "So what are your plans for today? Are you going to work on your book?"

"Yes, but I have to stop by the police station and see Mike." At my blank look, he said, "Mike Davis—Jenny's ex. I better get going if I want to catch him before he starts his shift." He patted Winston on the head. "You be a good boy while I'm gone." He turned to me and I half expected him to pat me on the head too. "See you later," he said.

After he left, it struck me how empty the house suddenly felt.

Chapter 11

The ringing of the phone pierced the silence. It was David Swanson.

"Hi, Della. I just got permission to get back into the building. If you have time right now, why don't you meet me there?"

I spotted him standing by the entrance to the building. He waved and I waved back. "How are—" I stopped short, shocked. "What happened to you?" His right eye was swollen shut, and his upper lip was crimson and crisscrossed with stitches.

"It looks worse than it is." He felt his lip carefully. "I was ambushed. Whoever the bastard was, he hit me from behind." He put the key in the door and pushed it open. "Okay, ready to see the place?"

"Whoa, not so fast. Tell me what happened."

He ushered me in, and I followed him up the stairs, being careful to avoid the nail he'd pointed out last night.

"There isn't much to tell. It was dark. I'd just turned onto the walk in front of my house when I heard a rustling in the bushes. And before I could see what it was—wham!—somebody hit me over the head."

I stopped at the top of the stairs and turned to look at

him again. "Are you sure you're all right? Those bruises look bad."

"After I came to—"

"You mean you passed out?"

He nodded cautiously. "I must have, because the next thing I knew, it was daylight, and I was lying facedown on the sidewalk, feeling like I'd just been mistaken for a football."

I was horrified. "Did you call the police?"

"What would be the point? They'd take down my statement and then forget about it. I went to the hospital and got stitched up. I'll be like new in no time." He tried to give me a smile, but it came out as a grimace. He slipped the apartment key into the lock, fiddling with it until it turned.

"Still, you should have reported it." I followed him in, feeling slightly uncomfortable about being there—no doubt a remnant of the confrontation I had witnessed the night before. I shook off the unpleasant sensation.

In my rush to get out of the building the previous day I was left with little more than the impression of a small-ish space. Now I took in the first room, a combination kitchen, dining, and sitting area. It held many of the same charming details as the other apartment: old-fashioned cupboards in the kitchen, leaded-glass windows in the living area and hardwood floors throughout.

"It's nice, but not as nice as the other apartment." I'd been right. It was much smaller—almost half the size.

"The bedroom is down the hall." He indicated the area from which Jeremy and Marsha had appeared. For some reason, I dreaded going in the room. But I decided

I was being silly, and so I marched over, the clickety-click of my heels echoing through the empty apartment.

"Do you know if the floors are sound insulated?" I asked over my shoulder.

"We can easily check that out later. After we finish in here, you can go downstairs and listen while I stomp around up here."

I pushed the bedroom door open and had just stepped in when I was overcome by a sickly sweet metallic odor. My eyes darted around the dim room and came to rest on a bundle on the floor. Gradually my vision adjusted and—I screamed. There, in the middle of the empty room, was a man lying in a pool of blood.

Feeling faint, I crouched down, my hands reaching out to the solid floor for support.

David bounded over and brushed past me. He gasped, and stood frozen while I tried to regain my breath. He took a few hesitant steps into the room and bent over the body. "Shit," he said, followed by a long list of other expletives. He crouched and picked up a limp hand, feeling for a pulse. A wave of nausea hit me.

"Is he dead?" I whispered hoarsely.

"Dead as a doorknob," he said, dropping the hand.

The room seemed to tilt, and I forced myself to breathe slowly, regularly. I dared another glance. There was something familiar, something—I squelched another rush of nausea and looked again. "Do you know who— Oh, my God!" I exclaimed, getting a look at the dead man's face. "Is this who I think it is?"

"It's Jeremy Fox," he muttered, and when he looked

up at me, his face was as pale as the dead man's. He took a shaky breath and said, "I think he's been murdered."

I got to my feet and on unsteady legs stumbled to the bathroom, where I braced myself against the counter. My head was spinning and my heart was thudding hard and fast against my ribs. I squeezed my eyes shut, trying to force the image out of my mind. I turned on the tap, wet my hands and pressed them to my face.

When David joined me a second later, the room was still spinning.

"Are you okay?"

I wasn't. But I nodded.

He pulled out his cell phone and punched in a number. "I'm calling to report a body." He answered a stream of questions while I struggled to calm my racing heart. "An ambulance?" He looked at me questioningly. I stared back, and shrugged. "I'm sure he's dead. There's an awful lot of blood."

He hung up and hurried to the door. I wasn't sure which of us was in more of a hurry to get out. He held the door open and I scrambled down the stairs. I didn't know how it happened, but one minute I was on my feet and the next I was rolling down, head over heels, thumping and bumping, until I came to a rib-crushing stop at the bottom.

I knew I was alive because I was hurting all over.

Chapter 12

My eyes fluttered open. "Owwww."

David leaned over me, his brow furrowed. "Are you all right?"

"I—I think so," I said, uncomfortably aware that the skirt of my little sundress was now somewhere north of the equator, exposing an indecent amount of thigh. I tugged it back down. And then I remembered my gorgeous sandals. "Did I break a heel?" I asked with sudden panic. I sat up. "I paid a fortune for those shoes." To my relief, my precious heels were intact. And then I remembered the dead body upstairs. "I want to get out of here. Help me up."

David was studying my sandals disapprovingly. "No wonder you fell. How can you even walk on those things? They're not shoes. They're stilts."

"I can walk perfectly well," I said, still woozy from my tumble. "I just lost my balance because of—you know." I indicated upstairs.

"Are you sure you want to try standing?" I nodded and he helped me to my feet, where I stood wobbling for a few seconds.

"Can you move your legs?"

I was in such pain that I was having trouble moving anything, but I took inventory, wiggling my right foot and then my left, and winced. "Ouch!"

"What's wrong?"

"My ankle," I squeaked.

"Can you move it?"

I shook my head, trying to rotate it. I succeeded only in wiggling my toes. "I think I sprained it," I moaned.

"Don't worry. I'm sure it's only bruised."

"Maybe you're right." I wasn't convinced. I took a deep breath and almost shrieked as I put my foot down. I grabbed the doorjamb to steady myself. I took a few shallow breaths and decided I'd be fine as long as I kept that foot off the ground. "If it's not sprained, it must be really badly bruised."

"Maybe you should go to the hospital. You look a bit pale."

I'd just found a body, tumbled down a flight of stairs, and he thought I looked a bit pale? All I said was, "That makes two of us."

Leaning on him, I hopped outside on one foot, just in time to see a police car careening around the corner. It came to a tire-screeching stop across the street, and two police officers jumped out and hurried over to us. One of them, a heavyset, dark-haired man with a mustache, shouted, "Did you just call in a body?"

David nodded and pointed up the stairs. "He's in the apartment on the right."

The second officer—he looked about sixteen, with his curly red hair and face full of freckles—called out, "Stay right where you are," in our direction. The way my ankle was throbbing, I couldn't have run away if I'd wanted to. Not to mention that I was still reeling from discovering the body. If I didn't sit down right now, I was going to pass out. I held on to David's arm as I lowered myself to the ground.

The officers took the stairs two at a time. I was still breathing shallow little breaths, holding back moans, when a moment later a second police car showed up. The driver—this one dressed in civilian clothes—stepped out and walked over to us. He was tall and thin—too thin—with sandy hair and piercing blue eyes.

"Did you call 911, David?" he asked officiously as he pulled out a small pad and a pencil.

David nodded. "I did." He looked as if he was about to be sick, which probably wasn't any worse than how I looked. My ankle throbbed painfully. Would I have to pass out from the pain before anyone took notice?

"Officer," I said, "I think I should go to the hospital. Would you mind calling a cab?"

He looked at me, raised an eyebrow as if to say, "Give me a break." Without bothering to answer, he turned to David, studying his injured face. "Care to tell me what happened?"

Already people were gathering, coming out of the surrounding buildings and forming a small crowd—if you can call half a dozen people a crowd. They craned their necks, studying David and me, whispering to each other. I heard the name "Mike" murmured, followed by, "chief of police."

So this was Jenny's ex-husband. I might have looked at him more closely, but whether from the shock of finding the body or from the tumble down the stairs, I was shaking uncontrollably, which only made breathing more difficult. The pain in my ribs now almost rivaled that in my ankle. Mike turned to look at me again, this time with a feverish intensity that suggested he was seeing clear inside my mind. It gave me the creeps.

I was sitting in the middle of the sidewalk in my Ralph Lauren floral sundress. Any moron should know that no woman would do that unless she was in real pain. I gritted my teeth. "Excuse me. I really think I should go to the hospital. I think my ankle might be broken."

Mike Davis smirked at me cynically and looked down at my ankle. "I'll get someone to drive you there in a minute. We have some important issues to take care of first." He repeated his question to David. "What happened?"

A sickly pallor covered David's face. "I have no idea. I swear. I was just showing Della the apartment when we found him."

"How'd you get those bruises?" He sounded suspicious. That was when it hit me. Poor David was sure to be the cops' first suspect. Wasn't that the way it always worked? Whoever found the body—especially since the whole town knew he had threatened to kill Jeremy just a few days ago.

He touched his stitches lightly with an index finger and explained about the previous night's ambush.

"What time was that?" asked Mike.

"I must have left the bar around eleven." He avoided Mike's eyes. "I went straight to the hospital as soon as I came to, and that's where I was from around six this morning until about nine, when I met up with Della."

"Why the rush? You say you just came out of the hospital. You could have arranged to meet her later."

"It would be just like my wife to put an offer on it just because she saw me showing it to a prospect. We ran into her last night," he said without going into any detail. "I wanted Della to see it before it was too late."

Mike looked at me as if for confirmation. I felt the intensity of his gaze again, like lasers boring into me. My shaking morphed into a shiver. He stepped closer and I just had time to register an odor. It reminded me of something, but I couldn't quite put my finger on it. And just when I decided that I would scream if nobody took me to the hospital, he said, "And you are?"

"Della Wright. I own Dream Weaver, just up the street." To my embarrassment, tears gathered in my eyes. I blinked them away. He either chose to ignore my loss of composure or was distracted by the arrival of the ambulance.

At that moment, the two officers came down the stairs. The freckled policeman nodded to Mike and said, "He won't be needing the ambulance. You better call the coroner."

Mike scowled. "Dead?"

"Oh, yeah. And it looks like murder."

The other officer grimaced. "There's blood all over the place."

Mike addressed the younger officer. "Why don't you drive Miss Wright to the hospital and get her version of the events at the same time?" To the heavier officer, he said, "You take David to the station." And then, dismissing us, he entered the building and disappeared up the stairs.

By now, the crowd had grown to nearly a dozen people, and one of them, an old lady, tugged at my arm. "What happened?" she asked. "Did somebody die?"

Officer Freckle Face turned to the group and said, "All right, folks. There's nothing to see here. Go on home, everybody." They moved back a few feet but kept staring.

He tilted his head toward the patrol car. "Can you walk?"

I shook my head and struggled back to my one good foot. If not for the officer catching me, I would have toppled to the ground. He picked me up and carried me—as if I was light as a feather—to the patrol car. This cop wasn't so bad—a real sweetie, in fact.

Chapter 13

Officer Bellows introduced himself during the drive (still Officer Freckle Face in my mind). He pulled up to the emergency entrance and walked around the car.

"Hold on to my neck." I wrapped my arms around him and he swooped me out of the car effortlessly. The painful throbbing of my ankle ran up to my calf. During the ten-minute drive it had swollen to almost double its size. I might not have been exaggerating when I said it was broken.

He carried me through the automatic doors to the reception area in the waiting room. The doughy blonde at the desk glanced from me to the officer and back at me with a veiled expression. She threw a furtive look at my wrists—checking for cuffs, I realized with a shock.

"Let me get you a wheelchair." She reappeared a moment later pushing a very worn and primitive contraption. She and Officer Bellows helped me into the stiff leather seat, and she hurriedly retreated behind her desk, clearly relieved to be putting some distance between the criminal (me) and herself.

"Name?" she said coldly.

"Della Wright." I explained that I'd fallen down some

stairs and that my ankle might be broken, just so she knew I hadn't been injured while running from the law.

She typed away on her computer, seemingly more concerned about my insurance coverage than my injuries. I fumbled through my bag for my health card. She copied down the information and said dismissively, "The waiting time will be about an hour."

For anybody who has ever been in the ER waiting room of a city hospital, a ten-hour wait is normal. An hour was like a gift from the gods. But I was wracked with pain, and even a minute would have sounded like forever. I stifled a moan and followed her finger to the area where she was pointing—clear across the room, as far from other patients as she could possibly send me.

"You can wait over there." What did she think I was, a murderer? "The doctor will call you when it's your turn." Without another word, she returned to her keyboard.

Officer Bellows wheeled me over to the far wall as a dozen pairs of eyes followed me. I would so be fodder for the gossip mill once news of the murder got out. As long as I wasn't a suspect, I could deal with it.

Now, if I could only get this cop to leave. "Thank you for taking the time to drive me." I was still shaking from finding the body. The last thing I wanted was to be forced to go over the details; all I wanted to do was to forget them. Bellows did seem nice enough, but after my brush with the law last year, cops were not up there on my list of favorite people. It was just lucky I'd been assigned to him rather than to the older one, who hadn't looked nearly as friendly. "I'll just call myself a cab when I'm done."

His eyes registered amusement. "I didn't drive you here out of the goodness of my heart." He pulled a pen and a small notebook from his breast pocket. "I need you to tell me your version of the events that led up to finding the body this morning. I have to do this while the details are still fresh in your mind."

"You mean you want to question me right here? Right now? While I'm in pain, and with all these people listening?" I whispered back, horrified.

"It won't take long and if you keep your voice low, nobody will hear."

I had serious doubts about that, but looking around now, I saw that people had already lost interest. They were reading or chatting, nobody so much as glancing our way. Or were they just pretending? Wasn't that what I would do if I wanted to eavesdrop?

"Why don't you start by telling me everything that happened this morning? Did David Swanson pick you up?"

I shook my head. "We met in front of the building." I went over every detail, from the sweetish metallic smell that greeted me when I opened the bedroom door to the pooled blood on the floor and my tumble down the stairs. I had to fight to keep the quiver out of my voice as I recounted the events. "And then you and your partner showed up. That's all I know. Now why don't you leave me alone and go find the killer?" I was praying for him to please just go away and let me erase the awful picture from my mind.

He ignored my last barb, writing as fast as he could. "So, what gave you the impression it was murder?"

I bobbed my eyebrows. "You're kidding, right? With all that blood, only an idiot would think it was a heart attack."

His face flushed and he busied himself jotting down a few more words. He cleared his throat. "Did you know the victim?"

A fresh image of Jeremy Fox's pale face flashed through my mind. "I'd heard about him, but the only time I ever met him was last night—if you can call that a meeting. He didn't exactly introduce himself."

He put down his pen and cocked his head, reminding me of Jack McCoy on *Law and Order*. "So if you'd already seen the building, why did you need to go back again?" He was becoming less and less sweet with every question. On the other hand, maybe I deserved the attitude, since I had given him a bit myself.

"I'd seen the other apartment, but we had only just walked into this one last night when Mr. Fox and his girlfriend unexpectedly came out of the bedroom. We didn't exactly stick around after that." I glanced around. To my relief, except for one little girl hanging over the back of her chair and picking her nose, all the other patients were absorbed in whatever they were doing— flipping through old issues of *Reader's Digest*, conversing in whispers or just nodding off.

I described the run-in with Jeremy and David's estranged wife.

"So the scene was confrontational—is that correct?"

"David didn't lose his temper, even though Jeremy goaded him. He kept his cool the whole time." The officer raised his eyebrows, and I already knew what he was about to say. "It only lasted about two minutes, and then we just turned around and walked out." I kept David's clenched fists and his reaction during the drive home to myself.

He tilted his head, waiting for my answer to his next question. "And whose idea was it to see the place this morning?"

"Mine, er, I mean, I'd asked David to take me back so I could see the second apartment."

"Why did you want to see it this morning? Why not later in the day?"

I shook my head. "I didn't ask to see it at any specific time, but when David phoned and said he could get me inside right away, I happened to be free. But he wasn't pushy about it. I mean, I could have asked to see it later and he would have been fine with it."

"You have no way of knowing that for sure, do you?" He saw me hesitate, and continued. "Who got there first?"

I wasn't sure where he was going with this. "David was waiting when I arrived."

"So for all you know, he could have entered the apartment before you got there, killed Fox and gone back outside to wait for you."

"That's ridiculous," I said a bit too loudly. A few people craned their necks in their seats to look at me. I adopted a casual expression and waited for them to turn around again. I lowered my voice. "I was right there when he unlocked the door." Tears trembled on my lashes. I blinked them away. "You're trying to put words in my mouth. And if I don't tell you what you want to hear, you'll twist everything around. That's it. I'm through."

He looked at me coldly. "He could have been inside and come back out before you got there, couldn't he?" I opened my mouth to argue, then stopped. Actually, David *could* have done that. I really didn't know, did I? Officer Bellows continued. "I'm going to ask you something very important. I want you to think carefully before you answer. Did you see David touch the body or anything else in the room?"

I hesitated. "He touched Jeremy's wrist when he felt for a pulse."

"Did he touch anything else?"

"Anything else?" I asked, not understanding. "Like what?"

"Like a weapon, for starters," he said.

My eyes grew wide. "No, absolutely not. I didn't see any weapon. There was nothing in the room—nothing but the body."

He studied me for a long moment, then looked down at his notebook and scribbled a few words. "Did *you* take anything from the scene?"

I gasped. "No, of course not."

"Was David alone with the body, at any point"—I started shaking my head—"even for a moment?"

"No." I suddenly remembered something, though. I had left the room a few seconds before he did, but he couldn't possibly have had time to take anything. "No," I repeated.

Bellows shrugged. "One second is all it takes to pick

up something and slip it in a pocket. He could have done that while he was checking the victim's pulse and you might never have noticed."

I shook my head, determined to appear convinced, but if Officer Bellows's goal had been to rattle me, he had succeeded. I wasn't at all sure of David's innocence anymore. He could have taken something from the crime scene and with my eyes focused on the victim as they'd been, I wouldn't have noticed.

At last he flipped his notebook closed. "Thank you for answering my questions, Miss Wright. I might need to talk to you again at some point. In the meantime, if you think of anything, please call me." He offered me his card, which I slipped into my bag. "Are you sure you can find a ride back?" he asked.

I refrained from telling him that I'd rather crawl all the way home than have to suffer one minute more with him. "Yes, yes, no problem."

"Have a good day." He nodded curtly and left. I had rarely been so relieved to see somebody walk away. I was just wondering how much longer I'd have to wait before getting a painkiller when a doctor stepped out of the emergency room, grabbed a file from the rack on the wall, looked at it and called out, "Della Wright."

Chapter 14

Dr. Green was in his early to mid-forties, with slightly receding dark hair, blue eyes and a kind smile. *Cute,* I thought. If not for feeling so awful, weepy and shaky all at once, I would definitely have flirted. On second thought, flirting might do me good. It would take my mind off the whole horrendous experience. Besides, it had been a long time since I'd flirted—too long.

But as I discovered while lying on the examining table, batting one's lashes at someone who is peering into your eyes with an ophthalmoscope is practically impossible. The only response I got from the good doctor was a request to stop blinking. I blushed all the way to the roots of my hair as he peered into my eyes for what seemed like an eternity and my mind went right back to the nightmarish events of the morning.

"No concussion," he said at last, and moved on to my ankle.

"I could have told you that," I said. "I didn't hurt my head. I hurt my ankle and my ribs."

"Well, you've got quite a bump on your forehead," he said.

I did? I felt around my forehead gingerly and—

ouch—he was right. I had a lump the size of a plum along the hairline.

"You should ice that as soon as you get home," he said, slipping off my sandal. He scowled. "No wonder you hurt your ankle. These aren't shoes. They're an accident waiting to happen." At least he hadn't called them stilts like Matthew and David had.

He examined the offending sandal with incredulity. "Do you know the damage this kind of shoe can do to your foot?"

It must have been a rhetorical question because without waiting for an answer, he set it on a chair and turned his attention to my injury. My nice shapely ankle of a few hours ago now looked like a fat sausage.

"It really hurts," I said, hoping he noticed that my other ankle was quite trim.

He palpated the swelling gently, and I bit my lip, trying not to cry out.

"I'm sending you down to be x-rayed," he said. "I think it's only sprained, but I want to make sure." He helped me back into the wheelchair and walked away.

So much for flirting.

Chapter 15

Four hours later, I was back in the emergency room, flying on a different table, while Dr. Green wound what seemed like miles of elastic bandage around my ankle. My sausage-looking ankle was now a pig in a blanket—which I truly enjoyed along with a cocktail, but not at the end of my leg. "Stay off that foot for at least a week and try to keep it elevated."

"A week?" I exclaimed, aghast.

"Consider yourself lucky it isn't broken, because you'd be looking at months instead of days," he said. "And if you want to get back to normal as soon as you can, you'll take my advice."

"I'll stay off my foot and keep it elevated," I repeated dutifully.

"I'll give you a prescription for painkillers." He attached metal clips to hold the bandage in place and then stepped away. "That should do it."

I looked down at my ankle. The swelling had spread to my foot, which now looked like a plump baby's foot. "I guess I can forget about getting my shoe back on," I said.

He grinned, picked up my shoe and handed it to me. "What is it about women and shoes?" he asked, and to my surprise he was looking at me teasingly. Was he flirt-ing? "I suggest you settle for wearing a thick sock on that foot until it's healed."

I grimaced. "Call me crazy, but I like my feet to match," I said, dropping the shoe into my bag. I was car-rying on a flirty conversation, as if the subject most on my mind wasn't murder and bodies and pools of blood. It helped, but not a whole lot.

"I could wrap your other foot if it'll make you feel any better," he countered, and I realized that, yes, he *was* flirting.

For a second, I felt a whole lot better. I laughed. "Thanks, but no thanks." I struggled off the examining table, carefully setting my left foot on the floor. I winced. "Ouch."

"What did I just tell you? Stay off that foot. Hold on a second and I'll get you something," he said, and walked away. I was praying for a nice wheelchair, one of those modern ones with motors and a speed stick. I had an instant vision of myself racing down the sidewalk with Winston chasing along. That could actually be cool.

Dr. Green reappeared, carrying a pair of wooden crutches. "Here, try these on for size."

I grimaced. "Crutches. Ugh."

"Crutches are your friend," he said.

I slipped them under my arms and tried a few steps. "Let me adjust the hand rests," he said, and something in his voice made me look up. He was looking at me with a smile and the kind of twinkle in his eyes that made me think that maybe—just maybe—the good doctor liked me. I smiled back.

"How are you going to get home?"

"Oh, um, I guess I'll call a cab." And then, feeling like an idiot, I remembered that I didn't have my cell phone. "Is there a phone I could use?"

"The receptionist will call one for you." And then, grabbing a pen and a prescription pad from the nearby counter, he scribbled a few words and tore off the page. "This is your prescription." I looked down at the paper in my hands. "Or, you can take two aspirin and call me in the morning," he said, his eyes twinkling with amusement. I laughed.

"And if I don't follow the doctor's advice?"

"Oh, I wouldn't take that chance if I were you. Doctors always know best." He gave me another smile. "You should be fine in a week. If it takes longer than that, come back and see me."

He looked so cute, I almost wished I would have to come back. And since I couldn't quite manage sexy walking on crutches, I tried for sexy hobbling—also impossible. Still, I felt the good doctor's eyes following me all the way out of the ER.

Well, well. What do you know? Even on crutches, I could still turn a man's head.

Chapter 16

At the reception desk, the same pudgy blonde looked at me questioningly—a marked improvement over her earlier suspicious gaze.

"I can call a cab for you," she said when I asked her, "but there aren't very many around these parts. If they happen to be busy, they can take as long as an hour to answer a call." An hour! Even Charlotte cabs were faster than that. "Wouldn't you rather call a friend?" she added.

To my surprise, the first person that popped into my mind was Jenny Davis, and I rattled off her number. I always did have a memory when it came to numbers—a talent that came in handy when I was a business analyst. The receptionist punched Jenny's number into the phone and handed me the receiver.

The phone rang a few times. Just as I was about to give up, she answered.

"Hi, Jenny. It's me."

"Della? Are you okay? You sound odd," she said, hearing my voice.

"Actually, I'm at the hospital and I—" That one sympathetic question was all it took to bring the emotions to the surface. Suddenly I was once again the quivering Della who had just found a dead body.

"I just knew something bad happened. I had that feeling all morning. Are you all right? Were you in an accident?"

I forced the tremor out of my voice. "No, no, nothing like that. I'm fine. Don't worry. But I need a ride home. Do you think—?"

"No problem." She still sounded worried. "Meet me at the side entrance. I'll be there in ten minutes."

I followed the receptionist's directions, hobbling along, trying to keep my purse from sliding off my shoulder—no small feat with both hands holding on to crutches. I still thought a wheelchair would have been a better idea—or maybe not, considering that the bathroom and my bedroom at home were on the second floor.

"Della? Is that you?" a voice called out. I stopped and maneuvered a clumsy turn. Joan Douglas, the neonatal nurse who was my contact for the charity blanket-weaving project, was staring at me wide-eyed. "What happened to you?" This was a question I might as well get used to. I would hear it a lot over the next few days.

I smiled crookedly. "I sprained my ankle. I'll be stuck using these for a week."

"Oh, poor you. Do you have a minute for a cup of coffee?" she asked, eyeing my crutches with a frown.

The last thing I wanted was to be drawn into an explanation of how this had happened. "Right now, all I really want is to get home."

"Of course. We'll do it some other time. Make sure you keep that foot up as soon as you get home."

"I will, if I ever find my way out of here." I glanced around. "Maybe you can help me. I was supposed to turn right at the oncology department."

As she came closer, I noticed an odd smell—a mixture of something musky like cheap men's cologne and a chemical like camphor—not the usual baby powder smell I had come to associate with the nursery. She pointed at a door. "You're standing right in front of the oncology department. If you're looking for the side entrance, it's that way."

She gave me a quick wave, and I headed down the corridor. By the time I reached the entrance, I had been on crutches for all of five minutes and I already thought my arms were going to fall off. I let myself collapse into one of the waiting chairs, as exhausted as if I'd just run a marathon—not that I'd ever run one.

Hey, on the bright side, I was getting the workout of my life. I was picturing myself with Jenny's lithe body when the door flew open and she appeared. She took one look at me and her face fell. "What in the world—?"

"It's a long story," I said. I pulled myself up on one foot, struggling with my crutches.

"Is it broken?" she asked, looking like she was on the verge of tears. "I just knew something had happened to you. I had a bad feeling all morning," she said, repeating what she'd told me earlier.

I was tempted to ask if her bad feeling had anything to do with murder, or even just death. "No, just sprained, thank goodness. I should be better in about a week, but I'm not sure my arms can take a week of this." By some miracle, I made it down the steps and around to the passenger side of her car without tripping. I climbed in and fell back against the seat.

Jenny threw the crutches into the backseat, slid in behind the wheel and took off.

She glanced at me from the corner of her eye. "How did this happen?"

I took a deep breath and plunged into the story. "Jeremy Fox is dead. I found his body."

She turned to gawk incredulously at me and the car swerved dangerously near the side of the road. "Watch out!" I yelled.

She veered back into the correct lane. "Tell me."

I told her about meeting David in front of the building, him looking like he'd been mistaken for a punching bag, me finding the body. "I tripped down the stairs, getting out of there." During the recounting, Jenny must have repeated "Oh, my God," half a dozen times. "And to top it all off," I concluded, "Officer Bellows questioned me for half an hour, right in the waiting room, within hearing distance of half a dozen patients. And you know what that means? I'll be the subject of conversation around town tomorrow."

She took her eyes off the road for a second and glanced at me, shaken. "I hate to be the bearer of bad news, but you're being way too conservative. Guaranteed, people are already talking about you."

I groaned. "Oh, well, that's one way to bring attention to my shop." Cheerfully, I added, "On a brighter note, the attending physician was a hunk and he was flirting with me."

This elicited a chuckle. "I don't believe it. You flirted while in the emergency room? That's too funny."

"He started it, not me," I said, choosing to forget about my unsuccessful attempt at batting my lashes. "Maybe you know him—Dr. Green?"

"I do know him. He's nice. His wife used to shop at Franny's." She caught a glimpse of my face and added, "He's a widower. His wife died in a car accident a few years ago. I like him. Every time I met him, I got good vibes." She turned off the highway and soon we were entering Briar Hollow. "How exactly are you going to get around on that ankle?" she asked, almost sounding like my mother for a second. "You won't be able to do anything on your own, and knowing Matthew, he's not exactly the kind of man you can count on to cook and clean."

"Don't worry. I can manage. I've still got one good foot."

She chuckled. "All kidding aside, I can come stay with you if you like."

I had a quick flash of Jenny and Matthew laughing over a glass of wine, and wondered why it left me feeling uncomfortable. "Don't worry. I'll be getting around like a pro on those crutches in no time. But I'm really worried about David. The cop who questioned me seemed convinced that he's the killer." That comment was answered by a long silence. "Jenny?" Her eyes stayed focused on the road ahead, but I could tell she was troubled. "What's wrong?"

"That would explain the negative energy I felt the night of the group meeting."

"What are you saying?" I was still struggling with my own doubts about him and had counted on her to dispel them. "You can't seriously think he could be a killer. He seems like such a nice guy."

There was a short pause. "Every time a killer is apprehended, those around him are stunned. They can't believe that the brother, friend or neighbor they knew and who seemed so nice could turn out to be a criminal. What we all seem to forget is that murderers don't look like monsters. They look like normal people."

She was right, of course. If anyone had asked me about my boss a year ago, I would have said he was the most honest and trustworthy person in the world. Nobody was more surprised than I was when I discovered he was an embezzler.

"But I was there, Jenny. I saw the look on his face. Believe me, he was just as taken aback as I was." I was quiet for a second, staring blindly ahead. "Also, it was my fault he was there this morning. I was the one who wanted to see the apartment again. The least I can do is help in whatever way I can."

She looked at me in disbelief. "That is the craziest thing I've ever heard. What have you got to feel guilty about? He called you, remember?"

"There is no way he could have done it. I refuse to believe it," I said with more conviction than I really felt. I hardly knew the man. It wasn't as if I had feelings for him. So why did I want so badly to believe he was innocent?—except maybe to continue thinking that Briar Hollow was a nice, peaceful town and that one of the few people I knew here was not a murderer.

"I don't think I've ever felt such negative energy as at the meeting. The atmosphere was so dark, it was almost

evil." That was what she'd told me yesterday while helping me dress the loom.

"But didn't you also say that you can't always tell the
source of the energy when there are a lot of people in a
room? Maybe that negative energy came from somebody else."

"Let's see now—you and I were there, and so were
Dolores and her daughter. Oh, I know," she added. "That
energy must have come from Marnie."

"Well, it's not impossible. Just yesterday, Marnie was
saying she'd like to . . . Oh, my God."

Jenny glanced at me, alarmed.

I cleared my throat. "You don't think she could have—"

"No, of course not," she said quickly. Maybe too quickly.

But the thought remained with me. It could have been
Marnie just as easily as it could have been David. Suddenly I didn't feel much like talking anymore. We drove
along in silence, both lost in our own thoughts. When she
pulled up in front of the house, I noticed that Matthew's
car was gone.

"Are you sure you don't want me to come in?" she
asked, helping me out.

"You can come in for coffee if you like—oh, shoot. I
forgot. I'm out of milk."

"I think I'll skip the coffee if you don't mind," she
said, and I realized that all this talk of murder was just as
upsetting to her, maybe even more so. After all, Briar
Hollow was her home, and every person in town was her
friend. "But I'll pick you up a quart next door. Be back
in two minutes," she said, and headed for the Mercantile
while I limped inside.

Chapter 17

I had just closed the door behind me when Winston came galloping over. He skidded to a halt and looked at my crutches, confused. "Are you alone again, Winnie?" I asked, making my way toward the kitchen. He lunged for one of my crutches, trying to bite it. "No, Winston. Down, boy! This is not a game." He tugged at the crutch, almost toppling me over. "Stop!"

He let go and looked at me with wounded eyes. "It's okay, Winnie," I reassured him. But he plodded off, offended. In the kitchen, I refilled his water bowl, gave him a liver treat, and we were friends again. I rummaged through the freezer for a bag of frozen peas, and with my makeshift ice pack against my forehead I hobbled to the table as the phone rang.

"Hi, David. I just walked in."

"I've been calling you for hours. Where were you?"

"I was at the hospital," I said.

"Oh, right," he said, and then without bothering to ask me how I was, he blurted, "The police think I did it."

Judging from the questions Officer Not-So-Sweet-Face had asked, I wasn't the least bit surprised. But there was no point in upsetting him more than he already was.

"I think it's a bit early for you to worry about that. You just happen to be the first person they questioned. By the time they finish their inquiry, they'll have questioned dozens of other people."

"I hope you're right." He sounded doubtful. When he spoke again he sounded even more concerned. "You know, that body was ice-cold when I touched it. That means Jeremy had already been dead for a long time when we found him. If he was killed sometime during the night, that means unless somebody can confirm I was lying on my front walk from around eleven o'clock last night until six o'clock this morning, I'm totally screwed."

"You're overreacting, David. Surely—"

His voice rose to a frantic pitch. "I threatened to kill the guy, Della. This whole town thinks I have an anger management issue. And to top it all off, Jeremy and I almost came to blows last night, and not twenty-four hours later, he's dead."

"Hold on. Jeremy was a swindler. He stole money from half the people in town. Trust me, you're not the only person around here who had a reason to dislike the man."

"Maybe you're right." He sounded only mildly reassured.

"The person you should talk to is Matthew. He knows how the police work. Maybe he can give you some advice."

There was a long pause. "Is he there?"

"No. But wherever he is, he shouldn't be long. Why don't you come over?"

"If you don't mind. I could use his advice."

"Come on over. Just let yourself in. I'll be in the

kitchen." I hung up, hobbled over to the front door and unlatched it.

I hopped around on one foot, making a fresh pot of coffee—perhaps not such a good idea for someone who was already shaky. A moment later there was a knock at the door, followed by the sound of it opening and closing. Jenny appeared, carrying a quart of milk.

"You're just in time for coffee," I said. "Are you sure you won't stay for a cup?"

"I'd like to, but I really have to get back to the shop," she said, tapping her wristwatch. "I'm already late."

"You had to leave work to pick me up? You should have told me. I would have taken a cab."

"Don't worry. Franny was back from her appointment, and I was just about to go on break." She turned to leave, but paused in the doorway and pointed to my forehead. "You really should ice that bruise."

I picked up the bag from the counter, where I'd left it. "Already am."

Jenny had no sooner left than David arrived. He opened the door and called out, "Hello-o."

"I'm in the kitchen."

Footsteps approached and a moment later he appeared. "You're looking a bit green around the gills," I said, in a weak attempt at humor. "It clashes with your burgundy bruises."

"I know. I know. But you don't look so great either."

"Gee, thanks. You sure are a charmer when it comes to compliments." He chuckled. "Can I get you something? Coffee? Tea?" I held up my makeshift ice pack. "Frozen peas?"

"Thanks, but it's too late for that," he said. "Ice packs only work within the first few hours. But I sure could use a cup of coffee."

"I just made a fresh pot." I pointed to the crutches leaning against the wall. "You'll have to help yourself, if you don't mind."

He stared at the crutches, and then bent down to peek under the table. "Damn. You really did hurt yourself. It's not broken, is it?"

"No, just sprained. I think I also bruised some ribs in that tumble. It hurts like hell when I breathe too deeply."

He rummaged around the cupboard and returned holding a mug. "Can I get you a cup too?"

I nodded. "Thanks."

He poured and carried the cups to the table. He pulled out a chair and sat, staring glumly into space.

I hated to see him so worried. "Hey. Right now, the police haven't even started investigating. They're probably still combing the murder scene. Matthew will tell you the same thing, trust me." Somehow that didn't seem to make him feel much better. I groped for something to cheer him up. "By the way"—the words spilled out—"I think I'll make an offer on that building."

I stopped. Why had I just said that, knowing that finding the body had put a damper on my earlier decision? Did I still want to live somewhere, knowing a murder had occurred there? I looked at David, wondering if maybe I should tell him that actually I still hadn't quite made up my mind.

"That's nice," he replied vaguely, not having heard a word I'd just said. With his elbows on the table, he dropped his face into his hands. "I can't believe this is happening to me. If I was a cop, I'd suspect me too." He groaned. "If it wasn't for bad luck lately, I'd have no luck at all." He sat there, looking miserable. I put down my ice pack and placed a sympathetic hand on his.

Suddenly, from behind me, I heard, "Oh, uh, sorry." I turned in my seat in time to see Matthew leaving. From where he stood, he probably thought David and I—

"Matthew," I called out. "Don't go." He spun around and his eyes stopped on David's face. "Jesus, man, what the hell happened to you?" He didn't even glance my way, never mind noticing the bump on my forehead, or the crutches leaning against the wall.

David gave a pained smile. "I wish I could tell you I creamed the other guy." Then he retold his story, but didn't mention anything about finding Jeremy's body. I opened my mouth to say something, and then closed it again.

Matthew came closer, scowling. "Oh, man. You look awful. Do you have any idea who did this to you?"

"None." He shook his head and grimaced, bringing a hand to the back of his neck. "Hell. Every little move hurts."

"Would you like me to get you some Advil?" I offered. I could use a few myself at this point.

"No, I'm fine. Don't worry."

"I don't know about you guys, but I'm starving. You should have something to eat too," I said. "It's nearly eleven and I bet you haven't had anything to eat since last night, have you?" Without waiting for an answer, I struggled to my feet and reached for my crutches.

Matthew's eyes widened. "What happened to you?"

"I decided to roll instead of walk down some stairs." I shuffled to the refrigerator.

"You sit," said Matthew. "Tell me what you want and I'll get it for you."

"I'd love a sandwich, if you don't mind. I have some cheese and lettuce in the fridge, and some tomatoes on the window ledge," I said, shuffling back to my seat. "But first, can you get me some Advil? It's on top of the fridge."

"Would you like a sandwich too, David?" he asked.

"That'd be great."

Matthew picked up the loaf of bread and dropped two slices in the toaster. He turned to David. "I bet the last thing you had was a few drinks too many. Am I right?"

"Well, I did have a few bourbons. And you're right—a few too many." At last he brought the conversation around to the events. "Something else happened this morning that I should tell you about."

"Er, actually, Matthew, I hope you don't mind, but it was my suggestion that David come and talk to you. You might be able to give him some advice."

"Talk to me about what?" Matthew glanced from him to me and back again.

David told him about finding Jeremy Fox's body, concluding with, "And now the police think I killed him."

"Much as I believe you had nothing to do with it, what do you think I can do?"

Misery washed over David's face again. "You've helped the police on a lot of cases. I was hoping you might have some advice."

Matthew looked thoughtful. "Why don't we have a bite first? Meanwhile, I'll give it some thought." He set the platter of sandwiches on the table, throwing me a reproachful look. The message was clear. I should have minded my own business. "Can I get you something to drink?"

"Got any bourbon?" David asked. His attempt at grinning succeeded in a lopsided grimace. "Just joking— I'll have a glass of water."

Matthew set it in front of him. "I didn't realize how hungry I was." He plopped into a chair. He picked up a sandwich and glanced at me at last. "Now tell me about you. How did you manage to fall down the stairs?"

"Well, my story isn't nearly as dramatic as David's. Nobody hit me over the head. I was just in a bit of a rush to get out of the building, and I took a tumble."

"You were wearing those elevator shoes of yours, weren't you?"

I smiled. "Guilty as charged."

"Jesus, kiddo, you could have really hurt yourself."

"Trust me, I have plenty of bruises to drive the point home."

Matthew turned back to David. "Why don't you tell me again exactly what happened? I want all the details."

David set his sandwich down and shrugged, saying, "It must have been, what, seven thirty?" He looked at me for confirmation.

"That's right." I nodded at Matthew. "You were here. That's when I came in, remember?"

"After I dropped Della off, I went straight to Bottoms Up," David continued, naming the local restaurant and bar.

Matthew wrinkled his forehead. "That's where I picked up the Japanese food last night. I didn't see you when I was there."

David shrugged, but I couldn't help noticing the flush that appeared on his face. "I was probably in the washroom. By the time I headed home, I'd had about half a dozen drinks, so I left my car there and walked back to my place, around, er, eleven, I think." He avoided Matthew's eyes as he said this, just as he had Mike's, earlier. Was it my imagination, or was David hiding something? Or maybe, after so many drinks, he simply wasn't sure of the facts. God knows, if I'd consumed anywhere near the amount of alcohol he had, I wouldn't even recall my own name.

He said, "The last thing I remember is turning onto the walk to my front door. I heard some rustling in the bushes, but before I could see who it was—wham!—something hit me in the back of the head. Next thing I knew, it was daylight, and I was lying on the sidewalk, feeling like Rocky after the fight. I went inside, called a cab, and went straight to the hospital. And that's where I was—under observation in the ER—until I met up with Della."

Matthew crossed his arms. "I hate to say this, but knowing the police, they can just claim you caused those injuries yourself, hoping to create an alibi. Will the doctor who treated you confirm you were attacked?"

"Hell, if the cops want proof, all they have to do is feel the back of my head. Go ahead. Feel it. I've got a lump the size of an egg."

Matthew pushed back his chair and walked around to David.

"Right here," said David, guiding his hand.

Matthew's eyebrows rose. "You're not joking. You must have been hit pretty hard to get a bump like that."

"That's why they kept me under observation so long—in case I had a concussion."

I cleared my throat. "I think we all might be worrying for nothing. It isn't as if Jeremy didn't have a lot of enemies in town." I looked at Matthew. "You told me yourself that Jeremy swindled dozens of people. I imagine a few of them might have liked to see him dead."

David helped himself to another sandwich from the platter. "Until I saw him lying there, I was sure he was the one who clobbered me. I can't think of anyone else who would want to hurt me."

Matthew was pouring me a second cup of coffee when the thought flashed through my mind. "You both know what we should do?" They looked at me. "Investigate this murder ourselves." There was a stunned silence.

Matthew found his voice first. "That is ridiculous."

I shook my head. "No, think about it. The police already suspect David. They won't look any further. What I can't figure out is why anybody would attack David." I turned to him. "You don't have any enemies, do you?"

"Not anymore," he said. "Haven't you heard? I knocked him off."

"Not funny." I smiled crookedly. "I think we should start by making a list of all the people with reason to hate Jeremy Fox."

They looked at me as if I had just sprouted an extra head.

"What?" I crossed my arms. "Why is it that men never

want to consider a woman's opinion? You give as much credence to our sixth sense as you do to Bigfoot and flying saucers—" I stopped, shocked. Holy crap, I had just expressed belief in women's sixth sense. I was turning into Jenny.

They looked at each other.

"You think I'm a little crazy, don't you?" I asked Matthew.

There was a long pause before he shook his head. "No."

"You had to *think* about it?" I blurted, offended.

"Hey, you said a *little* crazy."

David and Matthew laughed.

"Not funny," I said, struggling to keep the corners of my mouth from twitching. But a second later I was laughing along with them. "Ouch, ouch! Don't make me laugh. It hurts!" I winced, holding my ribs, which only made them laugh all the harder.

When the laughter quieted down, we returned to our sandwiches, and Matthew said, "Let's forget this nonsense about playing detective." He turned to David. "By the way, Della wants to put an offer on that building you showed her yesterday."

Matthew outlined his idea of making an offer for a lease-to-own, and David nodded cautiously, rubbing the back of his head again—poor guy.

"How about I come by and fill out the forms later, say around four or so?" he asked, looking in better spirits.

The whole murder thing had dampened my excitement for the building, but not enough to change my mind. "Okay."

He turned back to Matthew. "About the police—what am I supposed to do? Do I just sit around and wait for them to arrest me?"

"I think you should get yourself a criminal lawyer."

I gasped. "Won't that make him look guilty?"

Matthew shook his head. "Who cares how it looks? Anybody would be a fool to let the police question them without a lawyer present."

David suddenly looked exhausted. "I guess I can call the lawyer who's taking care of my divorce."

Matthew shook his head. "What you need is a criminal lawyer, not a divorce lawyer. I know a good one—John Pattullo. His practice is in Charlotte, but he lives about twenty minutes from here, in Belmont. He works from home, unless he has to be in court. Give him a call. If he's there now, maybe he can see you right away."

"Er, my car is in the shop. I got a flat tire this morning." It occurred to me that I hadn't noticed his car when I went to meet him. But if he was on foot, when did he pick up his car? Again I got that niggling feeling that he was hiding something.

Matthew pulled out his cell phone, punched in a number and handed it to him. "If he's available now, I'll drive you myself."

After arranging to meet with the lawyer in half an hour, the men left. I couldn't help noticing that they didn't ask me to join them. Not that I wanted to go, but it might have been nice to feel included. As it was, I was still shaky from finding Jeremy's body, and I hated being alone.

I helped myself to yet another cup of coffee and threw the bag of now mushy peas in the garbage. The bump on my forehead had all but disappeared, but my ankle and my ribs still killed. I got the bottle of Advil and took a second tablet, gulping it down with a mouthful of coffee. I returned to the table and closed my eyes, rubbing my temples.

Of course, the first thing that flashed through my mind was the image of Jeremy's body.

Here I was, miles away from Charlotte, in what I'd believed would be a safe little town, and I'd stumbled upon a murder. As awful as I felt, I didn't feel nearly as bad as I had last year when I'd stumbled upon the evidence of my boss's embezzling. Of course, the victim here was not someone I knew, and I was not considered a suspect — or at least I didn't think I was. The point was that I felt stronger these days. Strangely, it had taken this shattering event for me to notice that the burnout, or depression, or whatever it was I'd been going through, was gone. I was my old self again.

Welcome back, Della.

Chapter 18

I had been sitting quietly for about twenty minutes and the second pill was just starting to do its job when the phone rang.

"Hello, dear."

Oh, God, just the person I didn't need to talk to right now. "Hi, Mom," I said, hoping my voice sounded cheerier than I felt.

"I can't believe you didn't tell me, dear. I was just talking to June, and she announced that Matthew is back in Briar Hollow"—I cringed, imagining that conversation between my mother and his. Sure enough, the pitch of her voice rose to that of a lottery winner—"and living with you," she concluded excitedly.

"Don't get your hopes up, Mom. We're living in the same house, not living together. There's a big difference."

"Still, Della, if you play your cards right—"

"I'll only be here a few more weeks at most—until I get a place of my own, which, by the way, I've already found."

There was silence at the other end, and I imagined her biting her lips, trying to come up with an argument.

"How is June?" I asked, hoping to steer her away from the subject.

"She's well. Of course she's disappointed that Matthew left town. She loved having him live so close for a few months." It occurred to me that living farther away from June might have been an added enticement to Matthew's decision to move back here. His mother and mine were two of a kind.

"Are you sure you want to move out? I was thinking that maybe—"

"I know what you were thinking. It's not going to happen." If my meddling mother had her way, she'd probably wheedle him into marrying me.

"I don't understand why you won't at least try. You and he would make such a nice—"

"Mom, stop it."

I heard the disappointment in her voice. "Oh, all right," she said, giving up the battle if not the war. "About your condo—now that Matthew's moved out, what are you planning to do with it? Maybe you should try to rent it furnished. I was speaking to Mrs. Johnson—you remember her—she was—"

Before she could launch into one of her long-winded stories about some relative stranger, I cut her off. "Funny you should say that, because renting it furnished is exactly what I've decided to do. And that reminds me. I should call my agent right now. Otherwise I'll forget."

"Okay. I'll talk to you later. Love you."

"Love you too, Mom." After hanging up, I rummaged through my purse until I found my agent's business card. I picked up the phone and punched in her number.

"Samantha Altman," she answered on the first ring. On hearing my voice, she immediately launched into an apology. "I'm sorry, Della, I swear I haven't forgotten about you. Sales have been really slow lately. It's not only your condo. It's all real estate. I've hardly sold anything in months."

"I know. Real estate is in a slump all over the country. Which brings me to what I wanted to talk to you about. I'm considering holding on to it until the market turns around. What do you think of renting it furnished until then?"

"Fabulous idea," she said without hesitation.

"That's a better reaction than expected. Do you really think you can rent it more easily than you can sell it?"

"Absolutely. In fact, if that's what you decide to do, I have a client who's looking for a place just like yours. He's an IBM executive from New York. His company gave him a budget of three thousand dollars a month for a place to stay while he oversees a new project out here. His wife and children are staying in New York, so he'll be commuting back and forth weekly. All he needs is a one-bedroom, but it has to be in the heart of Center City. And your place is so beautiful. I just know he'll love it. What do you think?"

I was almost dizzy with excitement. "Three thousand a month? Are you serious?"

"I know it sounds like a lot, but it's still cheaper for him than the price of a hotel suite."

"Please, make him sign on the dotted line before he changes his mind."

She laughed. "Tell you what—I'll take him out and show him your condo this afternoon. If he likes it, the deal is as good as done." She reminded me that the first month's rent would go toward her commission, which was fine with me. I was still dancing on the ceiling at the thought of thirty-six thousand dollars a year, which was laughable, really, considering how much less it was than what I used to earn as a business analyst.

"I can't thank you enough."

"I'll let you know the minute I have news."

After hanging up, I let out a whoop. A few feet away, Winston jumped to his feet, startled, and looked at me as if I had just lost my mind.

"Three thousand dollars a month, Winston! Can you believe it?" He tilted his head, trying to understand— gave up and settled back down.

Three thousand dollars would cover the mortgage payments and utilities on my condo, and still leave some money—albeit not much—but maybe enough to cover a portion of the rent on my new place. It struck me then that my decision to move was firm.

Chapter 19

I was halfway through a beautiful green and white basket-weave strip, using only one foot on the treadles because of my bum ankle, when I heard a knock at the door. I put down my work, grabbed my crutches and shuffled to answer. By the time I opened the door, Susan Wood was stepping all over my bed of petunias, trying to peek through the living room window. She spun around to face me.

"Oh, hi," she said, not looking the least bit embarrassed at being caught snooping. "I waited so long, I thought nobody was home." She looked, in fact, delighted.

I checked my watch. To my surprise, it was already a few minutes past one. "Sorry. I forgot to put out the 'Open' sign. Come on in."

She stepped in and then noticed my crutches. "What in the world?"

"Sprained ankle," I said and led the way to my desk. "I'll be better in no time."

She seemed on the verge of asking me something, and then changed her mind. She went straight to Kate Radley's gift-wrapped parcels, but instead of picking them up, she stage-whispered, "I heard the news. You must have been terrified."

Good God, was everyone in town a gossip? "What are you talking about?" I asked, pretending not to know.

She looked startled. "I heard Jeremy Fox was murdered and that you found his body. Are you telling me it's not true?"

I shook my head. "No, it's true. Jeremy Fox is dead, and David Swanson and I found the body."

And then, adopting a tone almost identical to Officer Bellows, she said, "Of course it was murder, but how was he killed? Was it a gun? A knife?"

"I have no idea. He was lying in the middle of the floor. All I could tell was that he was dead."

"Was there blood?"

I grimaced, reluctant to go into details. "There was some."

She frowned. "Well, if there was blood, no one can claim he died of natural causes."

"Are you suggesting the police would want to cover up a murder? Why would they want to do that?"

"No, no, I didn't mean anything like that. But sometimes people make mistakes. This is the second murder in Briar Hollow this year, and the first was pegged an accident. Mark my words—one of these days it'll come out that Dolores's husband was murdered."

I didn't believe that for a second, and was rather shocked at how so many of the townsfolk participated in malicious gossip.

"The coroner declared it an accident," I said in a no-nonsense tone.

"The coroner!" She crossed her arms and smiled. "Dr. Cook must be eighty years old. He's lived here all his life and probably attended half the births around here. He sees nothing but good in people. He would never believe anyone from this town could be a killer." She grew thoughtful. "I spoke to Marsha this morning. She told me she was at Jeremy's when he got a phone call last night. He went rushing out the minute he hung up—around nine thirty—saying he'd be back in an hour. When he didn't return, she went home." She shook her head, smiling conspiratorially. "Probably slamming the door behind her, if you ask me."

"You talked to her today?" I was astonished. "You mean, after she found out about Jeremy's death?"

"She and I are next-door neighbors. When Mike broke the news to her, she was so distraught that he came banging on my door and asked me to keep her company."

Susan had stirred my curiosity. "Did she tell you who he was meeting?"

"Unfortunately, he didn't tell her. She checked the call display after he left, but it was a confidential number. Knowing Jeremy, he could have been seeing another woman"—she leaned in and whispered—"which is probably why she wanted to know who called, and why I would be willing to bet she left in a huff."

I scrunched up my forehead. "How well did you know him?"

"I worked for Jeremy until a couple of months ago. That was when I began suspecting his project was a scam. I couldn't in good conscience stay. When I gave him my notice, Kate and David asked me to stay with the company and work for them. I would've liked to warn people, but I couldn't without some kind of proof."

"It was you," I said, as it came to me. "You did it."

Chapter 20

Susan looked taken aback. "What are you talking about? Are you accusing me of something?"

"You leaked that environmental report, didn't you?" Her frown melted into a smile, but she admitted nothing. I was beginning to like this woman. "Tell me about Jeremy Fox."

She sniffed. "What can I say? The man was a sociopath. When the contamination report came out, he pretended to be just as shocked as his investors. He went around assuring everyone that this was just a temporary setback, that their money was still safe with him. I feel sorry for anyone who invested in that ridiculous project of his. They might as well forget about that money. They'll never see a dime of it again." She looked thoughtful for a moment. "I think something must have happened before Jeremy was killed, because his whole demeanor changed almost overnight. He stopped pretending that everything was just dandy. He got into this really foul mood and spent all his time having whispered conversations on the phone. And judging by the dark circles under his eyes, I don't think he got much sleep either." She nodded knowingly. "He was scared of something, if you ask me."

"Maybe somebody was suing him."

"Maybe," she said, making it sound highly unlikely, and looked at her watch. "Uh-oh. I should get back." She picked up the parcels.

"If you find out anything, let me know," I said, and then surprised myself by adding, "Anything I can do to help, just ask."

At the door, she turned. "Oh, I almost forgot. I'll drop off my loom tomorrow if that's okay."

"That would be great." I closed the door and hobbled to the kitchen.

The day's events were catching up with me. I felt sore, tired and gloomy. Not that I believed her theory, but hearing another person claim that Dolores's husband had been murdered was unnerving. I returned to my loom with murder on my mind.

The door swung open and Matthew stomped in, his brow furrowed. He waited for Winston to trudge in behind him and then shut the door hard, sending the bell into hysterics.

"Uh-oh, somebody is in a bad mood," I said, grabbing my crutches.

"If you're talking about me, you're wrong," he snapped back, unclipping Winston from his leash. "There's nothing wrong with my mood."

"And slamming doors is something you do just for the heck of it," I said teasingly.

He scowled at me. "I did not slam it. I . . ." He gave up. "Okay, fine. So I'm in a bad mood." He glanced around, seeming at a loss for a moment, and then marched off toward the kitchen.

I followed, working my crutches as fast as I could—which was not all that fast. "What's wrong?"

He wrenched the fridge door open. "Nothing's wrong." He grabbed a Heineken, dropped it on the counter with a bang. And then, yanking drawer after drawer open only to slam them shut again, he mumbled, "Why can't I ever find a damn thing in this place?"

I opened the knife drawer, got the bottle opener and brandished it. "Is this what you're looking for?"

He took it, embarrassed. He popped the top off his bottle and threw the opener into the dishcloth drawer. "Why is it that women always have to keep moving everything around?"

"Moody, aren't we? Whatever happened to 'Thank you'?" I fished the opener back out from where he'd just dropped it and waved it, opening the knife drawer again. "And by the way, the bottle opener goes in here, along with knives, can openers and scissors." I slammed the drawer shut. "If you kept any kind of order in this place, you wouldn't constantly be searching for things."

"You're right," he said sheepishly. He turned to face me and leaned against the counter, looking like an imminent thunderstorm.

"I stopped by the station to see Mike." He took a swig from his beer. He smiled crookedly and shrugged, mellowing slightly. "Let's just say it didn't go well. I guess I didn't exactly pick the best time to drop by—what with the murder and everything. His phone was ringing off the hook with people calling to find out if it was true and wanting to know how they're going to get their money back now that the bastard is dead."

"Gee. People are really broken up about the man's death, aren't they?" I leaned my crutches against the wall and sat, propping my elbows on the table. "I thought you and Mike were friends."

He gave me something between a smile and a scowl. "We had a disagreement last winter. I thought he'd be over it by now." He took another swig. "I was wrong."

"Why? What happened?"

He shrugged, and under his casual demeanor I sensed real conflict. "Since then, whenever I see him, he pretends everything is fine. Today he talked about stuff—football, baseball. He even talked about the case, but he wouldn't look me in the eye. I called him on it, and for a moment I thought he was going to punch me."

"That's more than just weird. That's scary," I said. And disregarding my little voice, which was telling me loud and clear to drop it, I said, "What was the disagreement about?"

He glared at me, grabbed his beer. "I don't want to talk about it," he said, and walked out. I struggled out of my chair and back onto my crutches, following him to the front room. Winston lumbered behind me. When I got there, Matthew was standing in the middle of what used to be his living room, looking frustrated.

"I keep forgetting that my La-Z-Boy is gone."

I might have made a derogatory comment about that chair, but this was perhaps not the right time. Besides, I was dying to hear more about Mike. But before I had a chance to say anything, he spun around and stormed back to the kitchen. Winston and I trailed behind once again. I got to the kitchen in time to see him pull out a chair and plop himself down.

"You've got to stop running around all over the house," I snipped, dropping into the chair across from him. "Walking isn't so easy on these things."

"You don't have to follow me."

I altered the tone of my voice. "Jenny told me that Mike's personality changed suddenly last fall. Do you know if anything happened around that time?" I'd already heard Jenny's version, and not that I didn't believe her, but I was curious about Matthew's take on the situation. "I mean, people don't just change for no good reason."

A thoughtful look appeared on his face. "Actually, he did change quite suddenly, and not just his personality, although that's what was most noticeable. He lost a lot of weight too, and was wound so tight he looked ready to explode all the time." He thought again. "That was about the time he asked Jenny for a divorce."

"That's another thing that doesn't make any sense." I folded my arms on the table. "Jenny said they were really happy together; then, out of the blue, he asked her for a divorce. I don't get it. Was he having an affair or something?"

"No." He seemed to weigh what he was about to say. "You have to promise you won't breathe a word of this to her. She has no idea about any of this."

"I promise," I said.

"He thought Jenny was having an affair."

"Why?"

"That's what my disagreement with him was about. I told him he was nuts to think she would ever cheat on him, that he was a real jerk for leaving her." He stopped suddenly and scowled.

"And?" I prompted.

His eyes turned dark. "He asked me if I was sleeping with her too."

My jaw dropped.

He took a swig of his beer. "That was the single most insulting thing he could ever have said to me. Jenny is a friend. I like her because she's open and honest, and because she made him happy. I know she can be a bit flaky with all her woo-woo stuff, but when it came to her husband, that woman was as straight as they come. She would have died for him, and he just threw her away like a rag." The sincerity in his voice was unmistakable. "How could he even imagine I'd be interested in his wife? He and I have known each other all our lives. Even if I was the kind of man—like Jeremy Fox—who doesn't think twice about seducing married women, I was never attracted to her. No offense to Jenny, but I think of her as a sister."

He let out a *pfft* of frustration. "I think Mike must have had some kind of midlife crisis or something." He shrugged. "Or maybe he's just nuts."

I turned that over in my mind for a bit. "If Mike didn't confide in you, maybe there's somebody else he talked to. Isn't there someone he's close to? A longtime friend, or maybe a brother?"

Matthew rubbed his chin. "He was always close to his father. If there was anyone he would have confided in, it was him." I nodded my encouragement. "But his old man died about five years ago—prostate cancer."

"What about his mother?"

He shook his head. "He's not close to her. In fact, I don't think he's spoken to her in years—not since she left his father shortly after he was diagnosed. She'd been having an affair with another man for years. Mike never forgave her."

"It sounds like he was devastated."

"Funny thing is, I don't think it hurt his old man nearly as much as it did him. His parents had been fighting for years. I think it came almost as a relief to his father when she finally left. But Mike didn't see it that way. He was convinced that if only his mother had stayed, his father would have survived the cancer."

There was a long silence before he glanced at me, his expression suddenly sullen. "By the way, you had no business offering my help to David that way. I'm not a lawyer. I'm a criminologist."

"I know, but you help the Charlotte police on all kinds of cases. Why wouldn't you want to help David? You told me yourself he's your friend."

He softened. "He is, but I told Mike I'd help him on this case. I can't very well help both sides."

"I don't get it. Isn't the police's job to go after the truth? It shouldn't matter who you help as long as the police find the real killer."

He scowled.

"Where is David now?"

He shrugged. "I dropped him off at the garage to pick up his car."

"He didn't tell you anything about his appointment?"

"No. He kept it all to himself. Lawyer-client confidentiality, remember?"

"Right, I knew that." If David told Matthew what had been discussed in private with his lawyer, the confidentiality bond would be considered broken, and Matthew could then be compelled to testify in court about what David had told him.

"Sure, you did," he said teasingly.

"I did too," I said, and then I saw the amused glint in his eyes and my breath caught in my throat. "Sometimes you irritate the heck out of me," I said, blushing furiously.

He chuckled, giving me the sneaking suspicion that he'd gotten a real charge out of getting me flustered.

Chapter 21

The phone rang, but before I could answer, Matthew reached over and picked it up.

"My house, my phone," he whispered. And then he spoke into the receiver. "Hello, Norah. How nice to hear from you," he said. He covered the mouthpiece with his hand and whispered, "Your mother."

Again? I had just spoken to her a few hours ago. I signaled for him to give me the phone. He shook his head, taking a few steps back. Damn it! If I knew my mother, she was already promoting her get-Della-and-Matthew-together campaign. I scrambled to my feet and scooped up my crutches. For every step I moved toward him, Matthew took one step back. To an onlooker, we might have looked as if we were doing some kind of primitive dance.

He chatted on, smiling, and stepping farther away from me: the weather was nice, his book deal was great, and then, much to my embarrassment, the subject turned to me.

He winked at me. "Don't worry. She's fine. She's right here with me. It's great having her here."

Oh, God. I could just imagine how my mother would interpret that. I lunged for the phone again.

He ducked. "I guess it was a shock, but don't worry. She's handling it very well." Another short silence, followed by, "I agree, and I told her so myself."

What were they talking about?—and even more frightening—what were they *agreeing* about?

"I know, but she saw a great place and she's decided to put an offer on it." Another silence and then, "Of course I told her that. But you know your daughter. When she decides to do something, nobody can talk her out of it. But I'll try again." All at once, I knew. Mom wanted him to talk me into staying. My blood pressure shot up. I was so going to kill her.

As far as mothers go, there was nothing wrong with mine, except that from the moment I turned twenty-five, she made it her duty to find me a husband. And with every new birthday, she got more focused on it. Last Christmas, I'd been mortified to overhear her trying to coax Matthew into taking me to dinner.

"She's been despondent since that whole embezzlement thing," I heard her say as I walked into the living room one day. "It would do her a world of good if you took her out for a nice dinner."

Without waiting for Matthew to come up with some excuse, I had stepped into the living room. "You're embarrassing him, Mother." And sure enough, when I glanced at him, he turned bright red. "Matthew doesn't want to go out with me. He's seeing someone—Amanda."

After Matthew snuck away, I gave my mother a piece of my mind. "I don't need you to find dates for me. I can get them on my own."

"Well, then," she'd said, pointedly, "if you can do it,

why don't you? If you won't listen to your biological clock, will you at least listen to mine? I'm sixty-nine. How much longer are you going to make me wait before giving me a grandchild?"

I had to hand it to her. She had a real talent for pushing my buttons.

Now, I prayed to heaven Mom didn't know Matthew and Amanda were no longer seeing each other; otherwise there'd be no letting up on her part. I tried to read his face and found amusement. It didn't make me feel any better.

"Let me put her on the phone." At last he handed the phone over to me, mouthing through a teasing smile, "It's for you."

I snatched it. "Hello, Mother." I moved both crutches to one hand and hopped away on one foot until I was out of earshot.

"What's all that thudding I hear? And why are you out of breath?"

"I sprained an ankle, and I can't hold the phone and crutches at the same time."

"Crutches? Does that have anything to do with the body you discovered?"

Oh, cr-rap. "How did you hear about that?"

"I may not be young anymore, but I can still use the Internet. Everything is so easy nowadays with Google."

"*You* search the Internet?" I chuckled at the picture of my silver-haired mother surfing the Web.

"Of course I do, dear. The Internet is the way of the future," she said, trying to sound knowledgeable. "I check the *Belmont Daily* online every day. How else am

I going to find out what's happening in Briar Hollow? Not from you, that's for sure." I didn't give her the satisfaction of replying. "Are you all right?"

"Of course I am, Mom."

"I hope the police aren't stupid enough to think you had anything to do with it."

"Not at all. I didn't even know the man."

"That's what Matthew said, but I wanted to hear it from you." And then in a low voice she said, "Did you know it's over between him and Amanda?"

Uh-oh. "So I heard."

"Why don't you hold off a little before moving out? This is no time for you to be alone, with a murderer running around. Besides"—her voice dropped to a whisper— "you never know, maybe you and he might decide you like each other." There it was, just as I had been dreading, that same old tune. "I just know you two would be happy together."

"Mom, please stop."

"I hope you're wearing makeup."

"Yes, Mother, I am."

"And you're wearing skirts. Men like to see a woman's legs."

"Yes, Mother, I am."

"And are you cooking for him? On second thought, maybe that's not such a good idea. You never were much of a cook."

"I'm going to hang up now, Mom. I have some work to do. I'll call you soon. Love you." I hung up before she could say anything else. I returned to the kitchen and put the phone back into its cradle.

Matthew was eyeing me with a teasing smile. "Did Norma talk you into having dinner with me?"

"No, but not for lack of trying." I covered my embarrassment with a weak laugh. "I'm sorry. She can be such a bug at times."

"She's no worse than my mother."

I looked up at him, surprised. "Are you telling me your mother is trying to . . ." I pointed at him and then at me. He nodded. "What is it about our mothers?"

He shrugged. "It's cute. Don't worry about it. One of these days I'll have to take you out." And in case I got the wrong idea, he added, "Just to make them happy."

"You don't have to do that." My face grew hot. "In fact, I can't think of a worse idea. Can you imagine? If we ever did go out together, they'd be sending out wedding invitations the next day." I gave a strangled laugh. "There'd be no stopping them."

Matthew looked at his watch, and—thank you, God—changed the subject. "By the way, I asked David to come over to prepare your offer."

"Oh." I took a deep breath. "I wanted to go over the financials one more time."

"If you're worried about money, why don't you rent out both apartments and live somewhere else? It would make good business sense. Here's an idea. If you set up your shop and studio there, there'd be plenty of room for both of us in this house."

I was stunned. I swallowed and nodded slowly, unable to meet his eyes. I wasn't sure why the idea of staying here made me so nervous—it actually could solve my financial problems. I answered as casually as possible. "I hadn't thought of that." He was searching my face. I changed the subject. "If I rented out both apartments, do you think I could make a positive return on the building?"

"Yes, I do, although certainly not a high one." He paused and studied me. "So you'll take my offer?"

He had asked me to stay! At the very least I could give it some serious thought. After all, I did enjoy his company, and apparently he liked mine. "I guess so," I said, struggling to keep the corner of my mouth from twitching. I was suddenly scared and excited all at once. I was almost afraid to believe everything was falling into place so easily.

"I'm glad." He looked at his watch. "Oh, shit. It's later than I thought. David won't have time to prepare the offer right now. He has to report to the police station for questioning before the end of the day."

"But he was questioned this morning. He already told the police everything he knows. Why does he have to go back?"

"Don't worry," he said patiently. "What they took this morning was only a preliminary statement. Questionings are much more official. First of all, they're generally held in an interrogation room and taped. And then they make him sign a copy."

"And that's it?"

"Pretty much—unless he gives them a reason to keep him there."

"What are you talking about? What kind of reason could he possibly give them?"

"Listen, I know you like David—" I started shaking my head. I wanted to say that sure, I liked David—as a friend—but he cut me off. "Remember, you've only known him for a short time. I know I told you I've known him all my life, but he and I haven't been close in a long time. I hope—for your sake—that he's innocent, but we won't know for sure until this investigation is over."

My mouth dropped open. "Do you really think he might be guilty?" My mind was already racing. If David was the killer, it would mean that he set me up as a false witness. Could he really be that manipulative? I'd been going around telling everyone that he couldn't possibly have done it, that I had been there when he first saw the body, that I had seen his face, and that nobody could be such a good actor. I swallowed hard. Had David really played me so convincingly?

Matthew shrugged. "Is it possible? Yes." And then, he seemed to take pity on me. "But likely? No." More seriously, he said, "Don't worry, kiddo. Anything I can do to help him, I promise I will."

"Listen, Matthew, I want to clarify something. I'm not in—"

Before I could finish, there was a knock at the door. Matthew hurried to answer and a second later, he returned, followed by David, who—though I would have believed it impossible—looked even worse than he had earlier. The bruising around his swollen eye had turned a deep shade of eggplant. His upper lip had swollen to double its size, and the stitches looked ready to pop.

"Oh, God, David, you look awful." I continued with as much authority as I could muster. "Well, that does it. I don't care what you say. I'm getting you an ice pack right now."

He chuckled, keeping his face stiff. "Yeah, maybe an ice pack isn't a bad idea after all." He opened his briefcase and pulled out a file, placing it on the table.

I got a bag of frozen mixed vegetables from the freezer, smashed it on the counter to break its contents apart, and wrapped it in a dish towel. "Sorry, but I'm all out of peas."

David gave me a lopsided smile and placed it carefully against the bruised side of his face. "Thanks. I hope you weren't planning to make these for dinner."

"Not anymore." He looked taken aback. "Just joking."

He sat, propping an elbow on the table to keep the bag in place. "Do you want to sit in while we prepare the offer?" he asked Matthew.

Matthew smiled apologetically. "Listen, man, I hate to tell you this, but the offer will have to wait until later. The police want to question you."

David looked stunned. "Oh." He just sat there, looking uncertain. "I guess this is where I should call my lawyer." It was more of a question than a statement.

"That would not be a bad idea," said Matthew. "Ask him to meet you at the station."

David took a shaky breath and pulled out his cell phone. A minute later, he turned it off. "He'll meet me there in half an hour." Turning to me, he tapped the file. "You might want to read through these papers in the meantime." He turned to Matthew. "What do you think? Be honest, man. Am I going to get arrested?"

"I don't know," Matthew answered solemnly. "But having your lawyer present will make it less likely."

Panic filled David's eyes. "This is a nightmare. I can't believe this is happening to me."

Matthew walked over to him and clapped him on the shoulder. "I'll tell you what — I'll walk over to the station and wait with you until your lawyer shows up."

David turned to me, handing me my makeshift ice pack. "Here. Put it back in the freezer. One of us might need it later."

"How long will this take?" I asked.

Matthew shrugged. "Every case is different. It could take ten minutes or ten hours."

David blanched.

"Isn't there something I can do?" I asked. "I mean, I was there this morning. How come they want to question David and not me?"

Matthew gave me the raised eyebrow. "You didn't even know the man. But, hey, if you insist, I can tell them they should question you too."

"Very funny," I snapped.

Matthew chuckled. "About dinner — don't wait for me. I'll grab something on my own."

So much for ribs tonight.

I waved them off and they left, David with his shoulders slumped and Matthew full of false cheerfulness. I tossed the bag of frozen veggies back into the freezer. Feeling helpless, I turned my attention to the file David had left on the table. I opened it. I must have stared at it blankly for a full ten minutes before slapping it shut and returning to my loom.

The next time I looked at my watch, it was five o'clock.

I had been sitting at my loom for an hour, but even weaving had not helped calm my jangled nerves. In fact, when I looked at the strip I had completed, I realized a beginner would have done a better job. The thread tension was all over the place, ranging from seventeen yarns per inch to about twelve. *Garbage*, I decided. I had no choice but to undo all the work I'd done in the last hour—but later. Anything I attempted now would only result in more sloppy work. I heaved myself up, grabbed my crutches and returned to the kitchen, where I stared at the telephone, willing it to ring. What the hell was taking them so long?

Suddenly I couldn't take it anymore. If I didn't do something—anything—right this minute, I was going to go crazy. An idea flashed through my mind and I hurried to my desk, forgetting all about how tired and sore I was. I rested my crutches against the desk, flipped open my laptop and typed in David's name. In seconds, the online directory gave me his phone number and—more important—his address. I jotted it down.

Anderson Lane was just a few blocks away, still a trek for someone on crutches. Could I really do it? Or should I call a cab? No, I decided. No need for a cab. I could get there by myself. I stuffed the paper in my pocket and picked up my crutches again. Almost as if he could read my mind, Winston, who a minute ago had looked about as lively as the rug on which he'd been sleeping, jumped up and dashed toward the door.

"Sorry, Winnie. You know I'd take you along if it wasn't for these." I pointed to my crutches. He eyed me with such a pained look that I swallowed a lump of guilt the size of a fist. I closed the door and hurried down the walk, turning toward Anderson Lane.

It was a gorgeous day, the kind of day that brought a smile to everyone—everyone except me, that is. My crutches were turning out to be a real pain. Literally.

Chapter 22

David's place was a modest but well-kept beige clapboard house, trimmed in taupe. I liked the color combination. It was crisp and elegant. But I wasn't there to admire the man's taste. I was looking for evidence—what exactly, I wasn't sure. Something that proved David was telling the truth about having been attacked. On his front walk, I turned my attention to the hedge that bordered the gate—American holly, about eight feet tall. It was thick enough to swallow an army. Stepping closer, I examined the immediate area on one side of the entrance. After deciding that it looked untouched, I crossed to the other side and repeated my inspection.

That was when I spotted it: a damaged area in the hedge. Branches were broken, creating a depression deep enough to conceal a person. I laid my crutches on the ground and bent down, balancing my weight on one foot—very inefficiently, I might add—to examine the soil underneath. Were those footprints? They were faint, but I could make out one imprint that might have been from a shoe. The edges, however, were so indistinct that I couldn't tell whether the shoe that had formed it was big or small, sporty or dressy. I stood up, wobbling until

I got the crutches under my arms, and proceeded to scan the damaged shrubs.

Matthew had once described the correct way to conduct a search as imagining the area as a grid and examining carefully along one imaginary line after another, first horizontally and then vertically. I did this until I got to about shoulder height and spotted something. It could have been just a piece of dried leaf, but I stepped closer, plucked it out and found myself looking at a piece of fine, dark yarn, three or four inches long. Whether it was black or navy was difficult to tell.

Feeling like Sherlock Holmes, I looked around for something to wrap it in and pulled out the paper on which I'd jotted down this address. That would do. I folded it around the thread and slipped it carefully back inside my pocket.

I continued searching until I was satisfied that I had found all there was to discover. As far as I was concerned, the indent in the hedge, the footprints and the thread all pointed to somebody having been here, somebody who had been hiding from view. That was all I needed to convince me that David was telling the truth about the attack.

"I was right," I told myself, feeling oddly relieved as I hobbled back home. "David couldn't be the killer. He just couldn't."

When I got home—or rather, to *Matthew's* house—he and David were at the kitchen table, drinking Heinekens.

"Hey, you guys are back. How did it go?" I tried to read David's face, hoping the police had been easier on him than they'd been on me when I was a suspect. The long and painful questioning they put me through was an experience I wasn't likely to ever forget.

"Don't tell me you were traipsing around town," said Matthew, eyeing my crutches. "You must be sore as hell."

I lied through my teeth. "I was just out for a short walk. I'm getting used to them."

He stared down at the running shoe on my good foot. "I'm happy to see you gave up on those skyscraper heels of yours."

I sighed. "Doctor's orders." I maneuvered my way around the table to the chair Matthew pulled out and collapsed into it, groaning in relief.

Matthew gave me a knowing look. "Getting used to them, are you?"

I ignored his teasing, turning to David as he plucked an olive from the bowl in the middle of the table. He tossed it a few inches above his head, then caught it in his mouth. *Oh, for crying out loud.* I bit back a comment and slipped a hand inside my pocket for the yarn I'd found. I hesitated. It was maybe not a good idea to let David know I'd been snoo— I mean, investigating. He'd think I doubted him, which I suppose I had until I'd looked at his front lawn. I'd better tell Matthew when we were alone. I left the yarn in my pocket.

"Don't keep me in suspense. Tell me everything."

David tried to smile, but managed only a pained grimace. "Turns out I had to pay my lawyer three hundred bucks for nothing. All they did was ask me a bunch of questions I had already answered—where I was last night, who I saw, what time I got home."

I chuckled. "That's good. Better to pay your lawyer

for doing nothing now than for defending you in court later. Don't you think?"

He gave an appreciative smile. "You've got a point. I sure hope that was the end of it."

"It might be if the police believed you. Do you think they did?"

He shrugged. "Who the hell knows? As I was just telling Matthew, they asked me for the name of the emergency doctor who treated me. I'm sure they'll question him and everyone who saw me at the bar last night." Fear flashed over his face again. Poor guy. Having once been wrongfully accused myself, I knew just how he felt.

"But unless somebody happened to see me passed out on the walk in front of my house," he continued, "nobody can swear that I spent the night there."

Matthew said, "The police have to determine the time of Jeremy's death before they can start throwing accusations around."

"Did they mention how he was killed?" I asked.

"That was one of the first questions they asked me — as if I knew, or as if I'd be stupid enough to admit it if I did. And they wanted to know whether I noticed a laptop in the room."

"A laptop?" Until he nodded, I wasn't sure I'd heard right. "But that doesn't make any sense. If you'd seen one, it would have still been there when they got there. A laptop isn't exactly the kind of thing a person can hide in a pocket."

"I know. I didn't get that either."

My mind went back to the question of a weapon. "Considering all the blood around the body, it's a pretty safe bet that he was either stabbed or shot."

"Oh, it was definitely a gun. They asked me if I owned one and tested my hands for gunpowder residue."

"That answers that question." I faced Matthew. "That's good, isn't it? Once they saw there was no residue—" I turned back to David. "There wasn't, was there?"

"Of course not," he answered vehemently.

"Well, then, I'm sure there aren't too many people in Briar Hollow who own guns. Do you own one?"

"No. I hate them. I never even had toy guns when I was a kid. But one thing that puzzles me is this: If Jeremy was shot, wouldn't someone have reported hearing gunfire?"

Matthew considered the question briefly. "First of all, having no powder residue on your hands doesn't prove anything. The police can argue that you washed your hands after killing Jeremy. As for the shooting, people might not have heard it," he said. "Don't forget, the murder was committed indoors and probably late at night when most people were sleeping. Also, that stretch of Main Street is commercial. The closest homes are three or four buildings away. And to anyone who isn't familiar with the sound of gunshots, they can easily be mistaken for a car backfiring." He looked at me and smiled, sending my pulse racing. "So, where did you go on your walk?" He said this in a perfectly nice tone, but maybe because I felt a bit guilty about my investigating, I felt put on the spot.

"What is this? Am I accountable to you now?"

He looked at me quizzically. "Don't be silly, Della." That was the second time he'd called me by my name rather than kiddo. "I was surprised you weren't here when I got back. That's all."

"I wasn't anywhere special. Just around," I said, sounding guilty.

"Why are you being so vague? Are you hiding something?"

I did what I usually do when I feel cornered: I attacked. "Instead of giving me the third degree, why don't you take Winnie for a walk for a change? In case you haven't noticed, I'm in no shape to take over your responsibilities anymore." What the heck was wrong with me? I wanted to charm the man into letting me stay here, not make him hate me.

David glanced from me to Matthew and back again, looking puzzled. He cleared his throat. "How about filling out the paperwork for the offer? Do you want to do that now?" he asked in an obvious attempt to change the subject.

"They're in the folder on my desk. By the way, I've been meaning to ask you. Do you think the apartments might be difficult to rent after a murder was committed there? Would I need to disclose it to prospective tenants?"

"Are you kidding? This is Briar Hollow. You couldn't hide it if you tried. Everybody knows everything that goes on around here." He looked pensive for a moment. "I suppose it might spook some people, but I still believe you could rent those units very easily." He paused, looking concerned. "Are you sure you want to do this?"

"Yes. Let's do it right now." I was sure the apartments were lovely enough to charm even the most nervous of prospective tenants.

He pulled his chair closer, spreading the forms out on the table. And then, leaning in, he explained each clause, filling in all the lines along the way. At last he pulled out a pen and handed it to me. "All I need now is for you to initial and sign."

I initialed the clauses—dozens of them, it seemed. I signed the last line with a flourish and handed David's pen back to him.

He picked up the forms, slid one copy into the folder and handed it to me. The remaining papers he slipped into his briefcase, grinning. I guess there's nothing like the prospect of a nice commission check to lift a man's spirits.

"The offer is conditional until three o'clock the day after tomorrow. If the seller is interested, he'll get back to me with either an acceptance or a counteroffer. If we don't hear from him by then, your offer becomes null and void. Then you can decide whether or not you want to make a new offer." He pushed back his chair and stood. "One way or another I'll give you a call." I struggled to my feet, scooped up my crutches and followed him to the door.

A second later he was gone. I began to shake. It started with my hands and spread to my knees; pretty soon my whole body was trembling. This time it had nothing to do with bodies and blood and murder. I was having what had to be the worst case of buyer's remorse in history. And I hadn't even bought the building yet. I held on to that thought. With any luck, the seller would refuse my offer.

Matthew looked at me and chuckled. "You look scared out of your mind."

"That's because I *am* scared out of my mind." I squeezed my eyes shut, grimacing. "That building represents a lot of money for someone just starting a business."

"Come on," he said cajolingly. "Trust me. You have nothing to worry about. This is a good thing you're doing."

"I sure hope so. Otherwise, I'll have to go live in a cardboard box under a bridge." And much to my embarrassment, tears welled up. I was a mess and had been since finding Jeremy Fox's body. On second thought, I had been a mess since Matthew had moved back in; stumbling upon the murder had only made it worse.

He chuckled sympathetically. "You know what you need? A hug." He moved toward me and wrapped his arms around my shoulders. I melted into his arms. My crutches tumbled to the floor with a loud bang, but I barely noticed. He smelled so good. His arms felt so warm, so solid.

"Matthew?" I whispered, my face buried near his shoulder.

"Yes," he replied in a strangled voice, and when he pulled away to glance down at me, his eyes were golden. His eyes lingered on mine for a moment, and then he pulled away.

Before I could say a word, he turned and marched out of the kitchen, his footsteps echoing down the hall. A second later a door banged shut, and I was left wobbling on one foot, shocked at the overwhelming rush of sensations coursing through my body.

Chapter 23

David breezed in at seven o'clock sharp. "I'm not early, am I?" he asked, seemingly in a good mood. Of all the members of the beginner class he was the last one I would have expected to show up on time.

"The others should be here any minute."

He grinned. "I faxed your offer to the seller. Keep your fingers crossed."

I raised a hand, displaying crossed fingers.

He crouched to scratch Winston's head and was rewarded with a slurpy kiss. "Do you mind if I use the washroom?" he asked, wiping the pooch saliva from his hand.

"Upstairs," I said, pointing. "First door on the left." I watched him bound up the stairs enviously. It would be a while until I could maneuver stairs so easily again. After only half a day on crutches, I was utterly exhausted. Now I had not only bruised ribs and a sprained ankle but also blistered palms and sore armpits. No matter what Dr. Green had said, these crutches were *not* very friendly.

I was about to go sit when the sound of loud voices outside stopped me. It was Mercedes and Dolores, I realized. I stepped closer to the door. They were having one doozy of an argument. What was that about? I pressed an ear to the door, but most of what they were saying was too mumbled for me to hear. Except for a few of Mercedes's words.

"Blah, blah, blah *pretend*—blah, blah, blah *hate you*," and "blah, blah, blah *divorce*."

Dolores answered with something sharp, but as hard as I tried to, I couldn't make out any of it. This was followed by some more angry words from Mercedes, ending with, "*and now he's dead too*." I gasped at the implications, and then, sensing that the argument was winding down, I tottered away. The doorbell jingled and, forcing a smile, I turned to greet mother and daughter.

"I thought I saw David's car out front," said Dolores, looking around. Then she noticed my crutches and wrapped ankle. "What in the world happened to you?" She asked this with more mockery than sympathy.

"It's just sprained," I said. "David is upstairs. He'll be down in a minute." I glanced from mother to daughter, amazed at how composed Dolores appeared, considering she'd just been in a screaming match with her daughter.

Mercedes, on the other hand, looked furious. She let out an exasperated grunt and glowered at her mother.

I pointed to the stack of papers on the desk. "I prepared some basic weaving instructions for everyone. You'll find them very easy to follow."

Dolores picked up a sheaf, looking at the words as if they were written in Chinese. "How am I—" She noticed Winston and blanched, for a second looking as if she might scream. To my surprise, Winnie had flattened his ears and raised the hackles on his back. And for just an instant I thought he was going to attack her.

Mercedes rolled her eyes. "You're being ridiculous, Mom. Winston is a real pussycat," she said, approaching to pat him. Winnie wiggled his behind with joy. "You're a good boy, aren't you? Don't mind my mother. She's nuts."

"Mercedes!" Dolores retorted.

"I'll put him in the next room," I said, hobbling to the kitchen and calling Winston to follow. He did so, reluctantly. "Winnie, what was wrong with you? No biting. You hear me? No biting!" I said sharply, wagging my finger at him. He lowered his head between his paws, doing a good impression of remorse. "You're such a faker."

I returned just as David came down the stairs. Suddenly Dolores's entire demeanor changed. She pulled back her shoulders, tossed her hair and smiled seductively. It was like seeing a tiger morph into a kitten. And then her mouth dropped open.

"Oh my God. Are you all right? What happened?" she said, looking horrified. I couldn't help but wonder if she was really as surprised as she seemed. I would have bet that every soul in town had already heard all about both the murder and the attack on David. I tried to read Dolores's eyes, but if she was acting, it was a performance worthy of an Oscar.

"It's nothing. I got into a bit of a fight last night," he said in a tone meant to put the subject to rest.

Dolores pursed her mouth, staring from David to me and back at him. "Bad day all around, I guess." She might have tried to arch an eyebrow at that point, but her Botoxed forehead refused to cooperate. She gave David a half smile. "I hope you gave as good as you got."

I decided that now was maybe not a bad time to change the subject. "I have some basic instructions printed out, David," I said, pointing him toward the remaining copy on the desk. I waited for everyone to sit, then began with a two-minute history of weaving, from Stone Age times to the modern era, going on to explain the different types of looms, their advantages and disadvantages. "Which brings us to the rigid heddle loom," I concluded. "Jenny and I have already dressed some looms for you so you can begin weaving right away."

"That's so cool!" exclaimed Mercedes, whose enthusiasm for the art seemed to be growing at about the same rate that her mother's was diminishing. "But it's such a weird-looking loom."

I laughed. "This loom is just as real as any other." Seeing her eyes fill with wonder, I said, "You can create just about any weave on this as on the more sophisticated looms." To demonstrate, I opened a book showing dozens of weaving projects, all of which had been made on primitive and heddle looms. I passed it around. David was interested enough to flip through a few pages. Dolores barely glanced at the open page and handed the book to her daughter.

Mercedes studied the first picture—a Mojave rug—and said, "How long would it take a person to make a rug like this one?"

"It would probably take a long time, more than a person might want to commit to until they were proficient. But you could work your way up to it." I picked up a long stick shuttle instead of the traditional boat shuttle I usually favored, and demonstrated the first line of weaving. "The machine does the work for you. Then you just move the heddle and you're ready for the next line or pick of weaving. And repeat."

"It's just like basket weaving," said Mercedes. "It looks so easy." Could it be that the girl was developing a love for the craft?

"It is," I said, chuckling. "In fact, this weave is called the plain weave. There's another pattern called the basket weave. I'll show it to you later." I returned to the group instruction. "The trick is to maintain the same tension for all the rows." Again I demonstrated, weaving another row of yarn across and pulling it loosely into the shape of an arc rather than in a tight, straight line. "Make sure you do not pull the weft too tightly. Let it form a bubble, as weavers call it. And then, when you pull the beater down" — I demonstrated — "it pushes your last row tightly against the previous one. See?"

Mercedes watched my movements with fascination. "I can do that," she said, almost grabbing the loom from me. I was happy to see how much she enjoyed the work. At least one person in this class was interested.

"David and I will work together," declared Dolores, without consulting him.

Next to me, Mercedes rolled her eyes in disgust.

I was about to say that it might make more sense for her to work with her daughter, but she was looking at David, and the expression that flashed through her eyes stopped me short. For a moment I was reminded of a cobra about to strike. Any theory I'd had about Dolores

Hanson having romantic feelings toward David vanished. What was the woman up to? The angry words I'd overheard between Dolores and Mercedes popped into my mind—"*and now he's dead too.*" I grappled for a logical explanation and didn't like what I was coming up with. Dolores? The killer? Much as I preferred that theory to the one the police had embraced, it didn't make much sense. She was the one who'd cried murder when her husband died. Sure, that could have been a ploy. As Jenny had pointed out, she stood to gain the most by her husband's death. But what possible motive could she have had for killing Jeremy Fox?

Suddenly I realized Dolores was talking to me. "I *said*, am I doing this right?" she repeated.

"Yes, yes, you're doing fine. Remember, change the shed, bring the weft through, then push it into place with the beater." I stood by, shoring myself up on my crutches until I was sure she had the knack of it, and then I turned to Mercedes. "You've already done two inches. You're doing very well."

She looked almost embarrassed, saying, "It's sort of fun," as if admitting this made her uncool.

"I was about your age when I first started, and pretty soon I was addicted to it." She scowled, and I remembered too late that girls her age don't want to be compared to women my age. *Oops*.

Back at my loom, I finished my first warp and cut it off the loom. I brought it to my desk and cut the yardage into three equal lengths. I threaded a needle and began joining the pieces with a decorative cross-stitch as I lent an ear to the conversation between Dolores and David.

"I heard about what happened to Jeremy Fox. You and little Miss Weaver found the body." Hah! I was right. Dolores had already heard. David must have nodded because she added, "You know what people are saying, don't you?" Without waiting for his reply, she went on. "They think you killed him. Lucky for you he was shot and not strangled. After all, you did wrap your hands around his neck not too long ago."

I had to stop myself from jumping to David's defense. What the hell was she trying to do? Get David riled up?

I glanced over my shoulder and noted his tight jaw. But to his credit, all he said was, "Some people don't have anything better to do than spread malicious lies."

Dolores instantly switched her tone from taunting to sympathetic. "I agree. It makes me so mad when people gossip like that. Trust me, I know what it's like to be on the receiving end of it. You can't believe the things that were said about me when Greg was killed. I even heard one rumor that I had a lover, and that he and I had Greg murdered so we could run off together."

My ears perked up.

"All you can do is ignore the gossips and go on with your business," David said. "Some people just love to hurt others. And then there are those who will say anything to get attention."

There was a short pause, during which she seemed to be considering her next words. "Don't you think it's odd that Greg and Jeremy would die within months of each other?"

That was when it struck me: Dolores was fishing for

information. If she suspected David of killing her husband, that meant she didn't kill him—right?

I stole a quick glance at Mercedes, who was weaving away, her face devoid of expression. But I could sense the current of fury behind her placid exterior. That was her father's death Dolores was talking about in such a cavalier way. My heart went out to the girl.

"How are you guys doing?" I asked, deciding a change of subject was in order. I picked up my partly assembled friendship blanket and beckoned to Mercedes. "I want you to see how your blanket will look once it's finished." I held it out to her.

"It's beautiful. Look, Mom."

When Mercedes brought it over to show them, David had the grace to at least pretend he was impressed. Dolores didn't. She grimaced.

Mercedes came back. "I love it," she said, fingering the different weaves. "You have so many different strips."

"That's because I'm using different patterns and colors. See this one? It's the basket weave I was telling you about. And this one is called a twill."

"Can you show me how to do those? I want my blanket to look as pretty as yours."

"Of course I will, and I promise your blanket will be just as lovely." She picked up her loom for me to inspect her work. "I'm impressed. You are much better than the average beginner." My small compliment brought a beaming smile to her face. She returned to her project with zeal.

I hobbled over to the loom where Dolores and David were weaving. "That's pretty good. But you skipped a few threads. Here and here, see? If you don't fix them, your work won't look very good."

Dolores gave me a who-cares look. I ignored it. "I'll help you," I said, demonstrating how to unravel the rows quickly. I showed them again how to do the simple weave, and by the time I finished, Dolores seemed to have forgotten her previous conversation. Thank goodness.

About an hour later Mercedes asked for a bathroom break, grabbed her purse and ran up the stairs. When she returned David was leaving, taking one of the looms with him. Mercedes picked up the other.

"I'll make sure I have a loom for you before the next class," I said to Dolores.

"Don't bother. I'll use my daughter's," she replied.

We both knew she would do no such thing.

Chapter 24

"How was the class?" asked Matthew, closing his laptop and jumping up to pull over a chair for me.

I tried to read his eyes, but saw nothing other than his usual friendly expression. If he was hoping to put the earlier episode behind him, I was happy to oblige. I was still in shock at my response and wasn't at all sure what it meant.

"Good," I said, handing him my crutches and plopping myself down. "Especially now that I'm sitting again."

"Listen, Della, I want you to know I'm sorry—"

I reddened and cut him off. "I think we should just forget about what happened. Er, not that anything happened. I mean—"

"If that's what you want, that's fine by me." He nodded emphatically. "You're right. Nothing happened." He smiled and made a wiping movement with his hand. "So, if nothing happened, what are we talking about?"

I chuckled. "I think we were talking about dinner. Have you had anything to eat?"

He leaned back in his chair. "No. When I write, I forget about everything else. But now that you mention it, I am starving."

"I'll throw something together," I said. At the look of incredulity in his eyes, I added, "I'm not entirely helpless, you know. But don't expect a five-course meal."

I struggled to the refrigerator, located the block of aged Cheddar I'd bought a few days earlier, and placed it on a board alongside a couple of sliced apples, a bunch of gorgeous grapes and some crackers. I set the board on the table and then pulled out a cold bottle of Chardonnay. As long as there was no cooking involved, I couldn't burn anything.

"See? I can put a dinner together, no problem." I handed Matthew the corkscrew.

"That looks terrific," he said, filling the glasses.

We ate in companionable silence, and after we finished, Matthew turned to Winston and said, "Okay, big fellow, I think it's time I took you for a walk. What do you say?"

Winston's eyes popped open and he jumped up.

"Before you go," I said. "I didn't want to bring this up in front of David, but I did a bit of investigating this afternoon." I fished in my pocket and triumphantly produced the small piece of black yarn still folded inside the piece of notepaper. At the confused look on Matthew's face, I said, "Look at what I found."

He stared at it, no less puzzled. "What is it?"

I explained about my visit to David's house, going into the details about the indentation in the hedge, the footprint in the soil and the small piece of yarn stuck on one of the broken branches. He sat through my recital, his eyes wide in disbelief, until I concluded. "See? That's a clue, isn't it?" I said, unfolding the piece of paper.

His disbelief morphed into anger. "Do you realize what you did?"

Winston startled at his sharp tone. He glanced from Matthew to me, as if waiting for my response.

"What?" I asked, deciding to play stupid. "I thought you'd be excited." Winston moved closer, protectively. I could hear a low growl in the back of his throat. "It's okay, Winnie," I said softly as I patted him. He quieted, but remained by my side.

"Excited? You just tampered with evidence. You should know better than to go bumbling around a crime scene—on crutches, no less. You probably erased whatever evidence was there. That was not only stupid but against the law. Didn't you learn a thing from what happened last year?"

Now *that* was below the belt. "I-I'm sorry," I said. "I didn't think—"

"Didn't think? Shit! When the police find out what you did, they'll probably charge you for interfering with a police investigation. That's if they don't charge you with being an accessory after the fact."

From the corner of my eye, I could tell Winnie was becoming agitated.

I tried to keep my voice calm. "That's just plain crazy. Why would they even think that?"

"Why? Because you and David Swanson have a personal relationship," he sputtered back. "In their eye, that gives you a perfect motive for protecting him."

"I don't have a personal relationship with—"

"Oh, don't you? Let's see now." He counted on his fingers. "David is taking weaving lessons from you. He's representing you in a real estate transaction. You have coffee together, and God knows what else. If that doesn't make it a personal relationship, I don't know what does."

I blushed. "There is nothing going on between David and me. And you don't have to bite my head off. It was just a mistake."

He scowled in silence for a minute and Winston returned to his spot on the rug. Matthew picked up the piece of yarn and examined it. "It could be wool, or acrylic; it's hard to say." He dropped it in disgust. "The police will have to send it to a lab."

"You don't have to send it to a lab. I can tell you exactly what it is."

He gave me a doubtful smile. "And how do you propose to do that?"

"Easy. All I need is a match."

And just like that, his anger came charging back. "Are you out of your mind? Now you want to destroy the evidence?"

Winnie jumped off the rug and came running over, barking. I patted his head and he relaxed slightly.

"I wouldn't destroy it. All I need is about half an inch." I pushed back my chair abruptly, grabbed my crutches and hoofed over to my studio. I chose a few spools of yarn and, finding it impossible to hold on to them and my crutches at the same time, I stuck them inside the front of my dress. Back in the kitchen I pulled them out and set them on the table—under Matthew's startled eyes. I hopped over to the sink on one foot, filled a glass with water, retrieved some matches and a pair of scissors from the catchall drawer, and placed everything on a plate alongside the spools.

"Look." I cut a small piece of yarn from the first spool, then lit the match and allowed the flame to lick the end of the yarn. It sizzled for a second, and a smell similar to that of burning hair drifted from the flame. I took the match away and the flame burned out. I touched the residue and watched it disintegrate into ashes. "That, my friend, is silk."

He was looking at the ashes on the plate. "How can you tell?"

"Well, Mr. Criminologist"—I flashed him a victorious smile—"as any experienced weaver will tell you, different yarns burn differently. Natural yarns like wool and silk have a distinct smell, very similar to that of burning hair. And when you pull the flame away they extinguish on their own. On the other hand, acrylic has a chemical smell and will melt into a ball. Cotton or linen yarns have a papery odor. And they burn more slowly, especially linen. Another difference between silk and wool is that silk burns into a soft gray bead that easily turns to ash when you crush it, whereas wool burns into a dark, irregular form." I paused, then said, "If you don't want me to test the yarn I found, I won't. But just out of curiosity, what would the content of a yarn tell us?"

He gave me a half smile. "It's not what it will tell *us*. It's what it will tell the police!" He softened a bit and said, "It wouldn't tell them much on its own, except the type of garment it's likely to have come from. For example, if this were silk, the person wearing it would probably not be poor. So we could eliminate the home-less and itinerants."

I rolled my eyes. "Briar Hollow doesn't have any homeless or any itinerants, for that matter."

He laughed, sending my heart into the chugga-chugga dance, and Winston returned to his spot by the door.

Matthew said, "Nothing gets by you, does it?"

"You're teasing me."

He smiled and his eyes went all gold. "You're easy to tease, kiddo."

I swallowed hard. Trying to hide my dismay, I said the first thing that came to mind. "How do you think it went for David at the station? Do the police still think he's a suspect?"

His eyes went dark. "They took down his statement, but you know how cops are. They never tell you what they're really thinking."

"I do know, unfortunately, and I'll be happy if I never have to deal with cops again." He smiled, nodding, and I asked, "What do you think of the theory that Greg Hanson was also murdered?" I paused. "And why wouldn't you answer my question when I called you?"

He studied the floor, and then said, "I know you don't want to hear this, kiddo, but at this point we aren't one hundred percent sure that David isn't the killer, are we?"

"We aren't?" I asked, my eyes widening.

"We aren't," he said firmly. "So I think it's a good idea for us to avoid discussing any of the details, or any theory we might have about the murder when he's around."

My thoughts took a sharp turn. "I'm surprised that

Briar Hollow has a coroner. I always thought coroners only worked out of big-city morgues."

"You're thinking of pathologists. Pathology is a science. To become a pathologist a person has to go through medical school first and then complete another four or five years of studying the specialty. Unlike medical examiners, coroners are elected officials. In some regions, the only credentials a person needs to become a coroner is a basic training course as simple as a weekend seminar. At least here, the coroner is the local doctor. I've met some coroners who knew less about medicine than a butcher."

I was aghast. "But, that's terrible. That means some murders probably go unnoticed."

He nodded. "And worse, sometimes a natural death can be pegged as a murder, resulting in an innocent person being sent to prison."

"Surely the doctor can tell the difference between an accident and a murder."

Matthew nodded again. "One would think."

I couldn't help but notice that he didn't sound all that sure.

He picked up the small piece of yarn again. "I'll have to think about how to explain this to the police." He scowled and went on. "Damn—as if Mike isn't already pissed off enough with me. Guaranteed he's going to blame this on me. And it'll be your fault, kiddo." He started walking away, then turned and said, "Come, Winston." Winston jumped up and raced over to him. Matthew clipped his leash on, and glancing at me, he said, "I have to ask you not to leave town until the police question you."

My jaw dropped.

And then he winked, making it clear he'd been joking, and walked out.

The next morning when I opened my eyes, a sunbeam filtered through the window, and I could hear birds singing outside. Winston had snuck into my room during the night, and he was now snoring not so softly at the foot of my bed. I pushed back the blankets and sat up, swinging my legs over the side, briefly forgetting about my ankle. *Arrrghhh.* I flopped back on the bed, gritting my teeth.

That was one mistake I wouldn't make again. I let the throbbing subside, and then, hopping around on one foot, I slipped on my Ralph Lauren safari-style shirt-dress, pulled out the vachetta belt—just another name for fake leather—and replaced it with my favorite Hermès scarf, tied around my waist with the ends draping over one hip. I checked the mirror and decided I looked, well, maybe not hot, but at least warm.

I was stumped for shoes, until—hold on—what about those gold ballerina shoes I'd bought on sale two years ago and never worn? I located them in my closet and slipped one on my right foot. On the other, I wore a khaki wool sock that sort of coordinated with my dress. I checked the mirror one more time and decided the ballerina slipper did nothing for my height but I looked nice enough.

I heard the telephone ring and after the third time, determined that Matthew wouldn't pick up the extension in his room. I grabbed my crutches and maneuvered down the stairs as fast as I could. Winnie brushed by so close he almost tripped me; but I made it without falling. After all that rushing, all I got when I picked up the receiver was the dial tone. *Sheesh!* And then the telephone rang again and I snatched it up.

"I didn't wake you, did I? I tried your cell phone, but I went straight into voice mail," a voice said. It was Samantha.

"I keep forgetting to recharge the battery." Besides, it wasn't as if I had very many friends calling me anymore. "You sound suspiciously upbeat for so early in the morning." Was she calling with good news? My hope surged.

"I thought you'd want to know as soon as possible. My client loves your condo! He's decided to take it."

I squealed. "He will? For three thousand dollars a month?"

"For three thousand a month—and I have the first and last months' checks in my hand right now."

I let out another whoop.

She laughed. "The lease is filled out and signed. But it won't be official until you sign it too. Where do you want me to fax it?"

"I have a fax right here. All I have to do is turn it on. Give me two minutes and you can send it to the same number."

"Will do," she said, and hung up

I hobbled about madly, getting the fax machine from under the desk and setting it up. Then I held my breath as I waited for the papers to come through, which they did about two minutes later. I ripped them out, reading them through until I got to the part where it said, "Three thousand dollars a month." I kissed the page.

From the corner of the room, where he had been snoring softly, Winston lifted his head and watched me with obvious disdain. "Sorry, Winnie. Go back to sleep." That dog could fall asleep faster than you could say "time for bed."

Chapter 25

A few minutes later Matthew padded down the stairs. I stopped my three-footed happy dance (two crutches and one leg) and turned to face him. He wore jeans and a T-shirt and had dark circles under his eyes, a two-day-old growth of beard and heavy lids.

"I've heard of dogs looking like their owners, but this is the first time I've seen an owner look like his dog."

He glowered at me, and I wiped the grin off my face. "Uh-oh. I woke you, didn't I?"

"What the hell was all that racket? First the phone, then the fax machine. Who were you talking to so early in the morning?"

"Sorry about that. Go back to bed. I promise I'll be quiet."

He rejected that suggestion with a frustrated wave. "Forget it. I'm up now," he said, heading for the kitchen.

"I made some coffee. Can I get you a cup?" I chirped, hobbling along. In the kitchen, I pointed him to a chair, grabbed a mug from the cupboard and poured.

He dropped into the chair, took a few gulps, and his scowl melted slightly. "Sorry. I didn't mean to snap your head off. I'm not much of a morning person."

"So I noticed."

He smiled sheepishly. "Was that fax from David by any chance?"

"No." I grinned. "Even better. My agent in Charlotte has rented out my condo. She sent me a copy of the lease."

He got up, went over to Winston, picked up his water bowl and filled it. Winston opened one bleary eye and closed it again. "Good for you—one less worry on your mind." He returned to the table. "Judging from the way you were jumping around when I came down, I'm guessing that she rented it for a decent price?"

I tapped a finger on the lease, which I'd purposely left in plain sight in the middle of the table. I always was a bit of a show-off. "See for yourself."

He picked it up and scanned it. I could tell exactly when he reached the dollar amount by the way his eyes suddenly widened. "Am I reading this right? She got you three thousand dollars a month?"

"She sure did," I said, grinning.

His eyebrows jumped up. "Hey, good for you, kiddo. For that kind of money, I'd consider moving out and renting my house too."

I smiled sweetly. "Eh, sorry, Matthew, but I doubt any big-shot executive will be transferring to Briar Hollow anytime soon."

He chuckled. "You might have a point there." He planted his hands on his hips and looked at Winston, who hadn't stirred since he'd plopped down there after my phone call.

"Has Winston been out yet?" I shook my head, and

he said, "Let's go, big fellow." Winston jumped up, instantly alert. Matthew got the leash and clipped it onto his collar.

"Don't you want something to eat first?" I asked, watching him walk toward the front door.

"I'll grab a bite along the way," he called over his shoulder.

"On your way where?" I yelled, but the door had already swung shut. The phone rang again. This place was usually so quiet. Lately, it was turning into Grand Central Station.

"Hello," I said into the phone, half expecting it to be Samantha calling to tell me the client had backed out.

"I can't find it. It's gone," a voice wailed. Who the heck was this? I had no idea. That meant, I guessed, that I was supposed to recognize the voice—only I didn't. "If you tell anyone about that threat I made against him, the police will be sure I killed him."

"Marnie? Is that you?"

Disregarding my question, she added, "I looked everywhere and I can't find it. Somebody must have stolen it."

"What are you talking about? What's missing?"

"My gun! It's gone."

"I don't understand."

"It's plain enough English! What is it you don't understand?" she snapped back.

"I'm sorry. I don't know what you're talking about. You had a gun and it's missing?"

"I'm sorry, Della. I shouldn't have made that crack. I'm just so worried." Her voice lowered to a whisper. I strained to hear. "After that comment I made—you know, the one about killing him—what if it turns out that he was killed with my gun?"

I was mute with shock.

"Did you hear what I just said?" asked Marnie plaintively.

"Yes, yes, I did," I said, gathering my thoughts. "When was the last time you saw it?"

"I—I can't remember." She sounded so frightened, and rightly so, considering the situation. "Do you mind if I come over? I'm just such a mess. I don't want to be alone right now."

"Sure, come on. I've just made a pot of coffee."

The front door opened and closed. "I'm in the kitchen," I called out, grabbing my crutches. To my surprise it wasn't Marnie but Matthew who walked in, carrying a bag of groceries and looking solemn.

"That was fast. Where did you—" I stopped short. Behind him was Mike Davis, in uniform, his mouth set in a grim line. My heart dropped.

"Della," Matthew said, setting the bag on the counter to unclip Winston's leash, "Mike wants to ask you a few questions."

Oh, shit. How could Matthew have done this without telling me first? I smiled tentatively. "Hello, Officer. Can I get you a cup of coffee?"

He looked back at me with that same intensity I'd noticed before, without bothering to so much as nod or smile hello. This was the man who had broken Jenny's heart? I *so* didn't like him. He was as stern and cold as she was sunny and cheerful. To each his own, as they say.

"I guess Matthew told you about my little visit to David's house," I said, faking confidence in the face of the hell awaiting me. I would rather have died than let on how nervous I really was. "Have a seat." I pulled out a chair, but again he ignored my offer, remaining in the doorway, glowering at me. Well, if he didn't want it that was fine by me. I propped my crutches against the wall and plopped down in the chair myself. I flashed him a smile.

Mike studied me as if trying to decide whether to strangle me or boil me in oil. How much trouble was I really in? He couldn't arrest me, could he? I took a sip of my coffee, feigning nonchalance as I squelched a feeling of dread.

He crossed his arms and said, "What you did was unconscionable. You know that, don't you? You tampered with evidence."

I swallowed hard. "I'm sorry," I said with as much sincerity as I could muster. I had apologized plenty for that yesterday and was getting pretty tired of it. "Matthew already pointed that out to me." I glanced at him as I spoke, throwing him a furious look. His mouth was still set in a straight line. I turned back to Mike Davis. "How was I supposed to know I shouldn't go there? Besides, all I did was take that one tiny little piece of yarn."

This didn't make Officer Davis look any happier. He frowned and said, "David Swanson is a murder suspect. A forensic examination of his front yard could have given us enough information to prove his innocence." I couldn't help but notice that he'd said, "prove his innocence." Did that mean Mike Davis believed David's story? He went on. "But now that you've trampled all over the place, whatever evidence might still be there has been compromised."

I was about to apologize again, but then remembered that the best defense is a good offense. "There was no yellow crime scene tape anywhere. What am I supposed to do? Stop going places *in case* they turn out to be crime scenes?" Okay, that last little bit was maybe pushing it, but to my surprise, Mike Davis dropped his scowl.

Looking down at my one good foot, he said, "Is that what you were wearing when you went traipsing all over Swanson's front yard?"

I shook my head. "Yes and no. I was wearing a running shoe on my right foot, but the same bandage on my left foot."

He gave me a tight smile that told me he didn't find my sarcasm the least bit amusing. "Would you please get that running shoe for me?" He glanced at my crutches. "Or, if you prefer, tell me where it is and I'll go get it myself."

"Don't bother. I can do it," I said, and then added, "Do you want the bandage too?"

He rolled his eyes at me, exasperated. Turning to Matthew he said, "Do you mind if I use the bathroom?"

This was obviously a ploy to follow me. I bit back a sharp retort. What did he think I would do? Jump out the window and hobble away? I hoofed it upstairs in a huff, stepped into my room and turned to give him a dirty look. But to my surprise, he had disappeared into the washroom. So he did need to go to the bathroom. Why was I getting so paranoid? Hah! After my experience last year, a person would be nuts *not* to be paranoid.

When Mike returned to the kitchen, I handed him my running shoe, and as he reached to take it, I smelled that same odd odor I'd noticed on him yesterday. And then it hit me. It was the same smell I'd noticed on Joan Douglas, the neonatal nurse—cheap cologne and mothballs. How very strange! Could he and Joan be involved with each other? I wondered how Jenny would react to that.

Mike took my shoe and dropped it into an evidence bag. "I'll get this back to you as soon as I can." He closed the bag, muttering something under his breath that sounded suspiciously like "of all the stupid things to do." He added firmly, "Don't ever let me catch you doing something like that again."

"I won't. I promise," I said, biting back my frustration. My tongue was getting sore from so much biting.

Mike gave me a curt nod, turned to Matthew and said, "Thanks for the heads-up. I'll see you around." And then he left.

The front door opened and closed. I planted my hands on my hips and glared at Matthew as he walked back into the kitchen.

"You told on me?" I sputtered. "Why'd you go and do that?"

He gave me an apologetic smile. "Did it ever occur to you that you could have incriminated yourself by going there?"

I frowned. "What are you talking about?"

"It was just a matter of time before the cops combed

the place for evidence. If they'd found anything indicating that you had tampered with evidence, you could have found yourself in a heap of trouble. They might think you did it to protect David—accessory after the fact. Or," he continued, his eyes lighting up as he imagined another possibility, "they might have thought you were the one who attacked him. I figured it was better to establish the facts. I didn't tell you ahead of time because I didn't want you to lose sleep over it."

"That's the craziest thing I've ever heard. Why would anybody think I would attack David?"

He raised his eyebrows. "You and David have been getting pretty chummy lately. Some people might think that you liked him enough to cover for him."

Before I could give him a piece of my mind, the doorbell rang.

"This place is turning into Grand Central Station. Maybe your condo wasn't such a bad place to write after all," he grumbled, heading for the front door.

Seconds later he reappeared, followed by Marnie, who wore a dress that looked suspiciously like old-fashioned blue chintz curtains. The blue of her eye shadow exactly matched the cornflowers in the print. "Why were the police here?" she asked, sounding falsely casual under the furious glance she threw my way.

"Mike is a friend of mine," said Matthew over his shoulder as he opened the cupboard. "He stops by to chat once in a while," he added, being surprisingly discreet—discretion he should have used toward me, as far as I was concerned. "Would you like a cup of coffee, Marnie?" he asked.

"Don't mind if I do," she replied, the scowl on her face softening only slightly. She pulled out a chair and then mouthed something silently, nodding toward Matthew.

I answered with a small head shake, and she brought a hand to her heart in relief.

Matthew set two cups of coffee on the table and said, "I'll go take a shower and let you ladies chat. I'm sure Della will tell you all about her exciting day yesterday."

The minute she heard him on the stairs, Marnie whispered, "You're sure you didn't tell him about the gun?"

"Of course I didn't."

"Thank God," she replied, collapsing against the back of her chair. "I thought I was going to pass out when I saw Mike Davis walk into your house."

"Have you been waiting out there all that time?"

Her eyes grew wide. "I wasn't about to come in without knowing why he was here. You could have told him about my missing gun." She shrugged apologetically. "And he could have been here to arrest me."

"Don't be silly. I would never do that. As a matter of fact, he came over to give me a speech." I explained about my little investigation of the previous day. But instead of making Marnie feel better, all my story did was excite her more.

"If the police eliminate David as a suspect, then they're sure to come after me," she said, tears hovering on her lashes.

"Don't be ridiculous. Do you really believe you and David are the only people in town with a grudge against Jeremy?"

She shrugged. "You might have a point," she admitted.

I leaned forward. "Tell me about the gun."

"I've had that gun for years. Jimmy—that's my ex-husband—he bought it for me when we moved to the city ages ago. After we moved back, I always kept it in a shoebox in the back of my closet. I haven't even thought about it since then. But when I heard that Jeremy Fox was dead, I went to check." Her chin trembled. "It's gone." She twisted her hands nervously. "I just had to talk to someone, so I told Jenny, and she has a really bad feeling about this."

I swallowed a chuckle. "Don't put too much credence in Jenny's feelings. I know she's intuitive, but I suspect many of her 'feelings' might be hindsight."

Marnie gave me a reproachful look. "I'm not so sure about that."

There was no point in arguing about it. "When was the last time you saw it?"

She shook her head, still wringing her hands. "It's been years. Somebody must have stolen it from my bedroom closet. Do you know how Jeremy was killed?" I shook my head. "What if he was shot? And what if my gun was the one that killed him? The police will think I did it."

"I doubt you have anything to worry about. It would take more than just knowing you used to own a gun and that it's gone missing. First, they'd have to know that your gun was the same caliber as the murder weapon. And I've watched enough *Law and Order* to know even that isn't enough. They'd have to find the gun and run ballistics. What caliber was it?"

She shook her head. "It was a small gun. I'm sure Jimmy told me what the caliber was, but I can't remember."

I thought for a moment. "Can you make a list of everyone who had access to it?"

She furrowed her brow. "Well, there's my ex-husband, Jimmy, of course. He moved out last summer. And then there's Norma Fischer. I gave her a key to my place after Jim left."

"Who's Norma Fischer?"

She rolled her eyes. "If you think Norma took it, you can wipe that idea right out of your head," she said forcefully. "Norma is my seventy-four-year-old neighbor. I gave her a key because I feel safer knowing someone can check on me if I get sick." She thought hard for a few more seconds and then shook her head. "I can't think of anybody else." She leaned back. "But guess whose car just so happened to be parked down the street from mine all night long? David Swanson's!"

I felt like a brick had dropped in my stomach. How close was her house to Bottoms Up? "You think David snuck into your house in the middle of the night, searched your closet and stole your gun?" I said, giving her the eyebrow.

She looked down at her hands, embarrassed. "It's crazy, I know."

"I think it's way more likely that your ex took the gun when he moved out. Why don't you give him a call?" I pushed the telephone toward her.

She took a long breath and nodded. "Maybe you're right." But she didn't sound convinced. "Me and my big mouth—I just wish I hadn't made that comment about how I'd like to kill him."

"Don't worry about that. Neither Jenny nor I took

that seriously. That's just the kind of thing people say when they're angry," I said. "Go ahead. Call him."

"I will, as soon as I get home." She took a long sip of coffee and seemed to relax a bit. "Thanks for listening." With that, she rose from her chair, rinsed her cup and saucer and put them on the drain board. "Maybe you're right. I know I sleep soundly, but surely I would have heard something if David had come into the house in the middle of the night." It sounded more like a question than a statement.

"And by the way," she whispered, sitting back down, "I've been meaning to have a talk with you. If you're in love with Matthew, why don't you make a play for him?"

"What?"

She gave me a knowing smile. "Don't bother pretending. You know what I'm talking about. Why don't you seduce him? You're a cute girl." I couldn't help noticing that she used the word "cute" rather than "beautiful." "Don't you know the first thing about men? You have to flirt with them, let them know that if they ask you out, you'll say yes. I bet he has no idea how you feel about him."

"Where in the world did you get the idea that I'm in love with him?" I whispered hoarsely.

She chuckled. "Sugar, anybody with eyes can see you're in love with him. Every time his name is mentioned, you turn beet red. And when you two are in the same room, you can't peel your eyes off him."

"You're wrong," I said. "I like Matthew, of course. He and I have been friends forever. But I'm not in love with him." I tried to laugh, but it came out strangled. My mind flashed to the way my body had reacted when he wrapped his arms around me. That did not mean I was in love with him—or did it?

"Anyhow," she continued, "it's none of my business, but if you want him, you can have him. Just remember: any man can be yours if you play your cards right." She stood and headed for the door. "Oh," she said, turning back to me just before walking out. "And get yourself some sexy clothes. Men like a woman in sexy clothes." She was starting to sound like my mother.

I stared at the door long after she was gone. Surely she was wrong. Me, in love with Matthew? That was laughable. As for sexy clothes, what did she want me to wear? Zebra pants and tight tops? Not likely.

"What do you think of that, Winston?" I asked, returning to the kitchen. "She says I should dress sexy. I thought I was already pretty sexy with my fitted jeans."

He opened one bleary eye, closed it and went right back to snoring.

"Gee, thanks."

Chapter 26

No sooner had the door shut behind Marnie than Matthew came charging down the stairs. "I heard the door. Is she gone?"

I looked at him, wondering if maybe I *did* feel more than just friendship for him. Nah. No way.

"Why are you looking at me that way?"

"You didn't take a shower, did you? You only said that as an excuse to leave."

He shrugged. "Guilty as charged. I wasn't in the mood to sit around and listen to gossip. What did she want, anyway?"

"Oh, nothing, really," I said. "She only stopped by to get more yarn for her project." Okay, that was an out-and-out lie, but the way I saw it, if Matthew had not hesitated to report to Mike about me, I wasn't about to tell him Marnie's gun was missing. He'd probably run right out and blab about it to Mike.

He opened the fridge and pulled out a carton of orange juice. He poured two glasses, handing one to me. "I hate to tell you, but Mike was right. It was completely stupid of you to go snooping around. I want you to promise me you won't ever do anything like that again."

So we were back to that again, were we? "Oh, for God's sake, I've already promised Mike."

Looking serious, he said, "This time I want you to promise *me*."

"Fine. I swear I won't do it again." It was an easy enough promise to make. "I don't know why you should worry. I mean, how many murder scenes am I likely to come across? This is Briar Hollow, for God's sake."

"All right," he said. "Let's talk about something more pleasant."

"Gladly," I muttered.

He picked up the grocery bag he'd left on the counter and plunked it on the table, pulling out a quart of milk, a container of yogurt and a box of cereal. "I picked up breakfast for us."

I stared at the box he had just placed on the table. "Froot Loops! Ugh!" I was halfway out of my chair. "You don't really want to eat those, do you? Let me make you something health—"

"Don't tell me what I want," he said brusquely. "Right now, this is exactly what I want."

I groaned, and hopping on one foot, I headed for the refrigerator. "You can have your Froot Loops if you like, but I'm making myself something else."

"You. Sit," he ordered. "I got something else for you."

I returned to my chair, pretending to be miffed, but the truth was I would have eaten just about anything if it meant not having to make it myself. Cooking while hopping around on one foot was no easy feat—pardon the pun. From the grocery bag, he extracted a smaller

brown one and overturned the contents on my plate—
two raisin bran muffins, still warm from the oven.

"I figured these might be more up your alley," he said.

Just when I had decided that the man was a Neander-
thal with the emotional development of a two-year-old,
he went and did something sweet. "That's so nice of
you," I said, feeling touched.

"Hey, it's only muffins, kiddo. Don't make a big deal
about it." He tore open the box of cereal and filled his
bowl. "When does your weaving group get together
again?" he asked, picking through the colorful mini rings
until he found a green one. He flicked it into the air,
catching it in his mouth. I bit my tongue.

"Tomorrow," I said. "And then maybe once or twice a
week until we have ten blankets. That's the number I
pledged for the hospital." I broke off a piece from my
muffin and bit into it, my thoughts taking a sharp turn. "I
just can't figure Dolores out. She likes weaving about as
much as I might enjoy playing with snakes. On the other
hand, Mercedes seems to enjoy it."

"Mercedes always struck me as a nice girl. Then,
about a year ago, she started getting into trouble."

"What kind of trouble?"

He scowled. "Forget it. I shouldn't have said that.
Mike told me in confidence. He'd be furious if I told anyone." He picked through his bowl until he found another
of the tiny green cereal rings. "I understand why David
joined the group. He just picked the better of two evils."
He shrugged. "Maybe Dolores is looking for activities to
do with her daughter."

I huffed. "More likely she's looking for activities to do with David."

Matthew's eyes lasered into mine. "Does that bother you?"

Every time I mentioned David's name, it somehow came out sounding like I had a thing for the guy. I rolled my eyes. "Don't be silly. I just think she could have thought of some other way of bumping into him."

He chuckled. "I have to agree with you there. She doesn't strike me as the weaving type."

"On the other hand, she hasn't exactly been flirting with him. It's more like she's trying to pump him for information; as if David might know something about her husband's death." I took a sip of coffee and settled back into my chair. "Would you happen to know if David ever went hiking with Greg Hanson?"

"Hell, a lot of people went hiking with him. Even I did," he said, and then, his eyes boring into mine, he added, "I don't want you going around playing detective. You hear me?"

"Of course." I took a bite of muffin. It wasn't nearly as good as Marnie's, but wanting to change the subject, I said, "Mm-mm, these are delicious. Where did you get them?"

"The coffee shop up the street," he said. He casually chose another cereal ring and tossed it up. I watched it fly a few inches above his head, back down, and straight into his waiting mouth.

"Tell me something. Why can't you just pour milk into your cereal and eat it like an adult?"

He grinned. "I thought women liked men to be boyish."

He repeated his performance with another Froot Loop. "But what do I know about women, right? I'm thirty-seven, and not one has ever consented to marry me."

This piqued my interest. "How many times have you proposed?"

He laughed. "Never. Which is just as bad, I suppose."

I bobbed my eyebrows. "Worse, actually. In my experience, men who haven't married by their late thirties have a problem with intimacy."

Matthew roared with laughter. "Are you telling me I have a problem with intimacy?" He looked pointedly at me. "What about women who haven't married by their mid-thirties?"

Blood rushed to my face. *Touché.*

Chapter 27

Matthew left the house, giving me a fresh warning on his way out. "You had better be here when I come back. I don't want you traipsing around town, looking for clues."

"I'm staying right here, I promise," I said. I swear, I meant it at the time—honestly. But, as it happened, I was just wiping the table when the phone rang. I put down the dish towel and answered.

"Hi, Della." It was Jenny. I was surprised at how happy I was to hear her voice. "Can I come over for a few minutes? There's something I'd like to run by you."

Suddenly an idea popped into my head. "Is it something we can talk about over lunch? Because if it is, maybe we could grab a sandwich at Bottoms Up."

Ever since Marnie had mentioned David's car being parked on her street the evening of the murder, I couldn't help but wonder if he had lied about his movements that night.

"Are you planning to play detective?" she asked, with a chuckle in her voice. "If you are, I'll be your Watson."

"Sounds like a plan, but you have to promise to not tell Matthew."

"Not a word, I swear. It'll be fun to do something exciting for a change. Nothing ever happens in this town."

Yeah, right. Nothing but murder.

As far as restaurants and bars go, Bottoms Up did not impress. It was on the opposite side of town, and from the looks of it, it could have been there for fifty years or two hundred years. It was that worn-looking. The first thing one noticed upon driving up was the large neon sign showing a shapely blond girl leaning over until her healthy behind was—you guessed it—pointing up. The building— surprisingly large considering the size of the town—was built of aged barn wood, and was set smack-dab in the middle of a gravel parking lot, which I imagined was filled to capacity on weekends with trucks, pickups and SUVs from every little town within driving distance.

"It's huge."

"People around here use it for weddings and parties. During the week it's pretty quiet," she said, as I noted the half dozen cars in the parking lot.

"We're in luck. That's Sam's car," Jenny said, pointing her chin toward a Honda with so much rust that guessing its original color would have presented a real challenge.

"Who's Sam?"

"A guy I know. I used to babysit him when he was a kid." She turned off the motor. "He's bound to know something. He's a regular here. It'll be easy to start a conversation with him without it looking like we're fishing for information."

"Good idea," I replied.

We got out of the car, and a minute later I followed

her into a dark room. My eyes took a moment to adjust to the dark. And then I almost wished they hadn't. I was in a wood-paneled room, facing a bar that ran the entire length of the back wall. Half a dozen patrons swiveled on their stools to look at us. I glanced to my left, where eight or so tables stood empty. To my right was the pool table, also unoccupied. To say the place lacked charm was an understatement.

"Not very elegant, is it?"

Jenny chuckled. "If you were planning to order anything fancier than a burger and fries, I suggest you rethink that." And then she marched over, calling out, "Hi, Sam. How are you doing?"

I followed on my crutches as fast as I could.

Sam looked to be in his mid-twenties, wearing painter's pants splattered with myriad paint colors. He set down his glass of soda, turned and smiled. "Hey, Jenny. I can't remember the last time I saw you."

"That's because you don't need babysitting anymore," she said, sliding onto the stool next to his. I took the next one over.

Sam chuckled politely and leaned forward to look at me. "What happened to your foot?"

Jenny answered for me. "Sprain."

He nodded. "What brings you and your friend to our watering hole?"

"My friend Della," she said, indicating me, "just moved here, and I thought I'd show her all the interesting spots around town."

Sam grinned. "I sure hope you took Della to see the local Laundromat."

At the look on my face, he and Jenny burst into laughter.

"Don't mind Sam. He's just pulling your leg. He used to tease me mercilessly when I was his sitter." She turned back to him and said, "How have you been, Sam? And how's your mother?"

"Ma's good. As for me—" He shrugged. "I'm working on a kitchen renovation for the Jordans down the street," he said, naming a family I had never heard of. "I was all set to start work on Jeremy Fox's project, but that job hit the skids when the contamination report went public." He turned to me. "You're the lady who owns the knitting shop, right?"

"Weaving shop," I corrected him.

He nodded, but I doubted he cared about the difference. His next words proved me right. "You could have knocked me over with a feather when I heard David Swanson was taking up knitting."

"Weav—"

Before I could say any more, he cut me off, saying, "And you're also the lady who found Fox's body, right?"

I nodded again. "That's right. Actually, David Swanson was with me," I added, thrilled that Sam had just brought up the subject.

"So I heard. He was here the night before, you know. The guys were teasing him mercilessly about him knitting baby blankets." I didn't bother correcting him. "But I have to hand it to him. He was a good sport about it and just let it roll off his back."

"I imagine the police must have been by to ask questions about that night," said Jenny.

"They sure did. I wouldn't want to be in Swanson's shoes," he said, dabbing a french fry in ketchup. "He picks a fight with the guy, threatens to kill him, and then a few weeks later the guy turns up dead."

Good thing he doesn't know about the confrontation the night of the murder, I thought.

He shook his head, continuing, "It's so obvious he killed the guy that it almost makes me think there's something fishy about it. You know?" He glanced back at Jenny. "Nobody could be that stupid, right?"

"That's what I think, too," I said. Sam gave me a long, measuring look.

"What did the police want to know?" Jenny asked.

"They wanted to know what time David arrived and what time he left."

"He was here all evening, wasn't he?" I said.

"I have no idea," he said. I interpreted this sudden reluctance to talk as neighborly loyalty. "He was still here when I left, but I was only here till eight or so."

Before I could ask another question, the bartender, a burly guy with curly red hair and a week's growth of beard, approached. "What can I get you two beauties?"

Jenny smiled. "You're such a charmer, Frank. I bet you say that to all the girls."

"Not at all." He winked. "I call it like I see it."

Without glancing at the menu, Jenny said, "I'll have a club sandwich, no fries."

I loved fries, but decided that maybe I should follow Jenny's example. "I'll have the same."

"Good choice," Frank said. And then he called over his shoulder in a booming voice, "Hey, Lorna. Two clubs, hold the fries." He turned back to us. "Coming right up."

I looked back at Sam, hoping he hadn't been distracted from my question. I was in luck.

He called after the burly man as he was walking away, "Hey, Frank, the police questioned you about David Swanson, didn't they?"

The big man turned around. "They sure did. Mike wanted to know what time David got here—what time he left—who he talked to—how many drinks he had. Man, that jerk kept at me like David was public enemy number one." All at once he realized that he was talking to Jenny and turned deep red. "Oh, uh, sorry, Jenny. I know you were married to the guy, but"—he shook his head—"you gotta admit, Mike ain't all there anymore." He said this apologetically, tapping the side of his head with an index finger. "He's just plain weird these days."

Jenny seemed taken aback at first, and then she recovered. "He tends to get a bit intense when he goes into police mode."

Frank looked like he wanted to say something more, but he closed his mouth and just nodded.

Sam broke the tense silence. "So what did you tell them?"

Frank ignored the question. "Do you ladies want something to drink with your sandwiches?"

We both ordered diet drinks and once he had brought them over, I repeated Sam's question. "If you don't mind my asking, what did you tell the police?"

Frank leaned his elbows on the bar and said, "Now,

why would you want to know what I told the police? I bet you got your heart set on David Swanson."

The other men along the bar stared openly, waiting for my answer. Suddenly I saw myself becoming the latest subject of gossip around Briar Hollow. "No, nothing like that," I said hastily, trying to cover my fluster. "I'm just curious. I was with him when we found the body, and he seemed so shocked. I just don't believe he could have done it. Nobody could be that good an actor."

Frank laughed. "In that case you haven't met Wayne here." He tilted his head toward the guy to his left. "He can be real convincing when he tells strangers that he never played pool in his life."

Wayne laughed. "Either of you two ladies wanna take me on for a game of pool? Never played the game in my life. I swear."

Everybody along the bar laughed, including Jenny and me.

"Very funny," said Jenny when the laughter quieted. "But I'm curious too. What did you tell the cops, Frank?"

Frank hesitated and then shrugged. "Like I told them, I can't keep track of everyone's comings and goings when I'm working. I couldn't say exactly what time he got here. But I checked the credit card charges, and his first charge was at exactly seven thirty and his last one was at ten past nine."

I was stunned, and struggled to keep a straight face. "But he didn't necessarily leave right after paying his tab, did he?"

Frank shook his head, giving me a knowing smile. "Hate to disappoint you, darling, but one thing I did see was that he paid and two minutes later he went straight to that phone," he said, pointing to an old-fashioned pay phone in the corner. He leaned closer. "I couldn't help but wonder why he would use a pay phone rather than the cell phone in his pocket."

My mouth went dry. *Unless he didn't want a call to be traced back to him*, I thought. After all, a phone call had sent Jeremy running out into the night. This amounted to no more than circumstantial evidence, but it was starting to stack up. Weakly I asked, "And did he actually use it?"

"He did. He made a call—oh—I'd say no more than two or three minutes before leaving." A bell rang from the back and Frank said, "That'll be your clubs," and walked away.

I took a sip of my soda, feeling stunned. None of what I had just heard would help David in any way—in fact, quite the opposite. The police would claim that he left the bar in plenty of time to meet Jeremy and kill him, and that the whole attack thing was staged.

Suddenly my own confidence in his innocence was shaken. Could I have been wrong about him? Could David be such a good actor that he could have faked his reaction upon seeing Jeremy Fox's body?

The thing was, I reminded myself, that I really didn't know the man. I'd only met him a handful of times. How could I expect to recognize when he was lying and when he was telling the truth? I looked at Jenny, remembering what she'd said about never really knowing another person. Matthew had said the same thing. In fact, if anybody could attest to the truth in that, I could. Just one year ago, I had been completely and utterly taken in by my boss, someone I had known for close to a decade.

Jenny leaned forward. "That doesn't mean anything," she said, as if reading my mind. I shivered.

At that moment Frank appeared, carrying our sandwiches along with two side orders of french fries. I said a silent thank-you to the absentminded cook. "I'm famished," I said, my stomach rumbling in anticipation. He set the plates before us. I picked up a wedge of sandwich and bit into it with enthusiasm. The place may not have been fancy, but it made a mean club.

Sam slid off his stool. "Well, I'll let you ladies enjoy your lunch. I'd best be getting back to that kitchen. Nice to see you, Jenny, Della," he said, turned and left.

Jenny waved good-bye to him, and then turned to me. "Okay, now that we did our investigating, there's something I want to talk to you about." I nodded, waiting. "I'm thinking of quitting my job."

"Whoa, when did you decide this?" I asked, smacking the bottom of the ketchup bottle over my fries.

"I'm still only thinking about it. It really depends on you," she said, looking nervous.

I had a sudden uncomfortable feeling, and hoped I was wrong about where this was going. "This is beginning to sound like a serious conversation."

Jenny twisted her napkin nervously. "I've been wondering whether you're still interested in buying that building. I mean after finding the body and everything, I would understand if you'd changed your mind," she said haltingly.

"I already put in an offer," I said, feeling more and

more certain of what she was going to say. "I admit, I almost did change my mind, but Matthew convinced me that it's an excellent investment. What is this all about?" I asked. "Does this have anything to do with you wanting to quit your job?"

She stared down at her fingernails. "You mentioned that the space was too large for your shop. Have you come up with any plans regarding that?"

"What are you getting at?"

She cleared her throat. "I've been thinking about what you said—you know—that anybody can run a business."

I had said that—me and my big mouth.

"And I was wondering if you'd consider subletting a part of that space to me so I could start my tea shop. It could be good for both of us. For one thing," she said, her eyes shining with excitement, "the tea shop would bring in more traffic, and even if my customers don't buy from you, at least they would help spread the word." I had been fully prepared to hate her idea, but to my surprise I was intrigued. And the more she explained her vision, the more I liked it.

She continued, "I could set up in the back of the space. All I really need is a counter where I can brew tea, make coffee and display baked goods. I could get a few tables and chairs, and I could use what used to be the clothing store's changing rooms to give private consultations—you know, read tarot cards or tea leaves for customers. The changing rooms are still there, aren't they?"

I nodded. "Yes, they are."

"So what do you say?" she asked, searching my face for an answer.

I thought quickly, adding up the advantages. "I could rent you the space on a monthly basis. That way, if it didn't work out you wouldn't have invested too much money. And you could get your baked goods from Marnie. Matthew brought home some muffins from the coffee shop down the street and they weren't anywhere near as good as hers."

Her eyes widened. "Does that mean it's a yes?"

I was getting excited about the idea too. "I don't even have an accepted offer yet, but if I do, I suppose—"

She squealed and jumped off her stool to do a subdued version of a happy dance. Heads along the bar turned to stare. "Oh, uh, sorry, guys. Della just promised to teach me a new weave pattern." She hopped back on her stool, stifling a giggle.

This explanation was followed by bemused looks and much rolling of the eyes. The men soon returned to their meals, clearly convinced that the two women at the end of the bar were certifiable.

Jenny whispered, "This is going to be so much fun! I can't wait."

"Hold on. I don't even know if I'll get the place."

She nodded knowingly. "Oh, yes, you will. I have a feeling about this, and I'm never wrong about my feelings."

I laughed. "Do you get feelings about lottery tickets too?"

"You're making fun of me," she said. "Go ahead. Laugh all you want, but I know what I'm talking about." She glanced at her watch. "I have to go. And you do too if you want to open your shop at one o'clock."

Chapter 28

I had no sooner walked in and flipped the sign to OPEN than Matthew came storming out of the kitchen, Winston at his heels.

"How did I know you would be gone when I returned? What kind of trouble did you get yourself in this time?"

"Hey, not fair. All I did was have lunch with Jenny."

Matthew's eyes went from angry to guilty to suspicious. "Lunch, eh? Where'd you go?"

"To Bottoms Up, not that it's any of your business."

"Aha!" He pointed a finger at me. "I knew it. You went there to do some snooping, didn't you?"

I was not going to defend myself. "Not snooping—investigating. And wait till you hear what I found out."

He suddenly became curious. "What did you find out?" He followed me to the kitchen. "Tell me."

"I found out that David lied. He lied to the police and even to us."

He was silent for a second. "And how do you feel about that?"

My mouth dropped open. "You knew!" I was shocked. "You knew, and you didn't tell me?"

"Listen, kiddo, I know how you feel about—"

"Will you please stop saying that? I do not *feel* anything for David. He's a friend, that's all. And maybe less of a friend than I thought."

I must have sounded sincere because Matthew's eyes widened. "You're not in love with him?"

"I don't know where you got that idea. I am not in love with him. I am not even attracted to the man."

"Oh." He was silent for a second, studying me. "Jenny told me you were in love with someone. I guess I assumed—"

Where did Jenny get that idea? Oh, right, my aura. "When did she tell you that?"

He waved my question away. "Not important."

"She told me *you* were in love with someone." A long silence followed, during which he looked uncomfortable. "I guess that proves she's not always right," I said.

"So what did you find out?" He seemed in a hurry to change the subject.

"Never mind what I found out. You tell me what you know."

He pulled up a chair, gesturing for me to sit, and took a seat across from me.

"Well," he began, "Mike seems to be getting over his anger with me. He told me a bit about the case. But everything I tell you stays here—right?"

I nodded.

"David lied about spending the entire evening at the bar. He left there much earlier than eleven—around nine thirty or so. I also know that he called his wife from the pay phone before leaving. Mike got the LUD from the phone company." I must have looked confused because he explained, "LUD is an acronym for 'local usage details.'"

I flopped against the back of the chair. "Oh, my God! He killed Jeremy, didn't he?" I was shocked that I could have been friends with a killer. "He really had me fooled."

He shook his head. "We don't know that for sure."

"But it's certainly beginning to look that way, isn't it?"

He hesitated. "Well, he did have motive and opportunity. But all the evidence is just circumstantial. There's nothing irrefutable yet."

"Yet," I repeated. "Isn't there some way we can find out for sure?"

"Yes. We let the *police* handle it."

At that moment the doorbell rang and I rose, hoping it was a client, but before I could get to the front, who should walk in but the devil himself.

"Well, well." I stifled my sarcasm. "Look who's here."

"Were you two just talking about me?" asked David. Behind him, Matthew was shaking his head furiously.

I ignored him. "You lied to us, David."

David's mouth dropped open and blood drained from his face. "I . . . uh."

I was beyond feeling sorry for him. "Where were you the night of the murder, David? And don't tell us you spent the evening at the bar, because we know that's not true."

"Oh, shit." He pulled out a chair, collapsed into it and buried his face in his hands. "I should have known people would find out sooner or later. I lied because the truth sounds so lame."

Matthew sat. "Try us."

Looking resigned, he sat up straight and glanced from me to Matthew. "I did have a few too many, but not at the bar. I was in my car." He sighed, then said, "After the run-in with Marsha and Jeremy, all I wanted to do was talk to her. I still can't believe that she left me for a jerk like him." He ran a hand through his hair. "After I dropped you off, I went to the bar and had a few drinks, which didn't help me feel any better. I tried to call her, but the call went into voice mail, so I figured she was probably at Jeremy's." He looked up at us again. "So I called there. I didn't get an answer, so I drove over and sure enough, her car was in the driveway."

"Why did you use the pay phone instead of your cell?"

"I was out of battery."

Matthew frowned. "If what you're telling us is true, that means you called Jeremy's number at the precise moment he was on the phone with whoever he was meeting. That would be one hell of a coincidence."

David nodded. "I know. I know. But I am telling you the truth. Anyhow, I left, determined to give her a piece of my mind. But first I picked up a quart of bourbon for some liquid courage. When I got to the house, I sat in the car and polished off the whole bottle, but in the end I didn't have the guts."

Matthew crossed his arms. "Did you see Jeremy leave the house?"

He nodded.

"Did you follow him?"

"I swear I didn't." He suddenly looked embarrassed.

"I would have, but I had a flat tire." Emphatically, he said, "You can check with the garage that installed the new tire the next day. Turns out my tire wasn't just punctured. It was slashed. Somebody had to have done it while I was right there, sitting in the car, because it was fine when I left the liquor store." He frowned. "But I don't know how the hell they did that without me seeing them."

Matthew and I were silent for a few minutes while we digested this.

"You're right," Matthew said at last. "That is a lame story." He scowled. "Maybe I should have my head examined, but I believe it."

"You do?" asked David.

"You do?" I repeated, shocked. I *so* didn't believe a word of it.

Matthew nodded. "Yes, I do. Spending hours sitting in a car and drinking in front of a rival's home is just the kind of stupid thing people do after a breakup."

He had a point. I remembered once sitting in a car for hours, watching the front door of a boyfriend's house because I was convinced he had been cheating on me. I hadn't made a very good spy—I fell asleep behind the wheel and woke up with him tapping on my window. So embarrassing!

Matthew frowned. "Did you speak to Marsha at all that night?"

David shook his head. "No, by the time Jeremy left, I was more sloshed than I was pissed. I must have dozed off for a while, because when I looked at the time next it was about eleven. I left the car there and walked home."

He looked at us, his palms spread apologetically. "And you know the rest. The ambush part is completely true."

Matthew was right. As lame as it was, David's story rang true. And studying his face now, all I could see was sincerity. I frowned. "You know what that means, don't you?" They both looked at me. "Somebody is framing you. Whoever slashed your tire is the person who ambushed you. They saw you watching the house and slashed your tire so you couldn't follow Jeremy when he left. And then after killing him, they waited until you got back to your place and ambushed you."

Matthew nodded in agreement. "That actually makes sense," he said, sounding surprised that a theory of mine could be plausible. "Did you happen to see anybody on the street that night?"

David frowned. "I saw Mercedes walk by on her way home."

I looked at David, surprised. "Dolores lives on the same street?"

David nodded. "Right across from Jeremy's."

I added this little tidbit to the rest of the puzzle. Marnie, Dolores and Jeremy all lived on the same street. *Wow*, Briar Hollow sure was small.

Another theory popped into my mind. Could Dolores have found a way into Marnie's house and stolen the gun? I'd have to ask Marnie about that. But what could have been her motive for wanting Jeremy Fox dead?

I opened my mouth to tell them about the gun, but then stopped myself. This was something I couldn't tell a soul, at least not until I figured out who had stolen it from Marnie's house.

Suddenly David blanched. Almost as if he had read my mind, he said, "Shit! Do you think whoever is framing me might also have planted the murder weapon at my place?" He glanced from me to Matthew. "That's what I'd do if I wanted to frame someone."

Matthew and I were quiet as we digested the logic of this.

David pulled his cell phone from his pocket. "I'm calling my lawyer."

A few minutes later he hung up. "He says he's calling the police right away. If they suspect me, it's only a matter of time before they search my place. For all we know, they could be on their way with a search warrant right now."

"So what are you going to do?"

David shrugged. "Cooperate. If they do find a gun, it'll look better for me if I invited them in than if I tried to stop them. I'm going down to the police department right now."

And without any further preamble, he got to his feet. "I better get going. See you later."

Matthew stood. "I'll go with you."

They took off without so much as a good-bye. What was it with these guys? Didn't I count for anything around here?

Chapter 29

David had convinced me of his innocence, for the most part. And I'd decided that I had to do something. The more I thought about it, the more it was clear to me that somebody was framing him—but who? The best way I could think of solving that was to make a list of all the suspects. I shuffled over to the desk and got a pencil, drawing a line down the center of a piece of paper. On the left, I wrote the names of everyone I thought might be the killer. On the right I would write possible motives.

The first name I wrote was David's. Just because Matthew and I believed his story, I couldn't ignore the facts. David did have motive and opportunity. Jeremy had seduced his sister and once she'd invested all her money with him, he'd dumped her and moved on to David's wife—both good enough reasons to have wanted the guy dead. Add to that the fact that David had threatened to kill the man in front of witnesses. Another thought occurred to me. Could David have also invested in Jeremy's project? That was something I had to find out.

I jotted all of this down.

Next on the list was Marnie. I knew in my heart that

she hadn't done it either, but by looking at all the possibilities and eliminating them one at a time, maybe I could get to the truth.

Jeremy had swindled her out of her life savings, and she had also uttered death threats. Add to that the possibility that the murder weapon belonged to her. She claimed the gun had been stolen, but for all I knew, she could have gotten rid of it herself after killing Jeremy. I closed my eyes, trying to picture Marnie pulling out her gun and shooting Jeremy. It would have been almost funny, if not for the fact that the man was very much dead. Still, I took note of it. I put the pencil down, and looked at Winston lying by the window.

"Who do you think did it, Winston? Was it the butler in the library with the candlestick? Or Marnie in the apartment with her gun?"

He didn't even budge. No sense of humor whatsoever, that dog.

I returned to my list. Next was David's sister. What was her name again? Leanne. She was supposed to be in New York, but she could have come back and killed him. There had to be some way I could confirm that. *Got it.*

I put down my pencil and rummaged through my purse for my phone. A moment later, I had Jenny on the line.

"Do you know David's sister, Leanne?" I asked.

"Yes, of course. This is Briar Hollow—"

"—and everybody knows everybody," I interrupted. "How can we be sure she was in New York the night of the murder?"

"Still investigating, are we? Well, you called the right person. Leanne isn't just an acquaintance. She's a good friend. And I know she was in New York, because I called her after work that day."

"You never told me that," I said.

"I didn't think it was important. I had a message from her on my answering machine when I got home. She'd heard that Jeremy had been killed and wanted details." I heard Jenny's shrug in her next words. "I guess she was too embarrassed to call her brother."

"And you're absolutely sure she was in New York when you called her."

"It was a two-one-two area code."

"It could have been a cell phone."

"It was her landline, and her roommate answered when I called, so I had to wait until Leanne came to the phone."

"Oh." Well, that killed that theory. We said good-bye and hung up, and I returned to my list.

There were many people who could have killed Jeremy. But my favorite suspect was still Dolores, which was why I'd saved her for last. I didn't have one single shred of evidence against the woman, but I wasn't about to let that stop me. Maybe because she made it so obvious that she didn't like weaving, I just didn't like her. But again, I kept coming back to the same question: What motive could she have had for killing Jeremy?

I had just written all of this down when it occurred to me that if Greg Hanson had indeed been murdered, what would have been David's or Marnie's motive for killing him? Proving Hanson had been killed could go a long way toward eliminating David and Marnie as possible suspects. But how was I supposed to do that?

All this thinking was giving me a headache. I slapped my pencil down in frustration. At that the phone rang, giving me a welcome respite.

It was Susan Wood. "Hi, Della. If you feel like a break, why don't you join me for coffee?" It would be my sixth cup of the day, but who was counting? I taped a note— BACK AT FOUR—on the door and left.

Chapter 30

The coffee shop was a small, pleasant room, furnished with the usual assortment of armchairs and tables. A few patrons sat around chatting, reading, or working on laptops. Behind a long counter at the far end, where baristas rushed about steaming milk and serving coffee, were shelves of goodies: cakes, muffins and pies.

I hobbled over to the counter, already salivating.

"What'll it be?" asked the barista, a pretty young girl with Goth makeup, black hair in pigtails, a star tattoo on her right hand and a moon tattoo on her left. I wondered if she was a friend of Mercedes's.

I swept my gaze along the row of goodies and settled on a cranberry-lemon muffin and a latte.

"If you'll have a seat, I'll bring it to you as soon as it's ready," the girl said, eyeing my crutches.

I chose a table by the window, waving at Susan as she walked in. "Can I get you something?" she mouthed. I shook my head.

A few minutes later the girl brought me my tray just as Susan joined me with her own.

"This place makes the best cranberry-lemon muffins

in the world," Susan said. She set her tray on the table. "I see you got one too. Good choice."

I broke off a piece and took a bite.

"Didn't I tell you they were good? I swear, I could come here every day."

"Really good," I said between bites. I'd now tried both the raisin bran and the cranberry-lemon, neither of which was nearly as good as Marnie's. I'd have to remember to mention this to her. The woman had every right to be proud of her baking.

I took a sip of coffee and sat back, readying myself for the gossip session that was about to ignite. "So, what's new?" I asked, hoping she had found out more about the murder.

Susan leaned forward conspiratorially. "I was just talking to Dr. Cook—he's also the town coroner, you know—"

"Yes." I nodded encouragingly.

Without pausing, she continued, "—and he says that Jeremy Fox had been dead for at least twelve hours when his body was found."

I counted backward in my mind. I had found the body shortly after nine. Twelve hours earlier brought the murder to before ten o'clock the previous night. Just as I had feared, the time of death didn't clear David. I took a quick gulp of coffee, covering my disappointment. "Dr. Cook told you that? How did you get him to talk?"

She smiled. "I made an appointment for this." She showed me a bandage on her little finger with a twinkle in her eyes. "I had a wart that needed to be removed."

I laughed. "A serious medical emergency if you ask me."

"He is also a bit of a blabbermouth. He told me that Jeremy had been shot four times with a small-caliber gun." She raised her eyebrows and leaned in to whisper, "Not that I'm any kind of expert, but I think if a woman uses a gun, she's likely to choose a small caliber." I held back a gasp as I remembered that Marnie had mentioned that her gun was small. I didn't know much about guns, but didn't small guns mean small caliber?

"I can't believe Dr. Cook told you all that. You must be a really good conversationalist for him to have opened up that way." Did I know how to butter a person up, or what?

Susan smiled with self-satisfaction. "You're right. People are always telling me their secrets for some reason. You would be surprised at the secrets I know. I know who's having an affair with whom. I know who's pregnant and by whom. I know who's getting chemo and keeping it a secret." She made a gesture, pretending to lock her mouth and throw away the key, looking self-righteous. "I know I like to talk, but if somebody tells me something in confidence, I'd die before I repeated a word to anyone."

Somehow I had my doubts about that. I suddenly had an image of Susan Wood miming, charades-style, "Three words. First word sounds like . . ." I stopped myself from laughing and put on my most earnest expression. "That's a rare quality. People must really trust you."

Susan beamed with pride. "They do. That's how I know that David Swanson's ex-wife wasn't Jeremy Fox's only girlfriend. I swear that man was a regular tomcat. He was always juggling two or three women at the same time." She shook her head. "But I don't feel sorry for Marsha Swanson. Those two are one of a kind. Her love life was just as active as his."

"She was seeing somebody else too? Are you sure about that?

She nodded solemnly. "That woman will sleep with any man as long as he has money." I must have looked shocked because she leaned forward and whispered, "Trust me. I know. She was having an affair with Greg Hanson shortly before he died, you know."

My mouth dropped open. "Really?" If that was true, Susan had just provided Dolores with a clear motive. "What about Dolores Hanson? Could she have been involved with Jeremy too?"

She nodded. "Maybe. I know Dolores was calling Jeremy regularly, at least until I quit working for him in May." She shrugged. "After that, I have no idea."

"What do you know?" I said reflectively. "Dolores and Jeremy, and Marsha and Greg. If Dolores suspected that her husband was involved with Marsha, it would be a motive for her wanting her husband dead, wouldn't it?"

She gave me a crooked smile. "Yes, but it also gives David a motive for killing Greg."

I fell against the back of my seat. *Crap*. I hadn't thought of that. "But," I said, thinking quickly, "if Dolores was jealous enough to kill her husband over his cheating, then she could have killed Jeremy over his cheating with Marsha."

Susan was studying me with an amused smile. "You really don't want it to be David, do you? I wonder why."

"It's just that he was with me when I found the body. It would be too awful if I thought he used me to fabricate some kind of alibi. Besides, I don't know very many people in town. I'd hate to think one of the few I consider friends was a murderer."

"Just between you and me, I'm convinced that Dolores and Jeremy were involved. You'd be hard-pressed to find any single or divorced woman in this town that wasn't involved with Jeremy at some point. A couple of married ones too," she added, her eyebrows doing the Groucho Marx wiggle.

"What a jerk! No wonder he ended up dead."

"Oh, and before I forget—guess whose house was broken into the night of the murder?" I looked at her blankly. "Jeremy Fox's."

"What?"

She nodded. "The police asked Marsha to help them figure out if anything had been taken. It turns out the only thing missing was his laptop."

Suddenly something David had said made sense. The police had asked him about a laptop, and I wondered why they hadn't asked me. Unless they already knew the laptop had been stolen from Jeremy's house and had only mentioned it to watch David's reaction.

"What could have been on that laptop?"

Susan shrugged. "I have no idea. He was very protective of it—never let me use it, even when it meant he had to e-mail me documents rather than let me work directly on his computer." She waved the subject away, continuing, importantly, "Just between you and me, I'm almost sure I know who killed him."

My eyes widened. "Who?"

She paused, and for a second I thought she was about to tell me. And then she shook her head. "As much as I'd like to, this is something I can't repeat unless I'm one hundred percent certain. I wouldn't want to get sued for defamation of character." She leaned forward again. "I'll tell you day after tomorrow. By then, I'll know for sure."

Of all the times to develop a conscience, she chose now. "Uh-oh. What are you going to do?"

She raised an eyebrow. "Oh, I have an idea."

"You're not going to do anything dangerous, are you?"

"Don't worry about me. I know how to take care of myself."

An idea occurred to me. "It isn't David Swanson, is it?" I was convinced she would say no.

"All I can say is that if I'm right, it would be just about the last person in the world anybody would suspect."

"So that means you don't think it's him?" Suddenly I thought of Marnie. She was probably the last person in the world anybody would suspect. I was tempted to ask, but then I would've had to explain about the gun.

"I think most people would be pretty shocked if it turned out to be David," she said, which still didn't tell me anything one way or another.

It was time to steer the conversation in another direction. "By any chance would you happen to have a list of the people who invested in Jeremy's condo project?"

She gave me a who-do-you-think-you're-talking-to

look. "Are you kidding? I was the one who did all of his company's bookkeeping. I know who invested and how much." She paused and gave me a piercing look. "You're sure asking a lot of questions. You're not working for the police, are you?" Before I could answer, she burst into laughter. "I'm just pulling your leg."

I chuckled. "What about Greg and Jeremy? Did they have anything in common—anything that linked them together?"

"Actually, yes. When Jeremy first launched his condo project, he tried to convince people that this was the best thing this town had ever seen, but not everyone believed him. Jeremy's biggest opponent was Greg Hanson, who made a huge stink about the project. He wrote an article for the local-news blog. And when that didn't work, I told you, he got a petition going. He went door-to-door himself, collecting signatures. About a week later he was dead."

Jenny *had* told me. How could it have slipped my mind? "That's the link," I said excitedly. "It does have to do with the condo project." Something stirred in my mind when I said this, but whatever it was escaped me at the moment.

"I thought about that, but it doesn't make any sense. Jeremy was in favor of the project. Greg was against. It would only have significance if they were both for, or both against the project."

I groaned. I hated to admit it, but she was probably right.

She started saying something as her gaze wandered to somewhere over my shoulder, and suddenly she blanched and looked at her watch. "Oh, no, I'm late," she cried. She jumped out of her seat, wrapped the rest of her muffin in her napkin and shoved it into her bag. "We'll have to do this again real soon," she said, smiling tightly.

"I'd like that." She turned to leave. "Hey, Susan, could you get me that list of investors?"

"You bet." And then, glancing sideways nervously, she whispered, "I'll drop it off as soon as I have a minute." A second later she was gone, the door closing behind her.

What had prompted her strange behavior, I wondered? The way she'd jumped out of her seat and run out was . . . well . . . odd. I turned around to scan the tables behind me, and I spotted them—Dolores, all dressed up in white linen, and Mercedes, wearing her usual black jeans and T-shirt. They were at the counter giving their order. Could Dolores be the reason Susan had left so abruptly? If so, it supported my theory that Dolores was the killer. I was still reflecting on this when, as I turned back around, I noticed Mike Davis sitting at a table near the door. He was watching Dolores with a measuring glare. And then he turned his eyes on me and smiled sardonically.

Shoot! If he'd overheard any of our conversation, Matthew would know by tomorrow that I was still playing detective. Rattled, I gathered my bag to leave. But when I swooped the crutches under my arms, Mike was already gone. From the bar, Dolores was staring at me coldly, leaving me with a bad feeling.

I was definitely spending way too much time with Jenny.

*   *   *

I hoofed it back to a dead silent house, no pun intended. I'd been gone no more than half an hour, but I still felt guilty about closing the shop in the middle of the afternoon. Still, the conversation with Susan had been interesting.

I was sitting at the kitchen table, attaching the satin edging to my yellow and green baby blanket—which looked spectacular, if you ask me—when the phone rang. I leaned over and picked it up.

"I just remembered," a voice I recognized as Marnie's cried excitedly. "You know who else had a key to my house? Mercedes Hanson! I gave her a key because she walked my Brutus every day until he died last summer."

Mercedes? My mind was grasping to make sense of this.

"Della? Did you just hear what I said?"

"Yes. Yes. But Mercedes is a just child. What would she want with a gun?"

"I don't know," came Marnie's frustrated response. "I called Jimmy, as you suggested, and he swears up and down that he never touched my gun. A .22-caliber is way too sissy for a man, he says. So I started thinking again—trying to recall everyone who had occasion to come into my house. That's when I remembered that I had a key made for Mercedes." She paused for a second. "And she never brought it back after my Brutus died." As if I were a slow child, she went on, pronouncing each word excruciatingly slowly. "That means Dolores had access to my house."

"Have you told anyone?"

"No," she replied plaintively. "I don't know if I should.

I don't want to cause any trouble. Mind you, I don't much like that Botox-injected woman. Just between you and me, I think she had her lips pumped up with something too. It's Mercedes I don't want to get into trouble. She's had a difficult enough time of it already."

"You mean, with her father dying?"

"Yes, that too," said Marnie. But before I could ask her what she meant, I heard the front door open and close.

"Oops, sorry, Marnie, I have to go. There's someone at the door." We rang off and Matthew walked in, looking exhausted.

"How did it go? Did the police search David's house?"

"They're conducting the search as we speak." He went to the refrigerator and pulled out a Heineken. "Join me in a beer?" I nodded, and he got a second one. He popped the top and handed it to me.

"Eh, would you mind? You may like swigging your beer straight from the bottle, but I prefer a glass."

He gave me a crooked smile and handed me a goblet.

"You know everyone around here, Matthew. If David didn't kill Jeremy, do you have any idea who else could have hated Jeremy Fox enough to kill him?"

He grew pensive for a moment, and then shook his head, looking baffled. "One thing that criminology teaches us is that sociopaths are masters of deceit. They can fool people for years. You've probably seen inter-views with friends and neighbors of serial killers. They invariably say how that person was always so nice—a paragon of the community. Meanwhile that person had a dozen kids buried under his house." He scowled, opening the fridge again and pulling out a jar of olives. He rattled around the cutlery drawer until he located a seafood fork. "You, of all people, should know that." He was referring—of course—to the boss I had trusted who had turned out to be an embezzler. Why didn't everyone just, please, let me forget about that?

I nodded, sighing. "I should, shouldn't I?"

"Mike says the weapon was a .22, which hardly anybody uses anymore."

I cringed. Marnie's gun was a .22-caliber.

Matthew continued. "And there was no stippling, which means Jeremy was shot from at least six feet away, which also suggests that the killer had experience with firearms."

I stared at him, confused. "You lost me at 'stippling.'"

"'Stippling' and 'tattooing' are both terms used to describe the circular pattern of dots created around a gunshot wound when a firearm is discharged from a close distance."

"Oh, and I always thought stippling was a painting technique."

He laughed. "Getting back to your question—at this point, I have no idea who killed him. I couldn't even hazard a guess." He frowned, looking thoughtful. "The problem with this case is that there are too many people with too many motives. The man was a Lothario."

I cleared my throat, but before I could speak, he cut me off. "I don't want you going around playing detective anymore. You hear me? I wouldn't want a pretty thing like you getting herself hurt."

He'd just done it again. He'd said I was pretty. I felt my face redden as I scrambled for something to say. I was still trying to think of a snappy comeback when the phone rang and Matthew picked up. "Hey, how'd it go?" he asked, and then he covered the mouthpiece and whispered, "It's David."

"Ask him if he heard anything about my offer."

Matthew repeated my question and then shook his head. I felt a flash of disappointment. I so wanted that building. Oh, well, it wasn't lost yet. I still had until tomorrow.

They talked for a few minutes, but Matthew's part consisted mainly of one-word answers—yes, no, really—and "see you tomorrow."

"What did he say?" I asked as soon as he put down the receiver.

"The police searched the whole house. They didn't find a gun, but they grabbed a bunch of his clothes."

"His clothes?" I said, frowning. "Why?"

"They were the clothes he was wearing the night of the murder. I suspect they want to test them for gunpowder residue."

"But didn't they already do that?"

"Yes, but he might have showered and changed into fresh clothes before meeting with you that morning."

"He has nothing to worry about, right?"

"Not unless he's fired a weapon lately," said Matthew. Judging from the expression on his face, he wasn't entirely sure whether David had done that or not.

Chapter 31

The next morning when I was in my studio, the door to the shop swung open and Marnie Potter walked in. Today she wore a floor-length orange floral dress, which looked surprisingly lovely with her red hair falling in loose curls on her shoulders. In her arms she carried a large shopping bag much the way one might hold a baby.

"What a nice surprise," I said, grabbing my crutches.

"Oh, don't get up," she said, approaching me. "I brought you something. Where shall I put it?" She looked around.

"How about right here?" I gestured toward a chair. She dropped the bundle on the seat with a thump and opened the bag.

"I've been so overwrought, I plumb forgot to bring you some of my pieces as I promised. Pretty stupid of me, considering I need the money." She wiped away the beads of moisture on her forehead.

Without waiting for her to comment on the heat, I went to the window, propped it open, and turned on the fan.

"That's better. Thank you." She swept her hair off the

back of her neck. "I don't know why I wore my hair down. I get way too hot this way."

"You look good with your hair down," I said, returning to my chair.

She waved away the compliment. "At my age, I'd rather be comfortable." She pulled an elastic band from her dress pocket and tied her hair into a loose ponytail. "There, that's better." She sat. "I've decided I should speak to Mercedes about my gun."

I put my index finger in front of my mouth in the international sign for "be quiet" and pointed to the kitchen. "Matthew is here," I mouthed.

"Do you think he heard? I wasn't speaking very loudly."

Actually, she had been, but all I said was, "He concentrates so hard when he writes, I'm sure he didn't."

She nodded with relief. Glancing toward the kitchen door, she opened her bag and pulled out a stack of beautiful handwoven items. Loudly, she said, "I know you like Jenny's work. I hope you like mine as much. It's very different from hers, you know." Regardless of the twinkle in her eye, I knew exactly what was going on. This was a contest between Jenny and her, and I was the judge.

I measured my words carefully. "There's room for all styles of weaving in my shop. Some customers will want modern, and others won't look at anything other than traditional."

She unrolled from a cardboard tube and tissue a beautifully woven linen bedcover, handing it over to me. "My work is most certainly traditional." Leaning forward, she whispered, "I would like you to be there when I speak to Mercedes. Do you mind?"

"No problem," I answered in a low voice. "When do you want to do it?" And then loudly I exclaimed, "This is gorgeous. You know, tourist season is just around the corner. I'll probably sell everything you give me. Do you have any more?" Her work was magnificent. I ran my hands reverently over the fine fabric. It was perfect in every detail. I looked closer. The yarns were very fine and tightly spun, resulting in an exceptionally fine texture. "This is probably the finest traditional work I've ever seen outside a museum." The smile on Marnie's face told me I had said exactly what she wanted to hear.

"Do you really think so?" Her hunger for praise surprised me. How could someone with such talent doubt herself?

"Absolutely. I had no idea your work was of this quality. I think these are exactly what my shop needs. Your style and Jenny's will complement each other perfectly."

"I can't see what you mean by that," she said, sounding slightly offended.

"In the same way art galleries sometimes show modern art next to classic art, to underline the contrast."

A light went on in her eyes and she grinned. "Yes, yes. I imagine you might be right about that."

"Come help me display them," I said, grabbing my crutches and heading for my desk.

For the next hour, she marked and tagged as I entered her pieces into my stock list. Meanwhile we carried on two conversations, the louder one for Matthew's benefit.

She raised her voice. "I'm so happy you like my table-cloths." And then whispering, said, "I was thinking of inviting Mercedes to come over tomorrow. I told her I already have three finished baby blankets and she asked to see them. It'll be the perfect excuse."

"What time do you want me there?"

"How about right after you close the shop—six thirty or so?"

I nodded. "By the way, did you ever go to the coffee shop up the street?" I said. "I stopped by yesterday and had one of their cranberry-lemon muffins. They do not compare to yours."

Marnie beamed. "I just made a batch of blueberry muffins. I should have brought you a few."

Actually, I did wish she had. "That's sweet, but trust me, I don't need the calories. I'm just telling you. You really could start a business with your baking, you know."

"Speaking of business, what's going on with your of-fer on the building?"

"If I don't hear by the end of the day today, that means my offer is null and void," I said. "I'll probably have to look for another place."

"That would be too bad," said Marnie.

"It would be. I really like the idea of moving my shop to that space." I was tempted to tell her about Jenny's idea of sharing it to open a tea shop, but thought better of it. If and when Jenny opened her business, she should be the one to announce it.

Soon we had priced and tagged every one of her pieces. Under my direction she set them up in various places: draped over the open door of the armoire, folded on the table. By the time she was finished, the shop looked amazing.

"This place is beginning to look like a real store," she said, standing back to admire the results. "I didn't want to tell you this, but you really needed more merchandise."

I laughed. "You're right. But Dream Weaver looks like a fully stocked high-end shop now. All I need is more customers."

"They'll come." She picked up the bag in which she had brought her wares, folded it and slipped it inside her purse. "Trust me, they'll come." And the door closed behind her.

Chapter 32

I looked at my watch—four o'clock. I hadn't heard from David all day, which surprised me. After Marnie left, I'd called his office and left a message asking him to call me back. If the deal was off, I wanted to know so I could start making alternate plans. At the sound of the bell, I looked up to see Susan Wood walking in.

"Here it is." She brandished a brown manila envelope.

She had no sooner said this than the door opened again and Jenny walked in. "Should I come back later?"

"No, no, come on in."

Susan swung around and Jenny smiled. "Oh, Susan, I didn't recognize you for a second."

Susan waved her in. "Don't mind me. I'm only here for a minute."

"You can stay for quick cup of coffee, can't you, Susan?"

She looked at her watch. "I wish I could, but I'm on break and I only get fifteen minutes."

I started for the kitchen. "It won't take long."

Jenny called out, "Would you mind if I had a cup of tea instead?" As an afterthought, she added, "If you make it loose leaf, I can read your fortunes."

"You read fortunes?" I heard Susan ask, and then the kitchen door swung shut and I lost the rest of the conversation. To my surprise, the kitchen was empty. Matthew was gone. He had left by the back door, God only knew how long ago, and during all that time Marnie and I had been carrying on our two-tone conversation unnecessarily.

I turned the kettle on and, not having loose-leaf tea, I tore open a couple of teabags and dropped the contents into a teapot.

"I told you it wouldn't take long," I said from the doorway. "Can one of you help me with the tray?" Jenny hurried. She passed the pot around and then helped herself.

Susan stirred a spoonful of sugar into her tea. "I was just telling Jenny about our conversation yesterday afternoon." She set her cup down and picked up the manila envelope from her lap, tore it open and handed me a sheet of paper. "I brought you that list you wanted."

I took the sheet from her and looked at it. She returned to her tea, taking a few long sips.

"Don't drink it too fast," instructed Jenny. "You have to sip your tea slowly until only the tea leaves are left. And hold your cup with your left hand," she added. Jenny continued her directives while I scanned the list.

It consisted of a dozen or so names, only two of which I recognized—Marla Jean Potter, Marnie's legal name, and Matthew Baker. This was disappointing. Under each name were dates, amounts and other details. I calculated quickly. "This adds up to a lot of money. But there are only two names I know."

Jenny leaned in, peeking at the list. "Is that the list of people who invested in Jeremy's project? How did you get it?"

Susan smiled. "Turns out that Jeremy never changed the password on his office computer. I went in and printed it off. Mind you, I could have given you my old list. It turns out he didn't have any new investors since I quit working for him. That was around the time the contamination report was leaked."

I chuckled. "And guess who did the leaking?"

Jenny glanced from me to Susan. Her eyes grew wide. "You?" Susan didn't reply. "Well, good for you." She looked full of admiration. "You saved countless people from losing their money."

"I wish I'd gone looking for that report sooner. Then I could have helped even more people."

I looked at the figures again. "I can't believe how many people he persuaded to part with their money."

"He could be a real smooth talker when he wanted to." She tilted her head and studied me. "You think Jeremy might have been killed by one of those investors, don't you?"

"I have no idea who killed him. But I do think there are lots of people here, all of whom had a darn good reason to want him dead." I took a sip of tea, wishing it were coffee, and set the cup down. "I never saw the project. I imagine it must have looked pretty impressive."

"I'll drive you by for a look if you like."

"Yes, I'd like that." I picked up the list of investors again. "Some of these people lost a huge amount of money. Do the police have a copy of this?"

Susan shrugged. "Probably. But it won't do them any good. I don't think Jeremy's murder had anything to do with his condo project." Looking at the list in my hands, she said, "You've only got one page? Where's the second sheet?" She picked up the manila envelope and looked inside. "Here it is." She handed it to me.

"How can you be so sure it had nothing to do with his project?"

"I think I know who did it," Susan announced as casually as if we were discussing the weather. She had already told me as much at the coffee shop, but I'd figured she was only bragging. She took another sip of tea and set the cup back in its saucer. She tightened her lips and made a locking movement with her fingers, pretending to throw away the key. "I told you, I can't talk about it until I'm sure." She turned to Jenny. "I finished my tea. Can you read my fortune now?"

Jenny put a hand on her arm, looking worried. "If you know who killed Jeremy, you have to tell the police. You could get in serious trouble if you don't."

Susan took a deep breath and expelled it slowly. "I can't, at least not yet. First I have to get the proof. If everything goes right, I should have that by tomorrow night. Then I can go to the police. But enough about that." Grinning excitedly, she held out her cup. "Tell me what you see."

For a moment Jenny seemed reluctant to drop the subject, and then she pulled herself together. "Turn your cup upside down on the saucer and spin it around three times. And while you do that, think about the questions you'd like answered."

Susan was almost hopping in her seat in anticipation. "Oh, this is so much fun!" She spun the cup, closed her eyes briefly, and then handed the cup back.

Jenny gazed into it silently. She turned it this way and that, studying the inside from all angles. "I see a snake near the rim. Look here. Do you see it?"

Susan nodded nervously. "Yes. What does that mean?"

"A snake is usually a warning, something you should be careful about. And see here?" She pointed near the head of the snake. "It seems to have something in its mouth."

Susan peered closer. "It looks like a dagger." She glanced up at Jenny. "What does that mean?"

"Generally a knife or a dagger means that somebody wishes you harm and that you should watch your back."

At that moment the telephone rang and I hobbled away, missing the rest of Susan's reading. It was David.

"Sorry I didn't call you sooner," he said. "I've been pretty busy."

"Hi, David. I guess you didn't hear from the seller?" I dreaded the news. "Maybe I should start looking at other options. I wouldn't mind looking at Mrs. McLeay's house again."

"Actually, I was planning to call you and suggest that, but . . ." He paused, and my heart pounded in nervous anticipation. "I just got a counteroffer from the seller. Are you free later?"

My hope deflated. A counteroffer? I couldn't afford more than what I'd already offered. Still, I said, "Sure. Around what time?"

"I can stop by after dinner. Say, sevenish?"

I hung up and returned to the studio in time to hear Jenny say, "Promise me you'll be very careful, Susan. You are in serious danger."

Susan looked stricken for a moment, and then she hooted. "Oh, my goodness, you are so good," she said between hiccups of laughter. "You really had me going for a second."

"That was David Swanson," I said, interrupting. "Turns out the owner of that building just made a counteroffer. He's coming over later to present it."

Susan jumped out of her chair. "Oh, shoot. What time is it? If he notices I'm gone, I can kiss my job good-bye." She raced out. A second later the door swung shut behind her.

Chapter 33

Jenny helped me take the cups to the kitchen. She set them in the sink and turned on the tap. Suddenly I remembered the second page of the list. "Where's that list of investors? I'd like to take a look at it again."

"You left it on the desk. I'll get it for you."

She disappeared down the hall and returned a moment later, brandishing the list. "Got it." She handed it to me. And then, peering over my shoulder, she said, "Well, well. Will you look at who we have here?" She pointed to a name—D. Symons. "Do you know who this is?"

"Not a clue. Don't forget, I'm still new in town."

"D. Symons is none other than Dolores Hanson. Symons is her maiden name."

My mouth dropped open. "Dolores Hanson is D. Symons? You're kidding."

"No joke."

"Just between you and me, something tells me the person Susan suspects is Dolores. She thinks she and Jeremy were involved. Mind you, Matthew is convinced Dolores didn't kill her husband. It turns out she has even more money than he did."

"Money isn't always the only motive." She sat across from me, worry lines appearing between her eyebrows. "If Susan plans to confront Dolores, she'd better be careful."

"You're really concerned for her, aren't you?"

She nodded, tears suddenly swimming in her eyes. "She thought my warning was all in good fun. If something happens to her, I, I—" She shook her head, at a loss for words. "I'm beginning to feel like Typhoid Mary. Everyone I go near gets killed. Maybe I should stop giving readings."

"Hey, I'm still alive." I grinned, and then more seriously, I added, "Don't be silly. It's not as if you're causing anything to happen." I was tempted to reason with her that all these premonitions of hers were—certainly in most cases—nothing more than hindsight. The perfect example was when I called her from the hospital. It was obvious that her "bad feeling" appeared the moment she saw where the call was from. And in Susan's case, anybody with half a brain would be at least somewhat concerned when she announced that she knew the identity of a killer. Even I had been—until I realized she was just trying to make herself important. "Look at it this way. What you're doing is warning people. If they took your advice instead of dismissing it, you might have saved them."

She nodded, the frown lines on her forehead softening. "Thank you for saying that. But I'd feel better if I'd been more insistent with Jeremy."

I glanced at her, puzzled. "What are you talking about?"

"I gave Jeremy a reading last week and I warned him that someone was wishing him harm."

"Are you telling me that you predicted both Greg Hanson's and Jeremy Fox's deaths?"

"Not *predicted*, exactly. I saw danger around them— *grave* danger."

"Are you serious?"

She nodded miserably.

I thought for a second. "Of course somebody was wishing him harm. The man had conned half the town. It's not as if giving him a reading caused his death, Jenny."

"I know you think I'm bonkers." She shrugged. "I shouldn't have told you. I just needed to get it off my chest."

"It's okay," I said weakly. "But I still think you're making yourself miserable for something you had nothing to do with."

"You're right, of course."

"If you're really worried about Susan, maybe you should tell Mike. He *is* a cop, after all. Maybe he can keep an eye on her."

Jenny cupped her chin in her hands, nodding pensively. "You call him. Mike won't talk to me. Besides, even when we were together, he never took my feelings seriously."

Talking to Mike Davis was just about the last thing I wanted to do—but what the heck. It wouldn't hurt me, and it might help Susan. "I can do that." I picked up the phone.

Jenny recited the number and I punched it in. A moment later I had her ex on the line.

"You're saying that Susan Wood knows who killed Jeremy Fox?" He sounded exactly the way I'd expected him to—skeptical. "Did she give you the name of this person?"

"No. She said she didn't want to get anybody in trouble in case she was wrong, but that she'd have proof tomorrow tonight. She sounded really sure of herself."

I heard the derision in his voice. "Ri-i-ight. Do you have any idea how many people have called to report that they know who killed Fox? I get at least one call an hour."

"But this is different. Susan worked with Jeremy. She knows everybody who invested in his company. She even knows everyone he was involved with romantically. I'm worried about her. If she confronts the killer—which I'm sure she's planning to do—and he's killed once, he won't hesitate to kill her."

He sounded sarcastically. "Maybe you should work for the police, Miss Wright." Or maybe I should hire Susan Wood to head the investigation."

Mike Davis was seriously getting on my nerves. "I'm sorry I bothered you." I knew I was being snarky, but I was beyond caring. "I was under the impression the police welcomed information from concerned citizens. I must have been wrong. Don't worry. I won't take up any more of your precious time." I dropped the phone into its cradle.

Jenny stared at me, her face drained of blood. "He didn't believe you, did he?"

I shook my head, scowling. "I guess I didn't do a very good job of convincing him."

"It's not you. Mike was always like that. He's a good police officer, but he never once considered my opinion, and whenever I turned out to be right—which was more often than not—it irritated him. In time, I learned to keep my mouth shut." She shrugged apologetically. "I guess our marriage wasn't quite as perfect as I like to remember it."

I smiled. "Congratulations. I think you just took the first step toward getting over him."

She grimaced. "I still have a long way to go."

Chapter 34

Jenny glanced at her watch. "It's five forty-five already. I have to get going. Do you want to take a look at Jeremy's condo project? It's only minutes away, on Mountain View Road, but I never go that way. I wouldn't mind taking a look at it myself."

I jumped at the chance. "And if you don't mind, could you drop me off at Marnie's on the way back? She asked me to come by after work."

"No problem," she said, picking up her car keys and her bag. Luckily she didn't ask me why Marnie had invited me over, which meant I didn't have to make up a story. I still couldn't bring myself to tell anyone about her gun.

Jenny clicked her seat belt in place and we took off. For a city girl used to driving half an hour just to get from downtown to the city outskirts, it never ceased to surprise me just how close everything was in Briar Hollow. One could drive clear across town, from one end to the other, in no more than three minutes.

This time Jenny drove north along King Street, a direction I had never taken. Minutes later we pulled up in front of a long trailer with a sign reading SHOWROOM AND

SALES OFFICES TO NORTH CAROLINA'S MOST EXCLUSIVE LUX-
URY DEVELOPMENT. In smaller letters it read, 17 OF 60
UNITS SOLD.

I couldn't see anything elegant or impressive about it.
In fact, it was quite the opposite. The trailer stood at one
end of the property jacked up on cinder blocks. Behind
it lay a large, rocky expanse of land with the mountains
rising in the background.

"It's not very impressive, is it?" I said, as she pulled to
a stop next to the trailer.

We sat in the car, taking it in for a few minutes. I tried
to visualize a modern building with beautiful landscaping, but the spot seemed all wrong for that kind of project. Sure, Briar Hollow attracted tourists, but these were
people who worked in the city. They flocked to Briar
Hollow and rented quaint cabins and cottages to get
away from their stressful lives. The last thing they'd want
would be to purchase city-type condos out here. A sixty-
unit building was an awfully large project for a small
town. Most of the locals were middle-class people and
couldn't afford luxury condos. I turned to Jenny. "Who
did Jeremy think would buy his condos?"

"I think the project was a con right from the start.
That's the only explanation that makes sense," she said.

"It certainly looks that way."

She climbed out of the car and walked around to the
passenger side. She opened the door and handed me my
crutches from the backseat. I hurried after her.

"I can't tell where the plot of land begins or ends," I
said. Swinging from my crutches, I kicked at a lump of
dry soil with my good foot and lost my balance.

"Careful there," said Jenny, grabbing my arm and steadying me. "Let's go back. This isn't the kind of terrain you should be walking around on."

I followed her to her car and climbed in. "Isn't it scary how a good salesperson can sell just about anything? Jeremy put up a billboard, printed a few floor plans and people fell for it," I said as she put the car in gear.

She nodded. "Thank goodness Susan leaked the environmental report or even more people would have lost money."

A few minutes later we pulled up in front of a bright pink house with white trim and black shutters. Along the front grew a wild medley of colorful flowers.

I chuckled. Marnie's house suited her to a T.

"Need help?" said Jenny as I climbed out of the car. But I was already scooping my crutches from the backseat.

"I'm good," I called out. "Thanks for the ride."

She took off with a wave, and I made my way up the path to the front door. It swung open just as I reached for the bell.

"There you are. I was worried you wouldn't show up." Marnie threw her arms around me in a bear hug. "I'm so glad you're here. I wouldn't have the nerve to bring up my missing gun all on my own." She took a step back. "Come in. Come in."

I crossed the threshold and stopped. My eyes darted around, jumping from one outrageous piece of furniture to another. In the middle of the room was a sofa shaped like a pair of giant red lips. On either side were Hawaiian hula-dancer lamps. In a far corner was a plastic palm tree with a stuffed toy monkey clinging to its trunk. Across the room was a penny arcade fortune-telling machine—a gypsy looking into a crystal ball. I walked over for a closer look.

"Oh, this is incredible. Jenny would love this."

"Everybody loves it. Can I get you a cup of coffee?" she asked. "And I just made some lovely chocolate cake. Would you like a piece?"

I didn't need any arm twisting. She disappeared into the kitchen and I settled on the lips sofa, still looking around. By the window I noticed a birdcage with a stuffed parrot. Next to it was a Victorian porcelain doll with a cracked face. This place was like a museum of oddities. It suited its owner perfectly.

I stifled a giggle just as Marnie reappeared.

She set the tray on the coffee table and poured. "Mercedes should be here any second," she said, handing me a generous piece of cake. "How do you think I should approach the subject?"

Before I could answer, the doorbell rang and she jumped up and rushed over. "Come on in, Mercedes," she said, opening the door. "I just made some cake. Would you like a piece?"

Mercedes appeared, dressed in black as usual, but today she wore safety-pin earrings instead of her usual skull and crossbones. "Oh, hi," she said, seeing me.

Marnie disappeared into the kitchen and returned with another piece of cake. "Here you go." She handed it to the girl. "I'll go get my blankets. In the meantime, maybe you want to take a look at this." She pointed to a stack of weaving magazines on the coffee table. "Feel free to borrow a couple if you like."

Mercedes took a seat next to me. She put down the cake and picked up a magazine. She flipped through pages, pausing at some of the pictures. "Do you know how to do all of these?"

"I do. It's not nearly as complicated as it looks. As long as you know how to read a pattern, you can do just about anything."

"I guess I need to practice."

"Yes, it's all about practice. If you like, I can give you a private lesson—no charge. Do you want to come over one evening?"

"Really? You mean it?"

Marnie reappeared, carrying a stack of folded blankets. "Here they are," she said, unfolding them on one of the armchairs.

I ran a finger along the length of the top blanket. The tension was impeccable, tight and even. "Oh, Marnie, these are beautiful."

Next to me Mercedes stared, mesmerized. "I don't think I've ever seen anything so pretty."

Marnie's blankets, like mine, were assembled from strips, but she had woven each strip in stripes or checks. The effect was gorgeous.

She smiled. "I'm glad you like them."

She settled in the armchair across from Mercedes and took a sip of coffee. Then she put her cup down and furrowed her brow, searching for the right words. "Mercedes, there's something I want to ask you. Would you happen to still have the key I gave you a couple of years ago?"

Mercedes took a bite of cake and answered with her mouth full. "Do you want it back?"

"Er, well, yes. But there's something else I want to ask you."

The girl's eyes darted from me to Marnie and back again, looking trapped. "What?"

"I used to keep a gun in the back of my bedroom closet. I went to look for it yesterday, and it's no longer there. Would you happen to know where it is?"

Mercedes's blush crept up her neck to the top of her head. Her pleasant expression of a moment ago disappeared. She put her plate down with a clatter and jumped to her feet, looking guilty, and then angry. "You think I have it?" she yelled. Before Marnie or I could react, she bolted to the door and flung it open. "For your information, I don't have your stupid gun."

"Wait," Marnie called, looking contrite. "Stop. I just—" But she was already gone.

Marnie walked over to the door and closed it with a sigh. "That went rather well, wouldn't you say?"

Chapter 35

I stepped into the house and Winston came galloping in from the kitchen, throwing himself at me, almost knocking me over. I should have seen that one coming.

"Whoa, there, big boy!" Luckily, he backed away. "Are you all by yourself?" I asked, following him into the kitchen, where Matthew was settled at the table, typing away on his laptop.

"Hey, look at you!" I exclaimed. "You started your book. That's great." I leaned my crutches against the wall, pulled out a chair and sat. "You'll never believe what I just found out."

Without taking his eyes off his screen, he put up a hand. "Can it wait? I'm on a roll and I'd like to keep going."

"Oh, of course," I said, already getting up.

He paused and looked at me. "Just give me half an hour. I've given myself a goal of a thousand words a day and I don't want to take a break until I'm done. It won't be long. I'm almost there."

"Of course—take all the time you need." I hobbled over to the studio and settled at my loom. I'd been surprised that Marnie had already completed three blankets, when I was only halfway through my second one. I set to work with a vengeance, and suddenly Matthew appeared, standing next to me. I'd been so concentrated on my work I hadn't heard him come in.

"Are you all done with your writing for the day?"

He grinned. "I did almost double what I was aiming for." He looked down at the yards of woven fabric wound tightly onto the cloth beam. "And it looks like you're doing well too."

"This is the last piece I need to complete my second baby blanket."

"If you need a break, I've got dinner ready and waiting."

At the mention of dinner, my stomach rumbled. "Coming," I said, putting away my shuttle.

I hurried to the kitchen, where—to my surprise—I found soup was simmering on the stove. I spotted an empty can of Campbell's vegetable soup on the counter and stifled a laugh.

I turned and noticed that the table was set for two, with a plate of crackers and cheese. "Not quite the dinner I expected, but it's sweet of you all the same."

"I know I promised you ribs tonight, but I forgot to do the shopping. Time flies when I'm writing. Tomorrow," he said. "I promise."

"Don't worry about it. I'm not all that hungry." That wasn't quite true. The smell of the soup had awakened my appetite. I was famished.

He took bowls from the cupboard and set them on the counter. "I've come up with a plan," he said, ladling soup into the bowls. "Tell me if you like it."

"Sure." I leaned my crutches against the wall and sat.

"I think the kitchen might not be the best place for me to work," he said, setting a steaming bowl of soup in front of me. "At least not until your shop opens in the afternoon. So here's what I propose. Mornings, I can write at the desk in the front room, and you won't have to tiptoe around me when you're in the kitchen. And if I haven't finished my writing for the day by one o'clock, I'll come and work at the table. What do you think?" He picked up his bowl and filled it.

His solution was logical, but I was filled with guilt. "This is your house, and here you are, trying to stay out of my way. It's not fair."

"Don't worry about it. I don't mind." Seeing the look on my face, he added, "I mean it."

"I guess if you're okay with it, but only until I can come up with a better solution. Speaking of which, David is coming over in a while to present the counteroffer."

"You got a counteroffer? That's great." He picked up a few crackers and crumbled them into his soup.

"I don't know what's so great about it. The offer I made was already the absolute best I could do. I can't offer a penny more." I finished my soup and stared at the bottom of my bowl. I glanced at him. He was gazing at his empty bowl too, looking even hungrier than I was.

He smiled ruefully. "I guess I should have made more food."

"Leave it to me." I pushed back my chair, opened the refrigerator and shuffled through the contents until I found some smoked turkey, a bottle of Dijon mustard and some more cheese. I popped bread into the toaster and said, "How about a smoked turkey sandwich?"

Matthew's smile was triumphant. He tilted his chair back, hands clasped behind his head. "I knew you'd come through. You're the best, kiddo."

"You rat." I wagged a finger at him, laughing. "You played me, didn't you? You knew I'd take pity on you. You totally took advantage of my good nature."

His smile became suggestive. "Sweetheart, if I took advantage of you, it wouldn't be for a turkey sandwich."

I swung around and faced the counter before he could see me blush. I busied myself buttering the bread and assembling the sandwiches, set them on a plate, and plopped them on the table. "Consider yourself lucky there's no arsenic in them."

He burst out laughing. "And that, my dear, proves a point. Women poison. Men stab and shoot."

Seconds later David arrived, brandishing the papers like a trophy. "Wait till you hear this counteroffer. You won't believe it." He handed me one copy and another to Matthew.

Judging from the satisfied smile on his face, he expected to close a sale today. I was not so sure. He sat down across from me, grinning.

I raised my brows. "I can't see how I can do any better than what I already offered." I picked up the offer, already prepared to reject it. The first thing I saw was the strike through the words "offer for a lease-to-rent" at the top, and handwritten over it, "offer to purchase."

I groaned. "Oh, for God's sake, David. We've already

been over this. I can't afford to buy. I don't have the money for a down payment."

Sitting next to me and leaning in so he could read along with me, Matthew was riveted on the offer. "Keep reading, Della."

I focused on the document, flipping pages until I got to the third one. My eyes widened. "Does this mean what I think it means?" I pointed to a section that was crossed out and above it was handwritten, "seller agrees to provide a first mortgage."

David's grin stretched wider. "What it means is that he's willing to finance the purchase. He'll lend you the money himself."

I frowned. "You're telling me that the seller will hold the mortgage on his own building. That hardly makes sense."

"It's not unusual, especially in commercial real estate."

I looked down at the document again. "But I still don't have the down payment."

All he said was, "Keep reading."

My eyes fell on the next line. "He's asking only twelve percent as a down payment? That's— that's—" I calculated quickly.

David nodded vehemently. "Not a lot. I know."

"It might not be much to you, but it's still a lot to me." I set the offer down. "But, why does he want to get rid of the building so badly? Is there something I should know?"

"Of course not."

"Then—I don't get it—why?"

"Don't forget he already sold the building once, which means he got a down payment from that buyer—a down payment that he kept when the buyer defaulted. So he's already made some money on the building. He's been trying to sell it for nearly two years and is probably fed up with it sitting there. Also"—he smiled wickedly—"the police contacted him and told him about the murder. When he and I talked later, I told him the truth: He might not get another offer for a long time."

I'd need—I calculated quickly—almost exactly the amount I had in my Roth IRA. "I'd have to cash in my retirement fund." That I would even consider that possibility shocked me.

"I don't know your financial situation, but in this case maybe cashing in would be the smart thing to do. Think of this building as your retirement plan. Once it's paid off, it will bring in good income." He paused. "What do you think?'

I was still trying to get my head around the idea of cleaning out all my savings. "I—I don't know."

Matthew, who had been keeping uncharacteristically quiet until then, spoke up. "You'd be crazy to pass this up, all the more now that the seller is willing to provide the financing."

David rose, shrugging. "Think about it overnight. But whatever you decide, let me know by three o'clock tomorrow. That's the deadline for the sign back."

I nodded slowly. "I can't believe I'm saying this, but I think you're right. This is a deal I can't pass up."

David beamed. "It sure is. And I'm not saying this because of the nice fat commission I'll be getting."

Matthew smiled. "I'm sure you wouldn't sneeze at it either."

"It'll make up for the slow year I've been having." He rose and headed for the door, calling over his shoulder, "Give me a call whatever you decide."

Matthew followed him to the front and reappeared a moment later. "Why do you want to think it over? I know how much you want that space for your shop."

I knew he was right, but I was still unsure. "I have until three o'clock tomorrow." I struggled with my fear quietly for a moment. "It's such a big commitment. I just want to sleep on it."

"I understand," said Matthew in a tone that said he didn't understand at all.

I clambered to my feet, and made it all the way to the stairs, when, all at once I decided. I returned to the kitchen, grabbed the phone and punched in a number.

Matthew looked at me, puzzled. "What are you doing?"

I smiled coyly. The phone rang once, then twice, and then somebody picked up. "Hello?"

I looked at Matthew and winked. "Hi, David. I changed my mind. If you want to come back, I'll sign right away."

Matthew whooped, and Winston, who had been snoozing again, jumped up, startled.

"Sorry, buddy. Daddy just got excited," I said, hobbling over to pet him. I set the phone back down, laughing.

"That's because Mommy just took Daddy's advice," added Matthew.

I looked at him, stunned. If I was Mommy and he was Daddy, that made us a couple, didn't it?

And then, almost as if Matthew knew what I was thinking, he blushed. "If you don't need me, I think I'll let you and David get your business done. I'll just go upstairs and do a bit of writing." He grabbed his laptop and hurried out of the room.

Chapter 36

I was at the stove scrambling eggs, one of the few dishes I did really well, and Jenny was setting the table when Matthew came in.

"What have we here?" he asked, looking around.

"Della called at seven o'clock, insisting that I come for breakfast," she said, and then smiling, she added, "It seems she has an announcement to make. Do you have any idea what that might be?"

Matthew glanced at me with a smile of his own. "I think I might."

I waved my wooden spoon at him. "Don't you dare tell her. This is my news." I pointed to the coffeepot. "How about you make yourself useful?"

Soon the food was ready and served. I opened the fridge and pulled out the bottle of sparkling wine that Matthew had bought the previous day.

"This is a celebration, so mimosas for everyone." I handed the bottle to Matthew and he popped the cork.

He poured wine into each glass, topping it off with a splash of orange juice.

Jenny waited expectantly. I raised my glass. "Here's to the new location of Dream Weavers."

"I knew it!" exclaimed Jenny. "You bought the building! I'm so happy for you!"

I laughed. "I just hope I don't live to regret it."

"Does that mean—?" She gestured from me to her.

I nodded. "You can quit your job at Franny's."

It was Matthew's turn to look confused. "What are you talking about? Why would you want to quit your job?"

She put her glass down, looking embarrassed. "I've always wanted to open a tea shop, and since the store space is way too big for Della's shop, she's agreed to rent me a part of it." She picked up her glass again—"I'm going into business"—and raised it. "To Tea and Destiny."

"Is that the name of your shop? I love it."

She grinned. "Good, isn't it?"

Matthew dropped bread into the toaster. "So when are you taking possession?"

"Well, since I have to cash in my Roth IRA, and that will probably take a few weeks, I asked for a first of July closing." I tried to read his eyes. "I hope you don't mind if I stay another few weeks, but I do need some time to get organized."

"What about your idea of buying Mrs. McLeay's old furniture?"

"I reminded David about that and he promised to speak to the nephew."

Jenny giggled. "You'd better dust off your paintbrush, Matthew. You offered to do all the work for Della when she moved, remember? I'm a witness."

Matthew laughed. "Don't worry. My word is my honor. We can do it in the garage."

"See?" Jenny turned to me with a teasing glint in her eyes. "He's already saying 'we.' Mark my word, you and I will do most of it." She glanced at her watch. "Oh, I better go, or I'll be late." She left the table and hurried to the front. Matthew followed. I scampered after them as fast as my crutches allowed, and stopped. At the door, Matthew and Jenny were having a whispered conversation, one of his arms wrapped protectively over her shoulders. And all at once I felt a sharp stab of jealousy. I turned and left quietly.

I sat at the kitchen table, reeling from the surge of mixed emotions. This was Matthew—my friend. Why would I care whether he embraced another woman? And not just any other woman—Jenny, who was also my friend. If they had found love with each other, I should be happy, not wracked with pain.

What the heck was wrong with me? I was reacting as if I was in love—I stopped, shaken. I had wondered about my feelings for him over the last few days, but the idea left me dazed, with my heart beating wildly. I tried to tell myself that I was wrong, but the more I thought about it, the more I was convinced it was true. It explained the ridiculous romantic thoughts I'd been having about him, the way I often felt flustered in his presence.

I was still sorting through my tangled emotions when I heard the door open and close and Matthew's footsteps going upstairs. A moment later he came back down. Settling into his work, I guessed, something I should be doing too. I shook off my distress and pulled out my cell phone.

I called my bank. After being put on hold while they transferred me from one department to another, I was finally connected to the right person.

"Sorry, but you'll have to come down to the bank to do that. We can't process any of the paperwork unless we have your signature."

After being told "No, an e-mail, a fax, not even a scan is acceptable," I hung up in disgust. I had just dropped my cell into my bag when the house phone rang.

From the front room I heard Matthew push back his chair and pick up. A second later, he called out, "It's David for you."

I grabbed my crutches and went over.

"David, hi." I glanced at Matthew, who was standing in the doorway.

"I've got good news for you," David said. "The nephew says that for a hundred dollars you can have the whole lot."

"Everything?"

"Everything in the house—furniture, drapes, kitchen utensils, pots and pans, all except the fixtures."

"That's great." I'd spotted an antique open-coil toaster on the kitchen counter. What other interesting things might I find?

"Frankly, if it had been up to me, I'd just give it to you for free. Even if he made a few bucks selling it at auction, it would cost him more than that to pay for shipping."

"I'm not going to argue about a hundred dollars. At that price it's a bargain."

"So when do you want to pick it up?"

I thought quickly. "How about a week from Saturday?

That'll give me time to get rid of these crutches and set up the garage for painting. But would you mind if I took inventory before then?"

"Sure. I have a couple of errands to do. How about if I pick you up in about an hour?"

"I'll be ready and waiting." It would be a relief to get out of the house.

I hung up, and turned to Matthew. "What was that all about?" he asked.

I explained about the furniture. "I know you offered to help, but you don't have to. I can set up an area of the garage and have it all done in no time."

"You've done so much work on this place. Doing a bit of painting in return is the least I can do."

"Er, I hate to break it to you, but it's not just a few pieces. There's a ton of stuff."

"Don't worry about it. I'll just lay plastic sheeting over the floors and the walls. Then I can spray-paint everything in no time."

"You can't just spray-paint without washing and sanding everything down or the paint won't hold."

He chuckled. "Don't worry, kiddo. I promise I'll do a good job."

He had just called me kiddo again. All at once, the emotions I'd been suppressing came surging forth.

"So we're back at that again, are we?" I snapped, more hurt than angry.

He looked at me in confusion. "Back at what? What are you talking about?"

"I'm sorry." I shook my head, feeling like a fool. I grasped for some excuse. "I-I just don't feel very well.

It—it's just the stress of . . ." Before he could see the tears that trembled on my lashes, I grabbed my crutches and hurried out of the kitchen, hobbling upstairs to my room. I closed the door and plopped down on the bed.

Damn it! There he was, offering to do something nice for me and instead of saying thank you I had behaved like an idiot.

Stupid, stupid, stupid.

I simply had to get a grip, control my emotions.

I was still lying there, berating myself, when Matthew knocked on my door. I sat up, wiped my eyes and finger-combed my hair. "Come in."

He pushed the door open and leaned against the jamb, looking contrite. "Listen, kiddo—"

I rolled my eyes. "You just can't help yourself, can you?"

"Wh-what are you talking about?"

"You've been calling me kiddo since we were children," I blurted. *So much for controlling my emotions.* "And just in case you haven't noticed, I'm not a child anymore."

He looked stunned. "Is that why you're angry with me?"

"No, er, yes," I said, getting off the bed. I picked up my crutches, trying to look aloof as I tucked them under my arms.

He dug his hands into his pockets, looking confused. "I'm sorry. I had no idea."

"That's not it, Matthew."

He put up a hand to stop me. "Tell me something. Are you uncomfortable living in the same house with me?"

Blood rushed to my face and I stumbled on my words again. "It-it's just that—"

He cut me off. "You don't have to explain. I should have known it wasn't a good idea to just barge into your life this way. Maybe the best thing for me to do is move back into your condo until your new place is ready."

"No!" I cried, taking a few steps toward him. "You shouldn't have to go. This is your house. I'll move."

"That's ridiculous. You have your store here. It'll only be for a few weeks."

"Wait." I grabbed for his hand. But as soon as our fingers touched, I forgot what I wanted to say. His eyes met mine and he looked as startled as I felt.

I took a step closer, or maybe he leaned in, but suddenly his eyes were staring into mine, golden and warm, like liquid honey. The spicy smell of his aftershave wafted up to my nose as I took a deep breath. My eyelashes dipped and my head tilted back.

The next thing I knew, he was halfway down the stairs, taking them two at a time. A second later, the front door opened, then slammed shut.

Chapter 37

Mrs. McLeay's house was even dustier than I remembered, but this time I was prepared. I wore jeans rather than my red linen dress. Besides, I remembered Matthew's comment about my dressing up for David.

David watched me taking notes for a few minutes. "If you don't mind, I'll wait for you in my car, where I can make some phone calls."

"Sure, no problem." Being freed from having to make conversation was a relief. I could barely hold my thoughts together. On my pad, I scribbled "six balloon chairs," checked under the dining room table and spotted a Victorian-style coffee table and a footstool. I added those to a quickly growing list and moved on. Soon I had itemized every piece of furniture on the main floor, and although I wasn't sure I could salvage the sofas and armchairs, I still had more than enough to fill a house. I continued on to the kitchen. In the top cabinets were two complete sets of dishes. I grabbed an old cloth and rubbed off enough dust to identify them as an old blue and white Chinese pattern. It was beautiful and would look gorgeous on my finely woven white linen place mats. On another shelf I found an assortment of heavy crystal glasses. I took note of those and moved on. In a far cupboard, I discovered a collection of milk-glass serving pieces. I couldn't believe my luck. I dug some more and found a set of bone-handled cutlery.

By the time I finished recording all the furniture on the second floor, I knew I had scored big. Obviously Mrs. McLeay hadn't cared much about furniture. Most of it was rather plain, but she sure had a thing for kitchenware. I returned downstairs, locked the front door and shuffled out to David's car.

I slid in, tucking my crutches between myself and the door. "You can't imagine everything I found. I haven't gone through the dressers and closets yet, but there's so much furniture I'll hardly need to buy a thing. Setting up will cost me next to nothing." I laughed. "Which is good because next to nothing is all I can afford."

He turned the key in the ignition and the motor roared to life. "Good for you. If you're happy, then that makes two of us. Now, with any luck I'll sell that house soon."

Three minutes later he pulled up in front of Matthew's house. "Here you go."

I looked at the front door, wondering what kind of greeting I was about to get. I thanked David and stepped out of the car, my heart already racing.

The first thing I saw as I walked in was a suitcase waiting by the front door. I swallowed the lump in my throat and hobbled to the kitchen.

"Oh, er, hi," said Matthew. He was on his hands and knees, pulling Winston's dog food out from under the counter. "Sorry, Della. I'm almost done here. I'll be out of your way in no time."

I could feel the heat in my face. "Honestly, Matthew, you don't have to go. You're not in my way. I think my nerves are just raw from everything that's been happening." I tried a chuckle, but it came out a squawk. "Finding a body isn't exactly an everyday occurrence. And for that matter, neither is cashing in all my life savings."

"I guess you have a point." He looked relieved and just as I thought everything was going to turn out all right, the doorbell rang. He hesitated, about to say something. Instead, he got up and disappeared down the hall.

"I'm back." It was Jenny. She appeared in the doorway, looking rushed. "I only have a few minutes—lunch break. I'm so excited, I just had to drop by and tell you my good news."

I hoped my smile looked genuine, but I couldn't erase the picture of Matthew's arm around her. "Come on in. What news?"

Matthew offered her a chair. She sat, throwing back her long sandy hair with a quick flick of her wrist. She was wearing her usual yoga pants with an off-the-shoulder silk knit in a soft blue that made her tanned skin glow. Rather than beautiful as she always was, today she was breathtakingly gorgeous.

"I just spoke to Marnie." Her eyes gleamed with excitement. "And she's agreed to provide all the pastries for my tea shop. Isn't that great?"

"Terrific. I was just about to make some fresh coffee. Would you like some?"

"Sure, I'll have a cup." She turned to Matthew. "Doesn't Della make the best coffee in the world? Maybe she should make the coffee for my shop?"

He smiled, but it didn't quite reach his eyes. "She sure does."

Jenny must have sensed the strained atmosphere, because the next thing she said was, "Did I drop by at the wrong time?"

Matthew shook his head. "No, no. Della and I were just talking about my moving back to Charlotte until she takes over her new place."

Jenny glanced at me, frowning. I kept my face impassive.

"Is that what that suitcase is doing in the front hall?" She looked from him to me and back again. "So your messiness finally caught up with you." She chuckled, but behind her casual demeanor her eyes were full of questions. "I don't blame her one bit for kicking you out. After all the work she did, getting this place in shape, you come in and mess everything up."

She should be getting plenty of vibes now, I thought as I measured beans into the coffee grinder.

"I know. I'm a slob. What can I say?" He played along.

Jenny snapped her fingers. "I have an idea. Don't move back to Charlotte. That's just plain silly. Why don't you move in with me? I have a spare bedroom. And you know me. I'm not at all like Della. I'm as much of a slob as you are."

Translation? You and I are the same. We'll fit together like a horse and carriage. I wanted to throw up. I kept my back to them and turned on the coffeemaker.

"You wouldn't mind?" he said, and I almost had a meltdown.

They went on talking about how this could work out.

He could use the back bedroom, blah, blah, blah. I tuned out in disgust and went shopping in my mind. I imagined myself trying on a sexy blue dress, the same blue Jenny was wearing now. I gave the dress a deep neckline, deep enough to reveal a bit of cleavage—not that I would ever wear something like that in real life, but this was a day-dream, so why not? And just for the heck of it, I gave it a tight skirt, with a slit up the side, and I looked sexy.

"Della?"

I snapped back to reality. Jenny was looking at me with a question mark in her eyes, and Matthew was no-where around. I heard his footsteps going upstairs. "Della?" she repeated.

"Uh, yes?"

"Is everything all right?"

"Of course. Why?"

She didn't answer, but from the way she was studying me, I knew I wasn't fooling her one bit. I also knew it had nothing to do with auras or feelings. I just knew my mis-ery was written all over my face. At last she said, "Did you and Matthew have an argument?"

I nodded, avoiding her eyes.

"I see." And when I looked at her, I thought she really did. "Don't worry. Whatever it was about, he'll get over it. In the meantime, he can stay at my place." She must have sensed my embarrassment because she changed the subject. "Oh, before I forget. Listen to this. Marnie was just coming back from the bank when I saw her, and guess what?"

I shook my head. "What?"

"The money she took out of the bank to invest with

Jeremy Fox? It's back in her account—the entire amount. When she asked the teller about it, the girl told her that it came in by electronic transfer from the Cayman Islands."

My mouth was still hanging open when Matthew rejoined us in the kitchen, looking uncomfortable. "So, you really wouldn't mind if I used your guest room for a couple of weeks?"

"Not in the least. The house has felt so empty since . . ." She waved vaguely. "It'll be nice having someone around."

He nodded, smiling. "In that case, I accept." I couldn't object without making a fool of myself even more than I already had.

Jenny jumped up, smiling at me reassuringly, as if telling me not to worry. "Great. Let's go." They took off, heading for the door.

I swallowed a lump in my throat the size of a fist. He had taken Winston, hadn't he? I went through the house, calling, "Winston," getting no galloping dog, not even a slobbering kiss in response.

I was all by myself, completely and utterly alone. And suddenly the house felt spooky rather than warm and safe. I wanted to be anywhere but here. But the shop was opening in—I glanced at my watch—twenty minutes. I couldn't just leave. I was running a business here. I hoofed it back to the kitchen, opened the fridge and rummaged through it.

I was hungry—but not. I slammed it shut again. And then I opened it and grabbed a container of yogurt. I sat at the table, dragging my spoon around in the yogurt without taking so much as a bite.

The phone rang and I jumped. But it wasn't Matthew. "Oh, hi, Mom."

"Don't sound so happy to hear me, dear." Her voice lilted in amusement.

"Sorry, Mom. I'm just having a bad day."

"That's why I'm calling, dear. I was just speaking to June and she told me that you and Matthew had an argument and that he was moving back to the city. What happened, sweetheart?"

I groaned silently. "He told her that?" He must have called his mother while I was taking inventory of the furniture at Mrs. McLeay's house.

"Well, June called him and he sounded so upset that she dragged it out of him. But he wouldn't tell her what the argument was about. So, tell me what happened."

I scrambled for some excuse. "I think, with my shop taking up all of the downstairs space, he's feeling a bit put out. This is his house, after all, and I changed everything around and now he doesn't even have a place to sit quietly and watch TV. And after stumbling on a dead body, I'm stressed out of my mind. We just got on each other's nerves."

"Is that what it was all about?" She sounded disappointed.

"What did you think the argument was about?"

She hemmed a bit, and finally admitted, "I thought maybe you two had a lovers' spat."

"A lovers' spat! That's ridiculous."

"Sometimes when there's tension between a man and a woman, you have to ask yourself if the cause is attraction." As my mother babbled on, I couldn't help but wonder at how she had hit the nail on the head. She was wrong in only one way. The attraction was all one-sided, and that was driving me insane.

"Della? Are you still there?"

"Oh, sorry, Mom. You were saying?"

"I was saying that I'd like to come for a visit one of these days. I haven't even seen your shop yet, you know."

"Tell you what, if you wait until the first of July, you can come and visit me in my new place." I went on to tell her all about the building and my plans for the new shop. But as exciting as I tried to make it sound, my mother took it like bad news. "Oh, well." She sighed. "I guess I should stop hoping you and Matthew—" Her thought trailed off unfinished.

"As disappointed as you are," I wanted to say, "I'm ten times more so." But all I said was, "That's exactly what you should do, Mom."

The rest of the day went by second by agonizingly long second. Every time I heard a car, my heart went into overdrive. Was it Matthew? Jenny's words had made me feel somewhat better. At least I knew she had no designs on him. But how could she imagine everything would be fine when she had no idea what had almost happened?

Meanwhile, I sat at my loom and continued weaving until I had not only completed the second blanket but also finished the warp for a third one. By six o'clock my back was screaming and my stomach was growling. And I was still heartsick over how I should best approach the matter.

I threw together a salad, added canned tuna and a

boiled egg for protein and sat down to a lonely dinner. I'd lived almost all of my adult life alone, and now, after only three days of Matthew being here, I missed him — and Winnie. On the bright side, I'd been so distracted this afternoon that for the first time in days, I'd thought of something besides the murder.

I went hunting for my cell and found it on the kitchen counter. I punched in Jenny's number. I was dying to know what Matthew was doing, but instead all I asked was, "What are you up to?"

"Nothing much. I'm almost finished with my second baby blanket. How about you?"

"I'm bored to tears." And then, before I could stop myself, I asked, "Is Matthew with you?"

"No. He dropped off his suitcase the moment he walked in and then took off. I haven't seen him since. Why don't you call Susan? If she has nothing to do, maybe you could ask her to come over. It would be a lot better than letting her go and do something dangerous. I'm still worried about her."

I'd been so busy feeling sorry for myself that I hadn't even thought about Susan.

Not having to spend an evening alone sounded great. "Good idea. I'll do that right away." I hung up, then punched in Susan's number. She picked up on the first ring.

"Hi, it's Della. I was just wondering if you happen to be free, if I could talk you into coming over."

"Normally, I'd be happy to, but I'm busy right now," she said, sounding preoccupied.

"Well, how about if I come over to your place?"

There was a long pause, and for a second I thought I

heard somebody in the background. "I don't think so," she said at last. "Maybe some other time."

"Uh, is somebody there with you?" There was another pause, during which I could have sworn she covered the mouthpiece. "Susan? Is everything all right?"

"Everything is fine, Della. I'll speak to you later, okay?" And then, before I could say anything, I heard her yelp, followed by a thud, and the phone went silent.

"Susan? Hello?" I stared at the receiver in my hands, filled with fear. It sounded as if someone had attacked her. I shook my head. I was just imagining things. I hung up and dialed again, getting a busy signal. I paused, questioning myself. Had I really heard someone in the background, or was it maybe just the television or radio? I was trying desperately to quash the panic that was quickly rising. I had to do something. Without pausing to think, I punched in Jenny's number.

"Susan's in trouble. We have to get there. Now," I shouted.

And, bless her for reacting so fast, it wasn't two minutes before she zoomed up in front of the house and screeched to a stop. I hurried out, jumped into her car and we took off. Two sharp turns later we pulled up in front of a pretty Cape Cod.

"I have a really bad feeling about this," she said, getting out of the car. This time, I tended to agree with her. I slid out and onto my crutches, and scrambled to keep up with her. By the time I reached the front door, she was pushing the buzzer repeatedly.

"There's no answer." She stared at me, her eyes wide with worry. "Do you suppose she went out?"

"She was here five minutes ago." I tried the doorknob and the door swung open. We stood frozen for a moment and then stepped in.

The inside of Susan's house was as neat and tidy as Marnie's was messy. A gorgeous half-moon table, covered with a handwoven cloth, decorated the entrance. On it was a brown leather bag.

"Her purse is here, so she can't be far." I wandered a few steps farther, stopping at the entrance to the living room and looking around. The walls were taupe, the furniture beige slipcovered cottage-style. My eyes traveled, taking in the blond wood desk in the corner. Susan had good taste. Suddenly the blood drained from my face as I noticed a pair of legs sticking out from behind the coffee table.

I staggered, almost dropping my crutches but regained my balance at the last second. "There she is!" I hobbled over. There was Susan, unconscious.

Jenny rushed past and dropped to her knees beside Susan. "Call an ambulance!"

Chapter 38

The paramedics appeared minutes later and soon were using words like "skull fracture," "intracranial hemorrhage," and "traumatic brain injury." By the time they sped away with Susan, siren blaring, Jenny was beside herself with guilt.

"All of this is my fault. I should have *made* her believe me," she said miserably. "If I'd insisted she take me seriously, none of this would have happened."

"You've got it all wrong." I patted her back. "What you did probably saved her life. Susan was going to do this whether you read her fortune or not. But the fact that you did is why we got here in time to call the ambulance."

She nodded hesitantly, but judging by the torrent of tears rolling down her cheeks during the drive to the hospital, she didn't believe a word I said.

The emergency room was swarming with doctors and nurses. A burly security guard stood blocking the doorway.

"I'm sorry," he said gruffly, "but you can't go in there."

"But that's our friend who was just brought in," argued Jenny. "We just want to see her."

"I'll ask her doctor to come talk to you as soon as he can." He pushed her gently but firmly away from the doorway.

I put an arm around her. "Come on, Jenny. The best thing we can do for her right now is let the doctors do their job."

She didn't look reassured, but she followed me to a corner of the waiting area and dropped into a chair, resting her elbows on her knees and her head in her hands.

Feeling compelled to comfort her, I said, "She'll be all right. Don't worry." My reassurance sounded false even to me.

We waited, watching the door to the ER almost as obsessively as we kept glancing at our watches. Every time it opened, we jumped to our feet, only to sit back down when it turned out to be a nurse or attendant. At last a doctor appeared. It was Dr. Green. We rose and he hurried over.

"How is she, Doctor?" Jenny wrung her hands with worry.

"Your friend hit her head pretty hard." He gestured for us all to sit. We did, and he leaned forward, looking somber. "She was brought in unconscious. She woke up for a little while, but seemed drowsy and confused. The good news is that, according to the MRI, she has no intracranial bleeding and no skull fracture. But we'll be keeping her overnight to continue monitoring her vital signs and the Glasgow Coma Scale."

I frowned. "What's that?"

"It's how we check for brain injury." He looked from me to Jenny. "I'm sorry there isn't anything I can add at this point. We should know more by morning."

"Can we see her?" I asked.

"She'll be kept in the ER for most of the night. I suggest you go home, try to get some sleep and come back in the morning." He glanced down at my foot. "How's your ankle? Are you still feeling a lot of pain?"

"No. I've been obeying your instructions to the letter."

"I'm happy to hear that. I think you can take off the bandages if all the swelling is gone. But don't try walking on it for another few days." With that, he nodded and hurried back to the ER.

"No bleeding, no skull fracture. That's good news, don't you think?" I said, scooping my crutches under my arms and heading for the door.

Jenny held the door open for me, still looking worried out of her mind.

And so was I.

Chapter 39

I finally fell asleep just as the sun began to filter through the window, only to wake up forty-five minutes before Jenny was due to pick me up. I swung my legs off the bed, testing my ankle gently. It still hurt, but the pain was hardly more than a dull ache. I raised my foot and examined it. It was now four days since I'd twisted it. The swelling was completely gone. Yay! I gave a silent thank-you to Dr. Green for allowing me to take off the bandages. If I'd had to wear a ballet slipper on one foot and a sock on the other for one more day, I would have screamed. As long as I kept using my crutches and didn't so much as set my left foot down, I could wear whatever I wanted, even heels, right?

I looked through the closet for my favorite midheight sandals, a pretty little pair of pink Manolos that had cost me a week's pay. After ten minutes on my hands and knees, I still couldn't find them. Had I left them behind when I'd moved all my stuff from Matthew's room to this one?

I hurried down the hall and, hesitating only slightly, entered Matthew's room. I gasped. This room was a mess: unmade bed with sheets and blankets bundled in a mass at the foot of it; an assortment of papers littering the bedside tables; jeans, sweaters and shirts piled on the corner chair; and loafers, running shoes and boat shoes littering the floor. I stood in shock, taking it all in. Good grief, Jenny was right. The man was organizationally challenged—if not a slob. But in all honesty, discovering this flaw of his only made him more endearing. What can I say? I covered the short distance between the doorway and the closet, got down on my hands and knees and rummaged around until I felt something hard and metallic. I froze.

It couldn't be. But even as I wanted to be wrong, I knew I wasn't. I held my breath and pulled it out. I was looking at a small gun!

I fumbled and dropped it. And in the split second before it hit the floor, I imagined it firing and saw my life flash before my eyes.

But the gun did *not* discharge, and I was *not* killed by a ricocheting bullet.

I stared at it for an eternity of seconds—unable to move, almost unable to breathe, my heart going like a jackhammer. A dozen thoughts raced through my mind at once, my mind locking on one. If he was David's attacker, it stood to reason that one of his garments would match the yarn I'd found. All at once I went into high gear. I wiped the weapon clean—I wasn't stupid enough to leave my prints on it—and pushed it deep in the back of the closet. I struggled to my feet and tore through the hangers, riffling through the few hanging sweaters and shirts at the speed of a cardsharp.

Nothing.

I crossed the room and went through a large pile of clothes on the chair.

Nothing.

The drawers, I thought.

In two swift crutch strides I tore them open, rummaging through underwear, socks and T-shirts.

Still nothing.

I paused, my eyes darting around. Where could he have hidden it? And then it hit me: Matthew knew about the yarn I'd recovered. If he was guilty, he was smart enough to have gotten rid of whatever garment matched that yarn. No wonder he'd been furious at me for investigating. He was afraid of what I would find out.

I returned to my room, shut the door and sat on the edge of the bed, my head spinning. Finding the gun in his closet did prove he was the killer, didn't it? I was in shock—sick to my stomach.

I thought back to the night of the murder, putting the events into sequence. Matthew had gone out to pick up dinner around nine, which was about the time Jeremy got that call. He could have made that call himself. He'd also gone out under the pretext of looking for Winston that night. My head spun as I added up all the evidence. I took a deep breath, trying to still my racing heart.

I shook my head again. There had to be a logical explanation.

I forced myself to think calmly. If Matthew had not put the gun in his closet, then the only explanation was that somebody else had. All at once I remembered David asking to use the washroom the night of the weaving class.

And then I remembered somebody else who had asked to use the washroom that night.

Mercedes Hanson.

Chapter 40

By the time Jenny pulled up in front of my house, I had made two decisions. First, I would keep quiet about finding the gun, at least until I talked to Matthew about it. And second, I would find out the truth about whether Mercedes had stolen it from Marnie. If I was correct, that put the gun in close proximity to Dolores—and made her my number one suspect. If she was guilty, that also meant that Mercedes was an accessory. What kind of a mother would involve her daughter in murder?

I locked the front door and hobbled over to the car.

"Nice shoes," said Jenny, as I slid into the passenger seat. I slipped my crutches between the seats, and raising a foot I wiggled it to show off my sandals. "Thanks. How'd you sleep?"

"Not a wink all night," she said, putting the car into gear.

"Me either." Ever so casually I asked, "So, did you find out where Matthew disappeared to yesterday?"

"He said he took Winston for a walk and ran into Mike." She sighed. "He made the mistake of telling him that he'd moved into my spare bedroom. It seems Mike didn't take it very well."

That was one heck of a long walk, I thought, remembering the call I'd made to her yesterday. By that time it had already been late afternoon and she'd told me Matthew had been gone for hours. I wondered what else he had done during all that time.

We sped along in silence until ten minutes later when Jenny tore into one of the hospital parking spots and came to a screeching stop.

"Oh, God, I hope she's all right." She hopped out, slammed the door shut and jogged toward the hospital entrance.

"Hey, what about the parking meter? You'll get a ticket." I fed the meter and hurried into the building as fast as I could. I caught up with Jenny at the reception desk, where the same chubby blonde was looking through admissions sheets.

She ran her finger down a list. "Susan Wood. Susan Wood. Ah, here she is—room 114."

Jenny took off again, with me in lobbing pursuit—one turn and she was gone. "Hey, wait for me!"

I hurried down a corridor, took a left, and realized I was lost. What was it about hospitals? They were all built like mazes. They should do something about that, like maybe paint their corridors different colors so they wouldn't all look the same. I stopped and looked around, trying to remember the directions the receptionist had rattled off. Suddenly I smelled the same odd odor I'd noticed on Mike Davis and on Joan Douglas a few days ago. That's when I noticed the sign above the door in front of me. ONCOLOGY DEPARTMENT, it read, and below in smaller letters, CHEMOTHERAPY. It hit me like a ton of bricks. The smell I'd noticed the last time I'd been here had come not from Joan Douglas but from this room. I'd been standing in exactly this spot when I noticed it.

I paused as a new thought began to form. Susan Wood had said something about knowing everybody's secrets. One of them had been about someone receiving chemo. And if Mike Davis was exuding that strange odor, it could mean he had cancer. Something niggled in the back of my mind. What had Matthew told me about Mike's parents? Mike's father had died from prostate cancer, and his wife had left him soon after he was diagnosed.

An orderly was walking by. "Excuse me. Could you tell me where I can find room 114?" I asked him. He pointed the way, and off I went, putting more of the puzzle pieces into place as I hurried along.

When I got to the room, Jenny was standing by Susan's bed, holding her hand.

She turned to me as I walked in. "She's still unconscious." And then she smiled. "But, I don't know, I have the feeling that she'll be fine."

I came closer and looked down at Susan. There were no bandages, no bruising. Her eyes were closed, her dark hair fanning over the pillow. But her color was good, her breathing regular.

"Are you sure she's unconscious? She looks like she's just sleeping."

From behind me a voice said, "That's because she *is* sleeping."

I swung around. "Dr. Green!"

He stood in the doorway, wearing a lopsided grin. "I see you're back to wearing high heels."

"I wouldn't call these high. They're only small heels."

He shook his head. "It's your neck," he said teasingly. He approached his patient and picked up the chart at the foot of the bed.

Jenny stepped back to give him room. "How is she, Doctor?"

"Pretty good. She was awake and alert for a few hours earlier. All her vitals are fine. As a matter of fact, if everything is still all right, she can probably go home when she wakes up."

As if on cue, Susan stirred. Her lashes fluttered and she opened her eyes. She glanced around, looking confused.

Jenny leaned over her. "It's okay, Susan. You're in the hospital."

"I am?" And then the cloud cleared from her eyes. "Oh, right. I remember."

Dr. Green stepped forward and said, "Let me take a good look at this patient." He did his flashlight-in-the-eyes thing. He listened to her heart and took her blood pressure. At last he smiled. "I think you'll live."

"She's all right?" I asked.

"Good as new." He smiled at Susan. "You can go home. Just make sure you stop by the nurses' station and sign the release forms." I couldn't help but notice that his eyes kept drifting over to Jenny. He liked her.

When he spoke, it was to me, but he was grinning at Jenny. "It seems to me that you and your friends are a bit accident prone. Are you involved in some kind of extreme sport?"

I chuckled. "This is my friend Jenny Davis." I watched

as they locked eyes again, smiled and shook hands. She
was looking rather intensely at the good doctor—
probably reading his aura. And then it struck me. No.
She wasn't aura reading. Jenny liked Dr. Green. That
raised the question of whether I should tell her my theory about Mike having cancer.

"I remember you. You used to work at that store," he
said.

"I still do."

He stood smiling at her, and then he looked at his
watch. "I was just about to have a coffee break. Would
you care to join me?" As an afterthought, he turned to
me. "You too, of course."

Jenny looked uncertainly from him to me.

"Good idea," I said quickly. "Jenny, you go ahead. It'll
take at least half an hour for Susan to get dressed and
sign the discharge papers. We'll join you when she's
done."

Dr. Green smiled and nodded. "Shall we?"

Jenny hesitated.

"Go, go." I shooed her away and watched them leave
the room, both smiling awkwardly.

"You have no intention of us joining them, do you?"
asked Susan, pushing off the blankets and swinging her
legs over the edge of the bed.

"You must have read my mind."

She nodded. "I think we may have just witnessed the
beginning of a romance." She stood, and holding on to
the back of her hospital gown, she looked around. "Any
clue where my clothes might be?"

I spotted a locker against the far wall. "Probably in

there." I went over and opened it, retrieving a pair of jeans and a T-shirt. "Are these your clothes?"

"Yes."

I carried them to her. "Now that we're alone"—I glanced toward the door to make sure it was closed—"can you tell me what happened? Did someone attack you?"

"Attack me?" She looked shocked at the suggestion. "Eh, do you mind?" She signaled for me to turn around—modesty. I did. "Of course not. I tripped. Silly me, I was on the phone talking to you and tripped on the telephone cord."

"So you didn't confront anyone about being the murderer?"

She paused. I could almost hear the wheels grinding as she tried to remember. "I was going to. I called Dolores, but before I could get to it, she went into a screaming fit, accusing me of spreading rumors about her having an affair with Jeremy Fox."

I swung around, just as she was pulling on her jeans. "Oh, sorry."

"Don't worry about it. I'm finished." She tucked her shirt into her jeans. "You know the old saying, 'The best defense is a good offense'?"

I nodded. "You think she already knew you were going to confront her?"

"If she thinks I'm just going to forget about that, she's dead wrong."

"You're convinced it was her?" Now, more than ever, I wanted her to be right about this. I wanted anybody to be guilty, anybody but Matthew.

She nodded. "I know she had a gun. I saw it in her purse a few months ago. She stopped by the office to see Jeremy one day and left her bag on my desk while I went to the washroom. When I came back, I didn't know whose bag it was, so I peeked inside. That's when I saw the gun. I was so startled I closed the bag and didn't tell a soul."

So my theory that Mercedes could have stashed the gun in Matthew's closet was plausible. A wave of relief washed over me. This theory could also explain the argument Dolores and her daughter had outside my front door. No matter how much mother and daughter argued, Mercedes was still Dolores's daughter, which could explain why she decided to hide the gun in Matthew's closet. She wanted to protect her mother.

"What should I do?" asked Susan. "I still don't have any proof."

Suddenly another piece of the puzzle fell into place. "I don't know why this slipped my mind," I said, sitting on the edge of the bed. "Did you know that Dolores is a dot-com millionaire?"

Susan nodded. "Yes, she invented some kind of software."

"And the only thing that was missing from Jeremy's house was his laptop." I looked at Susan and saw the spark of understanding. "What if she wanted to break into his computer for some reason? If anyone would know how to do it, it would be Dolores."

Chapter 41

We were at the nurses' station and Susan had just signed the discharge form when Jenny came striding over, wearing a wide smile.

"There you are. What happened to you? I thought you were going to join us."

"We figured you'd be perfectly fine on your own. Right, Susan? In fact, we thought you'd rather we left you two alone."

Jenny blushed. "He's nice." She shrugged. "But it was only coffee, for goodness' sake. I'll probably never see him again."

Susan opened her purse and dropped in her health care ID card. "Did he ask for your phone number?"

Jenny blushed even deeper. Before she could answer, I elbowed Susan. "Wait, wait, don't tell me." I closed my eyes, placing a hand to my forehead. "It's coming to me. Yes. Yes, I can see it now." I opened my eyes and pointed at her. "He's going to call and ask you for a date."

Jenny guffawed, slapping my finger. "You are so mean. You're making fun of me."

"You're easy to make fun of," I said, using the same words Matthew had once said to me.

*   *   *

As we headed toward the exit, I filled Jenny in on what Susan and I had concluded. "We still don't have any physical proof, but we have enough circumstantial evidence to make a pretty good case."

She pushed open the door, and we stepped outside. "So what are you going to do? Go to the police with what you know?"

We walked to the parking lot, trying to remember where Jenny had parked her car. "After the way Mike dismissed my tip before, I don't really want to go to him. But I think if Dolores is aware of everything we know, she might decide to turn herself in."

"There it is." Jenny pointed to a row of cars. She pulled out her keys, clicked to unlock the doors and we slid in.

She paused, car key in hand. "So what's the plan?"

I told her.

Ten minutes later we pulled up in front of a house that looked completely out of place on the quaint street. It was a large, modern stone structure that dwarfed all the neighboring houses. Except for that, it could have been on the cover of *Architectural Digest*.

"Her house suits her, don't you think?" I said, staring at it as I gathered my courage.

In the driver's seat, Jenny looked at Susan in the rear-view mirror. "Are you up to this? We don't have to do it now."

"I'm fine. Just a bit cold, that's all."

"Why don't you grab a sweater from the pile next to

you?" To me, Jenny said, "I was going through some old uniforms of Mike's to throw away, and then I thought of doing a new collection, pairing navy wool with sky-blue wool. What do you think?" She reached over the back-seat and grabbed a pair of pants.

I fingered the fabric. "It's nice, perfect for rugs and place mats. I bet it'll look gorgeous."

She looked pleased. "I'm glad you think so." And then she got back to the subject at hand. "Ready?"

A moment later we were on the front stoop. "Her shrubs look as plastic as she does." Susan smirked, look-ing at the immaculate landscaping. Bushes were clipped to perfection, flower borders in full bloom, automatic sprinklers spaced optimally. She pressed the buzzer and the sound of bells echoed through the house.

Jenny rolled her eyes. "Sounds like cathedral bells. A bit ostentatious, don't you think?"

A moment later Dolores appeared, perfectly coiffed and made up. Her gaze landed on Susan. "You! You have no business here."

Before she could slam the door in our face, Jenny pushed her way in. "We need to talk."

To everybody's surprise, Dolores moved aside with no argument. "We might as well get this over with." She led the way through a foyer that would have been better suited to a hotel lobby than a private home. I looked around, taking in the polished marble floors, the white silk window treatments and the dozens of paintings cov-ering the walls. This was not what anybody could call a cozy home.

She showed us into the kitchen. "I was just about to

make some coffee." She gestured toward the granite breakfast bar. "Anybody care to join me? Have a seat."

Jenny, Susan and I looked at one another uncertainly. I wasn't sure what I'd expected, but this was not it. We sat.

Dolores picked up a bag of Kona coffee and began measuring it into the coffeemaker. My eyes brightened. Kona was right up there with Jamaican Blue Mountain. "So what is it you want to talk to me about?" She did not look frightened as much as amused.

Susan raised her chin determinedly. "We know you killed Jeremy. And we have the evidence to prove it."

Dolores paused, and for a second I thought I saw her waver. But she continued measuring and then she laughed. "You think I killed Jeremy? Now why would you think that?"

This time Jenny spoke. "You were having an affair with—"

"Jesus!" Dolores cut her off. "Have you got rocks in your heads? I never had an affair with that jerk. I despised him."

"Then why were you spending so much time with him?"

She turned on the machine and spun around to face us. "Oh, what the hell, I might as well tell you. I've been spying on him—tracking the money he conned all those people out of."

But Susan wasn't about to be put off so easily. "You stole his laptop."

"You're right. I did." She came closer, not looking guilty in the least. If anything, she seemed proud. "I needed to get into his computer. How else was I going to track the money?" She crossed her arms, giving us a smug smile. "And as of yesterday morning, everything he stole is back in the bank accounts of his victims. Go ahead and check for yourselves if you don't believe me."

I was too busy staring at her in shock to notice whether everyone else in the room had their mouths hanging open like mine was. At last I found my tongue. "Uh, I think she might be telling us the truth. Marnie told Jenny that the entire amount was back in her account yesterday morning."

The coffee machine beeped and Dolores went to the cupboard, pulling out four mugs. She set them on the breakfast bar. "That, my dear ladies, was me."

"But . . . how?" asked Susan. I glanced at her, noticing that even wearing one of Mike's old uniform sweaters she was still shivering.

Dolores preened. "Jeremy Fox was greedier than he was smart. I invested in his project by way of international wire transfer. That's how I found out he had an account in Belize. Once I knew where the money was, it was easy enough to do the rest. All I needed was his laptop. Jeremy was set up for online banking and, being lazy, he never deleted his browsing history." She smiled. "He had a file with scans of all his victims' checks, so I had their bank account information. And then I figured out he used his birthday for his password." She smirked. "Such a moron! Once I was in, getting the money transferred back to everybody's account was a piece of cake."

"But, I heard you argue with him the day before he died." Susan no longer sounded confrontational—just wary.

"That's right. He caught me trying to log on to his laptop and he went ballistic. I'm pretty sure he didn't sleep too well that night."

There was another long silence. There were still a few things I didn't quite understand. "Did you call him the night he was killed?"

"I trust you won't tell the police about this." And then without waiting for a reply, she explained. "I had to get him out of his house long enough to break in and get his laptop. I called him and told him that I knew where he had hidden all the money, but that as long as he paid me back my own investment, I would destroy the evidence. I asked him to meet with me in that building, and then I hid behind his house, waiting for stupid Marsha to leave." She rolled her eyes. "I thought the woman would never go. She must have stayed there an hour. Anyhow, I never went near that building that night, so I have no idea who killed him." And then giving us another smug smile, she added, "But as far as I'm concerned, the murderer deserves a medal."

Susan cleared her throat. "I don't understand. You have lots of money. The amount you stood to lose was nothing for you. Why go to all that trouble?"

Dolores picked up the carafe and poured. "Nobody believed me when I said that my husband had been murdered."

"I believed you," said Jenny. "I had a feeling all along."

Dolores glanced at her, then said without pausing, "It didn't take me long to figure out that Jeremy Fox killed him." There was pain in her eyes when she went on. "I couldn't prove it. But if I couldn't get him for my husband's murder, I was bloody well going to make him pay somehow. And the next best way to hurt him was through his pocket."

"Why do you think he killed your husband?"

Dolores carried the mugs over and set milk and sugar on the counter. "Greg was a threat to Jeremy's project. He had organized a petition to stop it."

At last Susan said, "But what about the gun? I saw it in your purse."

For the first time since we arrived, Dolores blanched. "Wh-what gun?"

"That was Marnie's gun, wasn't it?" I asked. "Mercedes took it from her closet, didn't she?"

Dolores plopped down onto a bar seat, looking defeated. She dropped her face into her hands and haltingly explained. "Mercedes went through a bad time last year. She was caught stealing from a few stores. Mike gave her a good talking-to and scared the daylights out of her—or at least I thought he did because she seemed to be coming around. And then I found a gun in her backpack. When I questioned her, she admitted that the gun belonged to Marnie. The last thing I wanted was to get her into more trouble. I couldn't bring myself to tell anyone that she had stolen it, especially Marnie. She's one of the few people who like Mercedes. So I did the next best thing. I turned it in to the police and told them I found it."

Next to me, Susan said, "You gave it to the police?"

I swung around and looked at her. All at once my eyes fell on the police sweater she was wearing. I stared at the frayed edges of the collar. Something about the thread—then it hit me. The thread I'd found in the hedge at David's house— I felt the blood drain from my face. "You didn't by any chance give that gun to Mike, did you?"

"Yes, why?"

My heart went into overdrive. I turned to Jenny. "Do you know where Matthew is this morning?"

She looked at me, puzzled. "He said he was going to work on his car."

"I have to get there. Now!" I scooped my crutches under my arms.

Susan and Dolores stared at me, looking puzzled. Jenny ran out ahead of me, opening the passenger-side door and running around to slide behind the wheel. I closed the door and we took off.

Jenny raced down the street. "What's wrong?" Something in her voice made me think she already suspected. I had to keep my theory to myself until I was absolutely sure. I had never so much wanted to be wrong. "I'll tell you later."

We pulled up in front of Matthew's house and I pushed the car door open before we'd come to a full stop. "Do you want me to come in with you?"

If I was right about this, the last thing I wanted was for Jenny to be a witness. "No, you go on home. I'll call you later."

Before she could argue, I hurried to the house and let myself in, closing the door softly behind me. I leaned against the doorframe for a second, willing my heart to slow down. I took a deep breath, praying I was just being paranoid. And then something came charging at me and I almost screamed.

"Winnie," I whispered, as he covered me with slurpy kisses. "You nearly scared me to death. Is Daddy here?"

He titled his head, giving me a perplexed look.

"Shh. You stay here." I climbed the stairs as quietly as I could—which was not very, considering the crutches—followed by a disobedient Winston. That dog never was any good at taking orders. In Matthew's bedroom I got on my hands and knees and fumbled through the closet until I realized the gun was gone.

I stumbled back down the stairs with no idea what I should do. On my way to the door I spotted my stick shuttle. I grabbed it, jamming it in my pocket. It was as good a weapon as a gun I had no clue how to use. "Okay, Winston, let's go catch ourselves a killer."

Chapter 42

I made my way between the house and the garage without any semblance of a plan. Was I going to hit him over the head with my crutches? Or would I stab him with my shuttle? Or hide it behind my back, pretending it was a gun, and try to bluff a confession out of him? As I got nearer, I noticed the garage door was ajar. I moved closer. "Quiet, Winnie," I ordered in a low voice.

Winnie stared back at me, and I could have sworn he was nodding.

"Sit," I whispered. He dropped his butt to the ground with a thump, his eyes following me as I edged closer and closer to the door. I caught the end of something Matthew was saying.

"—you know I would never do that."

And then Mike's voice—"I have to hand it to you. You really had me fooled, but you can't talk your way out of it now." I gasped. Was Mike accusing him of murder? But Matthew's next words put a different spin on what was going on.

"I'm not living *with* her. I'm only using the guest bedroom. And don't worry. If it bothers you, I'll move out."

"Don't take me for an idiot. You told me yourself, back in January, that you were in love with someone."

"Yes, but I wasn't talking about Jenny! Why don't you put that gun away before somebody gets hurt?" My heart nearly stopped. Had I just heard correctly? Mike was holding a gun on Matthew? This time my heart nearly stopped.

Mike chuckled eerily. "You're not fooling me one bit. Jenny is just like my mother. I don't know how she guessed it, but as soon as I got sick, she started fooling around with every Tom, Dick and Harry—except in this case it was Greg, Jeremy and Matthew."

There was a brief silence, and then, sounding strained, Matthew said, "Medicine has come a long way since your father's cancer. There are brand-new treatments. You'll probably—" I edged a few inches closer, my heart drumming madly in my chest. I dared a peek, but my eyes were unaccustomed to the dark inside the garage.

Mike cut him off sharply. "It's too late for me. My cancer has metastasized. It's in my bones and in my brain now. I'm going to die—and so are you. Now get on that dolly."

Greg, Jeremy and Matthew. Jenny had told me that Mike had suspected her of having an affair with Greg Hanson, and then he had turned up dead. She'd given Jeremy a reading at a restaurant. Could Mike have spotted them and jumped to one of his paranoid conclusions? And then *Jeremy* had turned up dead.

And now Matthew was living with Jenny. He was next, unless I saved him.

"Hold on," Matthew argued, an edge to his voice.

"You don't want to do this, Mike. You're an officer of the law. You're not a killer."

"You brought this on yourself. You all did! What have *I* got to lose? Get on that dolly. Now!" *But why does Mike want Matthew to get on the dolly?*

My eyes were growing accustomed to the gloom. I could make out Mike, his back to me, pointing a gun at Matthew, as he obeyed Mike's order. Just behind him, the left front wheel of his TR6 had been removed and the car was jacked up.

In a flash I knew exactly what he was planning. He wanted Matthew under the car so he could kick the jack out of place. The car would fall and crush Matthew to death—another tragic accident, just as Greg Hanson's death had been.

I had to do something, but what? Point my shuttle from inside my pocket and pretend it was a gun? Or hit him over the head with it? Whatever I did, I would surely end up dead.

Suddenly Mike lifted his foot, placed it on the edge of the dolly and gave it a shove. Matthew rolled under the car. And then everything happened very fast.

I screamed, "No!" at the top of my lungs. Mike swung around, pointing the gun at me. Next to me, Winston growled and lunged for Mike's wrist, clamping his teeth down hard. The gun went flying.

Matthew rolled out from under the car, leaped to his feet and grabbed Mike's other arm, twisting it behind him.

I dropped my crutches and limped over. "Thank God you're all right!"

"Don't worry, kiddo. I'm fine. Could you please call the cops?" He winked at me, and his golden eyes made my fears melt away.

"Yeah," I whispered, not minding one bit that he'd just called me kiddo again. "Right away." I went inside and dialed 911.

Chapter 43

Three weeks later

News of Mike's arrest blew through Briar Hollow like a wildfire. But rather than feed the gossip mill, it left people stunned and asking themselves how someone so highly regarded could have done something so terrible. A pall settled over the community. A collective sympathy emerged for both Jenny, who locked herself away for days, refusing to speak to anyone, and Dolores, whose claims that her husband had been murdered had been ignored. She had only been wrong in suspecting Jeremy Fox.

Shortly after his arrest, Mike was transferred to the prison hospital, where it was determined that his paranoia had at least partly been caused by his brain tumors. This news seemed to calm everyone. It was the cancer, not Mike, that was to blame—easier to accept.

Three weeks later the members of the weaving group gathered in my shop to get ready for the official presentation of our baby blankets to the hospital the next morning. Soon I would be in my new space, where there was plenty of room for expansion. I already had plans for more classes. I'd put out feelers for more weavers to leave their goods on consignment. And I was sure I would find plenty of other opportunities. I could hardly wait. Still, I prepared for the gathering with a mixture of emotions—happy and sad all at once.

The first to arrive was Marnie, wearing a red polka-dot dress that did nothing for her figure. She carried a basket of cookies and cake on one arm and a large bag over the other.

She stepped in, dropped her bags and began fanning herself furiously. "It's so hot out there. I'm melting." And then seeing the numerous fans I'd set up all over the place, she broke into a smile. "Oh, it's so nice and cool in here now."

"I was afraid you wouldn't want to come visit anymore unless I got those fans I promised." I picked up the basket. "Mmm, something smells delicious."

"I brought enough goodies for everyone." She shrugged. "It won't hurt to do a bit of promotion ahead of time for Jenny's tea shop." She handed me the basket and opened her bag. "And here are the baby blankets. I made eight," she said proudly.

At that moment, the doorbell tinkled and Susan appeared in the doorway. "Hi, Della. Hi, Marnie." She carried a pile of folded baby blankets. "Where should I—?" And then spotting the chair where Marnie had set hers, she went over. "Good grief, you've already got a whole lot."

"Six from Della," Marnie said, "and eight from me."

Susan fingered one of Marnie's blankets admiringly. "And now we have another six. We did really well. The hospital should be thrilled."

Marnie went over to the coffee table I'd retrieved from the third bedroom and began setting up her cookies and cakes. Over her shoulder, she said, "I'll say. I'm sure they expected no more than half a dozen blankets and we already have twenty. By the time everybody brings in their projects we'll probably have nearly three dozen." She stood. "Hey, look who's here."

I turned around to see Dolores and her daughter arrive. Mercedes hurried over with her blankets, handing them over proudly to Marnie. "I made three. And they're pretty nice."

Marnie examined them carefully and nodded. "They're beautiful, child. I couldn't have done better myself."

Mercedes preened. "You mean it?"

"Absolutely."

I studied the girl, amazed at her transformation. She was wearing a pair of blue jeans and a pink T-shirt instead of her habitual black. Her skull-and-crossbones earrings were gone, in their place a pair of gold hoops. And most impressive, she had toned down her makeup to a soft blush, mascara and lip gloss. She looked beautiful.

Dolores wandered over to me. "Here. I have a little something for you to make up for not having any finished blankets."

"You didn't have to do that," I said, opening the box. Inside was a large bag of Kona coffee. "This is right up there among my favorites. Thank you so much." Call me silly, but Dolores's gift made me completely rethink my opinion of her. Anybody who gave me two pounds of luxury coffee couldn't be all bad. "That's very generous of you. I didn't think I'd be enjoying such a wonderful coffee again for a while—at least not until business picks up."

Marnie offered a plate of cookies. "Actually, you seem to be doing great. Every time I walk by lately, the shop is full of people."

It was true. Business wasn't exactly booming, but sales were good and consistent. "Tourists seem to have discovered my shop," I said. "You and Jenny will have to supply me with more merchandise. I can barely keep the shelves stocked."

"Speaking of Jenny, how is she?"

"As well as can be expected, I suppose. She's been keeping busy, making plans for her new tea shop, and I wouldn't be surprised if she starts dating soon."

Susan laughed. "I know. There's a certain doctor who's been calling her. The whole town is talking about it. If they start dating, I intend to take full credit for that relationship."

"How do you figure that?"

"If I hadn't tripped over my own two feet and cracked my skull on the coffee table, I wouldn't have gone to the hospital, and Jenny wouldn't have met Dr. Green."

I laughed. "Good point."

At that moment the door opened and David Swanson walked in, carrying his loom, with very little weaving completed. Apologetically, he said, "Here's my contribution. Not that it's worth anything. I did my best, but I just couldn't get the hang of it."

Mercedes giggled. "I think the bit you did weave would make a nice dishcloth."

He grimaced. "You can have it if you like. I'll be damned if I'll use a pink dishcloth." Everybody laughed.

David went to the second room and poured himself a cup of coffee, which he raised toward Winnie, who was snoring in the corner. "I propose a toast to the hero of the hour. If not for that big fella there, I wouldn't have been able to close the sale on that building."

I chuckled. "Nice. The only reason you're glad I'm alive is because I bought the building? I'm going to remember that."

He grinned. "Hey, without commissions I don't eat." He looked at Winnie again. "You understand that, don't you, Winston?"

Upon hearing his name, Winston jumped up.

"And I thought you were just a big ugly pussycat, but you are a hero," Mercedes said, earning herself a wet kiss. "Oh, yuck. That's gross." She wiped her cheek with the back of her hand. But for all her complaining, she looked happy.

Marnie leaned in and whispered in my ear. "Mercedes came over this afternoon. She apologized for taking my gun. God only knows why she did it — probably just a teenage prank. Whatever the reason, I forgave her. Everyone deserves a second chance." *Ah, that explains the girl's new attitude*, I thought. *There's nothing like forgiveness to give a person a fresh outlook on life.*

Mercedes wandered back to the chair where all the blankets were stacked. "I can't believe how beautiful they all are. I'm thinking of making a cream and white throw for my own bed."

The bell tinkled and Jenny walked in, looking lovely in a gauzy turquoise top and yoga pants.

I hurried over and gave her a hug. "I'm so glad you're here."

"I wouldn't have missed this for anything." She glanced over my shoulder. "Oh, hi, Matthew." I swung around.

Matthew was carrying a tray of coffee mugs from the kitchen. "I figured you might run out of clean cups."

Jenny's eyes traveled from him to me. In a low voice she said, "I have a feeling about you two. I can see it in your aura."

I gave her a look as if to say, "Give me a break."

She gave me a conspiratorial wink. "Don't play innocent with me."

I rolled my eyes. "Honestly, Jenny—my aura. You know I don't believe in any of that stuff." But I must have been spending too much time with my new friend, because I was really thinking, *I have a feeling too.*

A New Look at an Old Craft

Weaving for the Ages

For thousands of years weaving was the single most efficient way to produce cloth. From the lowliest of rough fabrics, like burlap, to the finest of silks, such as the intricately woven silk kimonos of the geishas, all were produced on looms. Today hand weaving is no longer a necessary craft, but in most cases it has become a pastime, an art and a ritual imbued with a meditation-like series of repetitive movements. A peaceful feeling accompanies weaving. For anyone wanting a vacation from the stress of modern life, escape is as close as the nearest loom.

Choosing a Loom

When it comes to choosing a loom, my philosophy is simple: First, determine your needs—what and how often you will weave—as well as your budget. Countless types of looms are available, most of which are relatively easy to operate. One word of advice: Be sure to try the loom before you buy it. You will want one that is comfortable for you. And whenever possible arrange for a weaving lesson from the person selling you the loom.

Tip: You can comb craigslist or your local classifieds for bargain loom deals. But take an experienced weaver with you before committing to a sale. Also, you can check local community centers for weaving classes—often they have looms available for member use.

Starting a Friendship Blanket

If you are a beginner, my best advice is to select an easy first project. I've seen many a new weaver grow frustrated when working on a project that is beyond his or her ability. Remember, you have to walk before you can run.

The friendship blankets Della and her weaving group made for the hospital nursery are a perfect example of an easy project for a beginner. If you think of quilt making and adapt its principles to weaving, this can be made on any loom, from the most simple—such as a frame loom—to the most advanced—such as a computerized loom. Woven friendship blankets are different from most other friendship crafts in one way: Instead of squares, the pieces assembled together generally are strips. This is because weavers make yardage rather than pieces.

However, rules can occasionally be broken (weavers are rebels!). A young weaving student I recently met was working with a frame loom and rather than make the standard long strips, she made squares, just like a quilt. She had to finish the raw edges of each square by weaving them back into the fabric. After completion, the effect was lovely. And each square was so easy and quick that she developed a love of the craft. When I last spoke to her, she was working on a set of place mats—a good moderate-level project that is great for gifting.

Tip: The easiest way to make a frame loom is to go through your attic, find an old picture frame, pop out the glass and voilà! you have a loom.

Assembling Your Friendship Blanket

Important: When you assemble your blanket, you must use the same material as you did to weave your fabric—cotton yarn with cotton weaving, acrylic with acrylic, and so on. My advice is to start with an easy yarn, something with plenty of stretch.

Tip: Although linen is lovely, it has less stretch than most other yarns and therefore is more challenging for a novice.

However you decide to make your friendship blankets, in strips or in squares, the trick to assembling is to lay your pieces on a flat surface, making sure the corners of your blanket are at perfect 180-degree angles. There are a few points to think about:

1. Decide whether you will crochet your pieces together or sew them. Whichever technique you are more comfortable with, the steps remain the same.
2. Make sure your strips are side by side (all the same length within one quarter inch) before you begin.

3. Before assembling, consider putting a row of single crochet along the strips, using the same color used for the strips. This is in no way necessary; it's just another way to embellish your design. Also, the seams will be that much less visible when using a matching color. Edging a large number of strips can be a time-consuming task, though, so you might prefer to assemble without edging, using an assembly method like a single-crochet join, which would become a part of the design.

4. If you assemble without edging, consider using a contrasting color when connecting your blanket, the same one throughout. This could be a nice added decoration to your work.

5. You can sew strips together with wrong sides facing, or right sides facing, depending on the look you want. You could also alternate wrong side, right side for a different look. Lay the strips side by side and work the stitches on top where you can actually see what is happening as you go.

6. Line your stitches up. If you crocheted or sewed three stitches in your corners, you might begin with the center stitch of each strip to assemble. Also, if your strips were done at different times, or are made of pieces contributed by different people, you may have to adjust for larger or smaller pieces. You might have to skip a stitch in some places or put two stitches in another. Skipping a stitch may leave a hole in your piece, so you want to avoid this as much as possible. Try to get your strips to line up for a pleasing finishing effect. I find it helpful to use

the joining between strips as a guide, so they are not off center. If you yourself are edging each strip, you can count the stitches and keep the same number on every strip before you get to the assembly.

7. Once your blanket is assembled, you will want to machine-wash it. Washing will shrink and tighten the material.

Tip: Throwing some color-absorbing sheets into the wash will stop the colors from ruining anything else you've added to the load.

8. Lay the blanket flat to dry. Finish with a quick ironing and your blanket will be ready to use and enjoy for years to come.

About the Author

Carol Ann Martin is an author and former television personality who divides her time between San Diego and the Canadian coast. She lives with her husband and an ever-expanding collection of dogs. When she is not writing, Carol Ann enjoys baking and beekeeping.